A Master of Deception by Richard Marsh

Richard Bernard Heldmann was born on 12th October 1857, in St Johns Wood, North London.

By his early 20's Heldmann began publishing fiction for the myriad magazine publications that had sprung up and were eager for good well-written content.

In October 1882, Heldmann was promoted to co-editor of Union Jack, a popular magazine, but his association with the publication ended suddenly in June 1883. It appears Heldman was prone to issuing forged cheques to finance his lifestyle. In April 1884 He was sentenced to 18 months hard labour.

In order to be well away from the scandal and damage this had caused to his reputation Heldmann adopted a pseudonym on his release from jail. Shortly thereafter the name 'Richard Marsh' began to appear in the literary periodicals. The use of his mother's maiden name as part of it seems both a release and a lifeline.

A stroke of very good fortune arrived with his novel The Beetle published in 1897. This would turn out to be his greatest commercial success and added some much-needed gravitas to his literary reputation.

Marsh was a prolific writer and wrote almost 80 volumes of fiction as well as many short stories, across many genres from horror and crime to romance and humour.

Index of Contents

CHAPTER I

THE INCLINING OF A TWIG

When Rodney Elmore was eleven years old, placards appeared on the walls announcing that a circus was coming to Uffham. Rodney asked his mother if he might go to it. Mrs. Elmore, for what appeared to her to be sufficient reasons, said "No." Three days before the circus was to come he went with his mother to Mrs. Bray's house, a little way out of Uffham, to tea. The two ladies having feminine mysteries to discuss, he was told to go into the garden to play. As he went he passed a little room, the door of which was open. Peeping in, as curious children will, something on a corner of the mantelpiece caught his eye. Going closer to see what it was, he discovered that there were two half-crowns, one on the top of the other. The desire to go to the circus, which had never left him, gathered sudden force. Here were the means of going. Whipping the two coins into the pocket of his knickerbockers, he ran from the room and into the garden.

During the remainder of the afternoon the half-crowns were a burden to him. Not because he was weighed down by a sense of guilt; but because he feared that their absence would be discovered; that they would be taken from him; that he would be left poor indeed. He kept down at the far end of the garden, considering if it would not be wiser to conceal them in some spot from which he would be able to retrieve them at the proper time. But Mrs. Bray's was at, what to him was, a great distance from his own home; he might not be able to get there again before the eventful day. When the maid came to fetch him in the coins were still in his pocket; they were still there when he left the house with his mother.

On the eventful day his mother had to go to London. Before she went she told Rodney that she had given the servant money to take him to the circus. This was rather a blow to the boy, since he found himself possessed of money which, for its intended purpose, was useless. He had hidden the half-crowns up the chimney in his bedroom. Aware that it might not be easy to explain how he came to be the owner of so much cash, there they remained for quite a time. So far as he knew, nothing was said by Mrs. Bray about the money which had gone; certainly no suspicion attached to him.

Later he went to a public school. During the third term he went with the school bicycle club for a spin. The master in charge had a spill. As he fell some coins dropped out of his pocket. Rodney, who was the only one behind him, saw a yellow coin roll into a rut at the side of the road. Alighting, he pressed his foot on it, so that it was covered with earth. Then, calling to the others, who, unconscious of what had happened, were pedalling away in front, he gave first aid to the injured. The master had fallen heavily on his side. He had sprained something which made it difficult for him to move. A vehicle was fetched, which bore him back to school, recovery having first been made of the coins which had been dropped. It was only later he discovered that a sovereign was missing. The following day a search-party went out to look for it, of which Rodney Elmore was a member. They found nothing. As they were starting back Rodney perceived that his saddle had worked loose. He stayed behind to tighten it. When he spurted after the others the sovereign was in his pocket. Mr. Griffiths was reputed to be poor. It was Elmore who suggested that a subscription should be started to reimburse him for his loss. When Mr. Griffiths heard of the suggestion—while he laughingly declined to avail himself of the boy's generosity—he took Elmore's hand in a friendly grip. Then he asked the lad if he would oblige him by going on an errand to the village. While he was on the errand Rodney changed the sovereign, which he would have found it difficult to do in the school.

At the end of the summer term in his last year Elmore was invited by a schoolboy friend named Austin to spend part of the holidays with him in a wherry on the Broads. Mrs. Elmore told him that she would pay his fare and give him, besides, a small specified sum which she said would be sufficient for necessary expenses. Her ideas on that latter point were not those of her son. Rodney's notions on such subjects were always liberal. Good at books and games, he was one of the most popular boys in the school. Among other things, he was captain of cricket. At the last match of the season he played even unusually well, carrying his bat through the innings with nearly two hundred runs to his credit, having given one of the finest displays of hard hitting and good placing the school had ever seen. He was the hero of the day; owing to his efforts his side had won. Flushed with victory, with the plaudits of his admirers still ringing in his ears, he strolled along a corridor, cricket-bag in hand. He passed a room, the door of which was open. A room with an open door was apt to have a fatal fascination for Rodney Elmore; if opportunity offered, he could seldom refrain from peeping in. He peeped in then. On a table was a canvas bag, tied with a string. He recognised it as the bag which contained the tuck-shop takings. Since the tuck-shop had had a busy day, the probability was that the bag held quite a considerable sum. He had been wondering where the money was coming from to enable him to cut a becoming figure during his visit to Austin. Stepping quickly into the room, he emptied the canvas bag into his cricket-bag; then, going out again as quickly as he had entered, he continued his progress.

He was on his way to one of the masters, named Rumsey, who edited the school magazine, his object being to hand him a corrected proof of certain matter which was to appear in the forthcoming issue. He took the proof out of his cricket-bag, which he opened in the master's presence. Having stayed to have a chat, he returned with Mr. Rumsey along the corridor. As they went they saw one of the school pages come hurriedly out of the room in which, as Rodney was aware, there was an empty canvas bag. Mr. Rumsey commented on the speed at which the youth was travelling.

"Isn't that young Wheeler? He seems in a hurry. I wish he would always move as fast."

"Perhaps he's tearing off on an errand for Mr. Taylor."

As he said this Rodney carelessly swung his cricket-bag, being well aware that the coins within were so mixed up with his sweater, pads, gloves, and other accessories that they were not likely to make their presence audible. At the end of the corridor they encountered Mr. Taylor himself. Mark Taylor was fourth form master and manager of the tuck-shop. Nodding, he went quickly on. Mr. Rumsey was going one way, Rodney the other. They lingered at the corner to exchange a few parting words. Suddenly Mr. Taylor's voice came towards them down the corridor.

"Rumsey! Elmore! Who's been in my room?"

"Been in your room?" echoed Mr. Rumsey. "How should I know?" Then added, as if it were the result of a second thought: "We just saw Wheeler come out."

"Wheeler?" In his turn, Mr. Taylor played the part of echo. "He just came rushing past me; I wondered what his haste meant. You saw him come out of my room? Then— But he can't have done a thing like that!"

"Like what? Anything wrong?"

"There seems to be something very much wrong. Do you mind coming here?"

Retracing their steps, Mr. Rumsey and Elmore joined the agitated Mr. Taylor in his room. He made clear to them the cause of his agitation.

"You see this bag? It contained to-day's tuck-shop takings—more than ten pounds. I left it, with the money tied up in it, on the table here while I went to Perrin to fetch a memorandum I'd forgotten. Now that I've returned, I find the bag lying on my table empty and the money apparently gone. That's what's wrong, and the question is, who has been in my room since I left it?"

"As I told you, Elmore and I just saw Wheeler making his exit rather as if he were pressed for time."

"And I myself just met him scurrying along, and wondered what the haste was about; he's not, as a general rule, the fastest of the pages. The boy has a bad record; there was that story about Burge minor and his journey money, and there have been other tales. If he was in my room—"

"Perhaps he was sent on an errand to you."

"I doubt it, from the way he was running when I met him. And, so far from stopping when he saw me, if anything, he went faster than ever. It looks very much as if—"

He stopped, leaving the sentence ominously unfinished.

"Master Wheeler may be a young rip, but surely he wouldn't do a thing like that."

This was Rodney, who notoriously never spoke ill of anyone. Mr. Taylor touched on his well-known propensity.

"That's all very well, Elmore; but you'd try to find an excuse for a man who snatched the coat off your back. This is a very serious matter; ten pounds are ten pounds. The best thing is for you to bring Wheeler here, and we'll have it out with him at once."

Rodney started off to fetch the page. It was some little time before he returned. When he did he was without his cricket-bag, and gripped the obviously unwilling page tightly by the shoulder. That the lad's mind was very far from being at ease Mr. Taylor's questions quickly made plain.

"Wheeler, Mr. Rumsey and Mr. Elmore just saw you coming out of my room. What were you doing here?"

Wheeler, looking everywhere but at his questioner, hesitated; then stammered out a lame reply.

"I—I was looking for you, sir."

"For me? What did you want with me? Why did you not say you wanted me when you met me just now?"

Wheeler could not explain; he was tongue-tied. Mr. Taylor went on:

"When I went I left this bag on the table full of money. As you were the only person who entered the room during my absence, I want you to tell me how the bag came to be empty when I returned?"

"The bag was empty when I came in here," blurted out Wheeler. "I particularly noticed."

To that tale he stuck—that the bag was empty when he entered the room. His was a lame story. It seemed clear that he had gone into the room with intentions which were not all that they might have been—possibly meaning to pilfer from the bag, which he knew was there. The discovery that the bag was empty had come upon him with a shock; he had fled. As was not altogether unnatural, his story was not believed. The two masters accused him point-blank of having emptied the bag himself. A formal charge of theft would have been made against him had it not been for his tender years, also partly because of the resultant scandal, perhaps still more because not a farthing of the money was ever traced to his possession, or, indeed, to anyone else's. What had become of it was never made clear. Wheeler, however, was dismissed from his employment with a stain upon his character which he would find it hard to erase.

Rodney Elmore had an excellent time upon the Broads, towards which the tuck-shop takings, in a measure, contributed. The Austins, who were well-to-do people, had a first-rate wherry; on it was a lively party. There were two girls—Stella Austin, Tom Austin's sister, and a friend of hers, Mary Carmichael. Elmore, who was nearly nineteen, had already had more than one passage with persons of the opposite sex. He had a curious facility in gaining the good graces of feminine creatures of all kinds and all ages. When he went he left Stella Austin under the impression that he cared for her very much indeed; while, although conscious that Tom Austin, believing himself to be in love with Mary Carmichael, regarded her as his own property, he was aware that the young lady liked him—Rodney Elmore—in a sense of which his friend had not the vaguest notion. Altogether his visit to the Austins was an entire success; he had won for himself a niche in everyone's esteem before they parted.

When he was twenty Rodney Elmore entered an uncle's office in St. Paul's Churchyard. Soon after he was twenty-one his mother died. On her deathbed she showed an anxiety for his future which, under other circumstances, he would have found almost amusing.

"Rodney," she implored him, "my son, my dear, dear boy, promise me that you will keep honest; that, under no pressure of circumstances, you will stray one hair's breadth from the path of honesty."

This, in substance, though in varying forms, was the petition which she made to him again and again, in tones which, as the days, and even the hours, went by, grew fainter and fainter. He did his best to give her the assurance she required, smilingly at first, more seriously when he perceived how much she was in earnest.

"Mother, darling," he told her, "I promise that I'll keep as straight as a man can keep. I'll never do anything for which you could be ashamed of me. Have you ever been ashamed of me?"

"No, dear, never. You've always been the best, cleverest, truest, most affectionate son a woman could have. Never once have you given me a moment's anxiety. God keep you as you have always been—above all, God keep you honest."

"Mother," he said in earnest tones, which had nearly sunk to a whisper, "God helping me, and He will help me, I swear to you that I will never do a dishonest thing, never! Nor a thing that is in the region of dishonesty. Don't you believe me, darling?"

"Of course, dear, I believe you—I do! I do!"

It was with some such words on her lips that she died; yet, even as she uttered them, he had a feeling that there was a look in her eyes which suggested both fear and doubt. In the midst of his heart-broken grief the fact that there should have been such a look struck him as good.

CHAPTER II

HIS UNCLE AND HIS COUSIN

Mrs. Elmore's income died with her. She had sunk her money in an annuity because, as she had explained to Rodney, that enabled her to give him a much better education than she could have done had they been constrained to live on the interest produced by her slender capital. But her son was not left penniless. She had bought him an annuity, to commence when he was twenty-one, of thirty shillings a week, to be paid weekly, and had tied it up in such a way that he could neither forestall it nor use it as a security on which to borrow money. As clerk to his uncle he received one hundred pounds a year. Feeling that he could no longer reside in Uffham, he sold the house, which was his mother's freehold, and its contents, the sale producing quite a comfortable sum. So, on the whole, he was not so badly off as some young men.

On the contra side he had expensive tastes, practically in every direction. Among other things, he had a partiality for feminine society, mostly of the reputable sort; but a young man is apt to find the society of even a nice girl an expensive luxury. For instance, Mary Carmichael had a voice. Her fond parents, who lived in the country, suffered her to live in town while she was taking singing lessons. Tom Austin, although still an undergraduate at Oxford, made no secret of his feelings for the maiden, a fact which did not prevent Mary going out now and then with Rodney Elmore to dinner at a restaurant, and, afterwards, to a theatre, as, nowadays, young men and maidens do. On these occasions Rodney paid, and where the evening's entertainment of a modern maiden is concerned a five-pound note does not go far. Then, although Miss Carmichael might not have been aware of it, there were others. Among them Stella Austin, who had reasons of her own for believing that Mr. Elmore would give the world to make her his wife, being only kept from avowing his feelings by the fact that he was, to all intents and purposes, a pauper. Since she was the possessor of three or four hundred a year of her own, with the prospect of much more, she tried more than once to hint that, since she would not mind setting up housekeeping on quite a small income, there was no reason why they should wait an indefinite period, till Rodney was a millionaire. But Rodney's delicacy was superfine. While he commended her attitude with an ardour which made the blood grow hot in her veins, he explained that he was one of those men who would not ask a girl to marry him unless he was in a position to keep her in the style a husband should, adding that that time was not so distant as some people might think. In another twelve months he hoped—well, he hoped! As at such moments she was apt to be very close to him, Stella hoped too.

The young gentleman was living at the rate of at least five or six hundred a year on an income of a hundred and eighty. He did not bother himself by keeping books, but he quite realised that his expenditure bore no relation to his actual income. Of course, he owed money; but he did not like owing money. It was against his principles. He never borrowed if he could help it, and he objected to being at the mercy of a tradesman. He preferred to get the money somehow, and pay; and, somehow, he got it. Very curious methods that "somehow" sometimes covered. He was fond of cards; liked to play for all sorts of stakes; and, on the whole, he won. His skill in one so young was singular; sometimes, when opportunity offered, it was shown in directions at which one prefers only to hint. His favourite games were bridge, piquet, poker, and baccarat, four games at which a skilful player can do strange things, especially when playing with unsuspicious young men who have looked upon the wine when it was red.

Rodney's dexterity with his fingers was almost uncanny. He could do wonderful card tricks, though he never did them in public, but only for his own private amusement. When reading "Oliver Twist," he had been tickled by the scene in which Fagin teaches his youthful pupils how to pick a pocket. He had made experiments of his own in the same direction upon parties who were not in the least aware of the experiments he was making. His success amused him hugely, while the subjects of his experiments never had the dimmest notion as to how or where their valuables had gone.

In very many ways Rodney Elmore obtained sufficient money to enable him to keep his credit at a surprisingly high standard. Everyone spoke well of him; he was a general favourite. Nor was it strange; he looked a likeable fellow—indeed, ninety-nine people out of a hundred liked him at first sight. Over six feet in height, slightly built, he did not look so strong as he was in reality. Straight as an arrow, head held well up, there was something almost feminine in the lightness with which he seemed to move. Many girls and women had told him to his face that he was the best dancer they had ever had for partner. Indeed, in a sense, he flattered his partners, having a knack of making a girl who danced badly think she danced well. He had light brown hair, which seemed as if it had been dusted with golden sand; grey eyes, which, with the pleasantest expression, looked you right in the face; an Englishman's clear skin; mobile lips, which parted on the slightest pretext in a sunny smile; just enough moustache to shade his upper lip. Altogether as agreeable looking a young gentleman as one might hope to meet. And his manners bore out the promise of his appearance. Always cool, easy, self-possessed, ready to perform little services for women, the aged, the infirm, in a fashion which, so far as our present-day young men are concerned, is a little out of date. With the pleasantest voice and trick of speech, no chatterer, it seemed impossible for him to say a disagreeable or an unkind thing either to or of anyone. It was a standing joke among his intimates that, when scandal-mongering was in the air, Elmore would spoil the fun by pointing out the good qualities of those attacked and refusing to see anything else but them. He had ever an excuse to offer for the most notorious sinner. It was not wonderful that everybody liked him. On his part, he seemed incapable of disliking anyone. He might rob his friend of all that he had, but he would not regard him as less his friend on that account.

To this rule, so far as he knew, there was only one exception, and as time went on this exception surprised him more and more. There was only one person who he felt sure disliked him, and why he disliked him was beyond his comprehension. This person was the uncle in whose office he was a clerk—

Graham Patterson. Mr. Patterson was Mrs. Elmore's brother. Rodney quite understood that his uncle had not offered him the position he held, but had only received him at his mother's particular request. There had been that in his uncle's manner which had struck him as peculiar from the first, as if he were prejudiced against him before they met, regarding him with suspicion and dislike. As, for some reason which he would have liked to have had explained, he had never seen his uncle till he entered his office, his relative's attitude struck him as distinctly odd; but, in his light-hearted way, he told himself that he would gain his uncle's esteem before they had been acquainted long. However, they had been acquainted now nearly three years, and he was conscious that his uncle esteemed him as little as ever. He wondered why.

Mr. Patterson's appearance was against him; he was big and bloated. A City merchant of the old school, he was addicted to the pleasures of the table and fond—for one of his habit of body unduly fond—of what he called a "glass of wine." He liked half a pint of port with his luncheon and a pint for his dinner, he being just the kind of person who never ought to have touched port at all. Nor, when his health permitted, was his daily allowance of stimulants by any means confined to his pint and a half of port. The result was that he suffered both in mind and body. The "governor's temper" was a byword in the office. When, to use his own phrase, he was "a little below par" he would fly into such fits of passion about the merest trivialities that those about him used to regard his "paddies" as part of the daily routine; so soon as he was out of his "paddy" he had forgotten all about it.

Although his methods were a little old-fashioned, he was still an excellent man of business. The staple of his trade was silk, but latterly he had added other lines. In these days of shoddy the quality of his goods was above suspicion; he did a remunerative trade in everything he touched. In the trade no man's commercial integrity stood higher than Graham Patterson's; whoever dealt with him could be sure that everything would be all right. His books showed every year a comfortable turnover at fair rates of profit. There were those in his employ who were of opinion that if only a younger and more pushing man could have a voice in the management of affairs, the business might rapidly become one of the finest in the city of London.

Rodney Elmore had not been long in his uncle's office before this opinion became emphatically his. He was conscious of commercial abilities of the most unusual kind, and was convinced that if he could only get a chance he would double both the turnover and the profits in so short a space of time that his uncle could not fail to be gratified. Since he was the nephew of his uncle, and, indeed, his only male relative, he did not see why he should not have a chance. When he first went to St. Paul's Churchyard he had hopes, but these hopes had grown dimmer. His perceptions on such matters were keen; few persons, no matter what their age, could see farther into a brick wall than he. He felt certain that his uncle only kept him at all because Mrs. Elmore had wrung from him a promise that he should have a place, of sorts, in his office. So far from having an eye to his nephew's advancement, it seemed to Rodney that his uncle even went out of his way to let him have as little as possible to do with the conduct of his business. It was true that he had a room for his separate use, and, though it was but a tiny one, on this foundation, at the beginning, he built much. But before long he understood that what he had reared were castles in the air. It seemed to Rodney before long that it must have been Mr. Patterson's intention to keep him apart from the others in order that he might know nothing of what was going on. His own work was of the simplest clerical kind; occasionally he was sent on an errand of no importance. He seemed free to come when he liked, and leave when he chose; nobody appeared to care what he did, or left undone. For these onerous labours he had been paid the first year eighty pounds, the second a hundred, then a hundred and twenty; now, after three years, he wondered what was going to happen next. Obviously an office boy could do what he had to do for five shillings a week.

Under the circumstances, the fact that he had acquired such an insight into the ins and outs, the pros and cons, of his uncle's business transactions spoke volumes for his keenness and acumen. He often smiled to himself as he pictured the expression which would come on his uncle's rubicund countenance if he guessed what an intimate knowledge his office boy had of his affairs. Rodney was perfectly aware that the expression would not be one of pleasure; that his knowledge would not be regarded as the fruit of promising zeal, but as something which could only be adequately described by a flood of uncomplimentary adjectives. What was at the back of Graham Patterson's mind the young man, with all his shrewdness, had still no notion. He was one of the few men he had met who puzzled him. But of this much he was clear—that, while for his sister's sake Mr. Patterson was willing that his nephew should have a seat in his office, the less active interest the young man took in the duties he was, presumably, paid to perform the better pleased his employer would be. Elmore was of a hopeful disposition, willing to persevere if he saw even a remote chance of ultimate gain. But so convinced was he that his uncle, if he could help it, would never, on his own initiative, advance him to a position of trust that, before this, he would have cast about for a chance of improving his prospects—had it not been for a young lady.

He had already been more than two years in his uncle's employment, and was meditating leaving it at a very early date, when one afternoon, Mr. Patterson being out, he heard an unknown feminine voice speaking in the outer office, and unexpectedly the door of his own den was opened, and someone entered—a girl. Slipping the papers he was assiduously studying into his desk with lightning-like rapidity, he rose to greet her.

"Are you Rodney Elmore?" He smilingly owned that he was. "Then you're my cousin. How are you?"

His cousin? He did not know that he had such a relative in the world. She held out her hand. Almost before he knew it he had it in his; whether willingly or not, she left it in his quite an appreciable space of time. He admitted his ignorance.

"I didn't know I had such a delightful thing as a cousin."

"Isn't that queer? I didn't till the other day. I'm Gladys Patterson; your uncle's my father."

For once in his life Rodney was taken by surprise. His researches into his uncle's affairs had been confined to their commercial side. He knew practically nothing of his private life. He had never heard it spoken of, and had asked no questions. He had a vague idea that his uncle was a bachelor. He knew that he lived in rooms, and—accidentally—had learnt that he had relations with certain ladies of a kind which one does not associate with a family man. That he had ever had a wife and, still less, a daughter he had never guessed. Even in the midst of his surprise he reproached himself for his stupidity that such an important point should have escaped him! As he regarded the girl in front of him he perceived that she was her father's child.

She was about his height, he being short and fat. One day, if appearances were not misleading, she also would be plump. Already she had something of her father's rubicund countenance; her cheeks were red, even a trifle blotchy. She had dark hair and eyes, both her mouth and nose were a little too big. Yet he did not find her disagreeable to look at. On the contrary, there was something about her which appealed to him, just as he was conscious that there was something about him which appealed to her. Where a girl was concerned it was strange how some subtle instinct told him these things. He was moved to audacity.

"If you're my cousin, oughtn't I to kiss you?"

Her eyes lit up. Her lips parted, showing her beautiful teeth; if they were a little large, they were very white and even.

"As I've had no experience of cousins, how can I say?"

"I shouldn't like you to feel that I'm beginning by evading what, for aught either of us can tell, might be my duty."

Stooping, he kissed her on the mouth. Though it was little more than a butterfly's kiss, her lips seemed to meet his with a gentle pressure which he found agreeable.

"You are a cousin!" she exclaimed.

"I'm glad you are," he replied.

"Didn't you really know you had a cousin?" He shook his head. "Nor I; isn't it queer? I only found it out the other day by the merest accident; in some respects dad is the most secretive person. I've been abroad for the last five years. How old do you think I am?"

There was a frankness, a friendliness about this cousin which amused him. In that sense she could not have been more unlike her sire.

"Twenty-two."

"I'm twenty-five—isn't it awful? How old are you?"

"I regret to say that I am only twenty-three. I'm afraid you'll regard me as only a kid."

"Shall I? I don't think I shall. You don't look as if you were 'only a kid.' I've been what papa calls 'finishing my education.' Fancy! at my time of life! If my mother had been living I shouldn't have stood it; but, as you know, she died when I was only a tiny tot; and I knew dad—so I lay, comparatively, low. I've been living here and there and everywhere with the queerest duennas, though they really have been dears; and now and then I have had a good time, though I've had some frightfully dull ones. But at last I have struck. You know we've got a house in Russell Square?" Again he shook his head. "What do you know?"

"So far as you are concerned—nothing. I know that I'm clerk to my uncle, and that's all."

"Well, we have got a house in Russell Square. It's been shut up all these years—papa's been living in rooms. But I've made him refurbish it, and he's made it really nice—when he does undertake to do a thing he does it well—and I'm installed in it as mistress. Of course, I know Russell Square's out of the way, but they are good houses, and, if I can only manage dad, I'm going to have a real good time."

"Did he tell you about me?"

"Not he. Don't I tell you that I only discovered your existence by the merest accident? Do you remember a boy named Henderson who was at school with you?"

"Alfred Henderson—very well; we moved together from form to form."

"I know his sister Cissie; we were at school together, years ago, and she knows you. She told me the other day that you were in your uncle's office in St. Paul's Churchyard, and that his name was Graham Patterson, and was he any relation of mine. I nearly had a fit. When dad came home I bombarded him with questions— What have you done to offend him?"

"Nothing of which I'm conscious. Ever since I've been in the office I've been aware that he dislikes me, though I assure you that I've done my best to please him and give him no cause of complaint."

"Well, he does not like you, and that's a fact. He as good as forbade me to make your acquaintance; but, as he wouldn't give any reasons, I decided to find out for myself what sort of person you were, and— then be guided by circumstances. The truth is, I've had enough of obeying dad, and that's another fact. If I'm not careful I shall end my days in a convent, and the conventual life has not the slightest attraction for me. I've got a will of my own, and when a girl is twenty-five it's about time that she should let such a very unreasonable parent as mine seems to be know it. I'm sure Cissie Henderson is a girl who knows what she is talking about, and as she said all sorts of nice things about you, and nothing else but nice things, I made up my mind that, since I had a cousin, I'd find out for myself what kind of cousin my cousin was. There is dad. Now you see how I manage him."

A heavy step and a loud voice were heard without; then the door was thrown back upon its hinges.

"Gladys! What does this mean?"

"I've come to see my cousin, dad, as I told you I should do."

"Come into my room."

"Directly, dad. I want Rodney to come and dine with us to-night."

Her father perceptibly winced at his daughter's use of the Christian name.

"To-night? Impossible! I'm engaged."

"Are you? Then in that case he can come and keep me company while you are out. We ought to have heaps of things to say to each other. Do you mind?"

The question was put to Elmore. Mr. Patterson glared.

"Gladys, I want you to come with me to the theatre to-night."

"My dear dad, this is the first time I've heard of it—and, if you don't mind, I'd much rather not. One can go to the theatre any night, but one can't discover that one has a cousin, and meet him for the first time, every day. I'd much rather Rodney would come to dine. Won't you?"

Again the question was put to Elmore.

"I'd be very glad to come—with Mr. Patterson's permission."

"You hear, dad? He'll come, with your permission. Nothing would please you more than that he should come, would it?"

The father looked into the daughter's eyes, seeming to see something in them which kept him from uttering words which were at the tip of his tongue. He spoke gruffly.

"Perhaps he has an engagement."

"Have you?"

"Not any."

"And if you had, you'd throw it over to dine with us, wouldn't you?"

"I certainly would."

"You see, papa, what a compliment he pays you. Come, since it seems that he doesn't regard my invitation as sufficient, will you please ask him to dine with us to-night?"

Again the father eyed his daughter. The observant youth, as he glanced from one to the other, was struck by the unmistakable evidence that this young woman was her father's child. He did not doubt that she had more than a touch of the paternal temper. He saw that Mr. Patterson, fearful of an exhibition of it then and there, as the lesser of two evils, yielded, not gracefully.

"He can come if he likes."

"Thank you, papa. You haven't a very pretty way—has he?—but as my invitation couldn't possibly be warmer, I'm sure you'll regard dad's endorsement as more than sufficient. So you will come?"

"I shall be only too delighted."

"Now, then, Gladys, come to my room. I want to speak to you."

"Coming, dad. Remember, Rodney, our address is 90, Russell Square, and we dine at eight; but if you come any time after half-past seven you'll find me ready. You can't think how dad and I will look forward to your coming."

CHAPTER III

RODNEY ELMORE THE FIRST

That was a curious dinner party. Elmore quite expected that when he had rid himself of his daughter his uncle would come and tell him that he was not to regard the invitation as having been seriously intended, and that he was not to present himself in Russell Square. But nothing of the sort occurred. He saw and heard no more of Mr. Patterson until he quitted the office, and just before a quarter to eight he entered the drawing-room at No. 90. Miss Patterson, who was its sole occupant, rose as he entered.

"It's very good of you," she said, while she continued to allow her hand to remain in his, "to take the hint, and come early. Dad never shows till dinner's served, so that I shall have a chance of finding out before he comes what is the meaning of the extraordinary attitude he is taking up towards you. He simply poses as the father who has got to be obeyed, and as that sort of thing appears to be ridiculous, as I ventured to tell him, I expect you to tell me all about it."

He told her all he had to tell, which was very little, in such fashion that inside fifteen minutes they were on terms almost of intimacy. He was one of those men who have a natural attraction for contrasting types of women; emphatically for that type of which Gladys Patterson was an example. The master of the house did not enter till dinner was served, and by the time they were seated at table Elmore was already aware that his cousin offered a pleasant and promising field for such experiments as he might choose to devise.

Conversation was almost entirely confined to the two younger members of the party, the initiative being taken by Gladys, Elmore acting as a sort of chorus. The meal was of the solid, plentiful, well-cooked order, which one felt would appeal to the host. Beyond replying shortly to an occasional inquiry addressed to him by his daughter, Mr. Patterson's whole attention was given to his food, and wine. When dessert was on the table his daughter asked him:

"Going out to-night, dad—as usual?"

"No," he responded briefly, "I'm not."

The young woman looked at her cousin with a twinkle in her eyes.

"Dad follows the good old-fashioned custom of sitting over his wine. He thinks that a glass of port gives a proper finish to a meal. If you don't think so you can come into the drawing-room with me."

"He'll stay here," observed the sire succinctly.

But the damsel was equal to the occasion.

"Very well, dad; then I'll stay too. And since this table really is too big for three, I think, Rodney, it would be more comfy if I were to bring my chair closer to yours. Are you fond of the theatre?"

Having brought her chair to within a foot of Elmore's she entered with him into an animated discussion on the subject of favourite plays and players, while the host, practically speechless, sat at the head of his board drinking more port than was good for him. Elmore, who could be abstemious enough when he liked, had followed his cousin's lead, and drank nothing but mineral water. At last the young lady used his self-denial as a pivot to gain her own ends.

"Really, dad, as Rodney won't join you in drinking, it's absurd our stopping here, especially as I want some music, so please, sir, will you come with me at once into the drawing-room?"

Before the slow-witted host, whose brains had not been rendered more active by his libations, had awoke to the meaning of his daughter's proposition, she had borne the guest with her from the room. They were alone together in the drawing-room for more than half an hour. If the music of which Gladys had spoken was not much in evidence, their acquaintance moved at a rate which was only possible in the case of a young man who was willing—nay, eager—to take advantage of the peculiarities of a young woman's temperament. So that when his uncle did appear, with eyes a little dulled and feet a little unsteady, Rodney was quite ready to make his adieux and his cousin to excuse him.

The acquaintance, thus commenced, not only continued, but advanced by leaps and bounds. Mr. Patterson's habits being those of a bachelor of a not too strait-laced kind rather than those of a family man, he did not find his daughter's society so congenial and satisfying as he might have done. Being desirous of doing as he liked, he left her with more freedom than he himself was perhaps aware of. She would even have not been without justification had she chosen to regard herself as neglected. But for what seemed to her to be sufficient reasons, she was content that her parent should amuse himself as he liked, though his doing so resulted in his practically overlooking her altogether.

Rodney Elmore never went again to the house in Russell Square as his uncle's guest, but he went there more than once as his daughter's, and that sometimes at hours and under circumstances which were, to say the least, unconventional. More frequently their meetings were not in the neighbourhood of Bloomsbury. Mr. Patterson had a fondness for week-ending, without informing his daughter with whom he spent his time or where. It was not strange if, during such absences, his daughter did her best to avoid being too much alone. More than one such Sunday she and Rodney spent together from quite an early hour to quite a late one. Before long they were on terms which certainly could not have been more intimate had they been an engaged couple. But they were not, on that point they supposed that they understood each other thoroughly. Gladys had less than two hundred a year of her own, left her by her mother; and Rodney was pretty sure that if she married him her means would not be materially increased for many a day to come—if ever. He was by no means sure that he cared for her enough to marry her if all he got with her in marriage was her person; no one could be clearer than he was that she would not make the sort of wife who would be likely to be in any way whatever of assistance to a struggling husband. Her attitude was almost equally practical. That she liked him much more than he liked her was sure; there was hardly anything he could ask of her which she would not be willing to give. She believed in him much more than he believed in her; in her eyes he was nearly a hero. But, not being quite blind, she realised that, as things were, marriage for them was out of the question. She knew her father, and was aware that while up to a certain point she could do with him as she liked, if on a matter of capital importance he bade her not to do such and such a thing, and she did it, he would cut her as completely out of his life as if she had not been in it, and never miss her. She was conscious that she was as unfitted for love in a cottage as Elmore was; was, perhaps, even dimly alive to the fact that in such a position her plight would be worse than his was. So that their association was based on that quite up-to-date article of faith which sets forth that though a young man and a young woman can never be husband and wife, they may still be "pals."

Elmore's position in the office was not improved by the incident of his having been a guest in Russell Square. Though his uncle never spoke to him upon the subject—nor, indeed, if he could help it, on any other—his nephew's acute perception realised that he had not grown to like him any more. As time went on a doubt began to grow up within him as to whether his uncle had not some inkling of the relations which existed between him and his daughter. That his doubt was well founded he was ultimately to learn. One morning, soon after his uncle's arrival, a request came to him to go to him at once in his room. When he went in he was struck, not by any means for the first time, by certain points about his uncle's appearance. He felt convinced that his relative's was not, from the insurance point of view, a good life. Rodney Elmore knew little of medicine, yet he hazarded a private opinion that Graham Patterson was a promising subject for an apoplectic stroke—the kind of man who, at any moment of undue stress, might have cerebral trouble from which he might not find it easy to recover. He caught himself wondering whether if, by any mischance, his uncle became the victim of such a catastrophe, it might not be worth his while to marry his cousin, if, indeed, that would not be the lady's own point of view. Were Graham Patterson to have such a stroke, it was at least within the range of possibility that he might never again be in a condition to manage his own affairs; in which case who would be so likely to be appointed administrator as the husband of his only child?

While such gruesome imaginings occupied his mind, the subject of them continued to regard him with a stolid silence which at last struck him as singular.

"I was told, sir, that you wished to speak to me."

He said this with the little air of pleasant deference of which he was such a master and which became him so well. His uncle still said nothing, but continued to glare at him with his bloodshot eyes as if he were some strange object in an exhibition. He really looked so odd that Rodney began to wonder if that stroke was already in the air. He tried again to move him to speech.

"I trust, sir, that nothing disagreeable has happened."

Yet some seconds passed before his uncle did speak. When he did it was with a hard sort of ferocity which his listener felt accorded well with the singularity of his appearance.

"You took my daughter to the Palace Theatre last night."

Rodney wondered from whom he had learned the fact, being convinced that it was not from his daughter. However, since he could scarcely ask, he tried another line, one which he was conscious went close to the verge of insolence.

"I hope, sir, that the Palace is not a theatre to which you object. Just now it has one of the best entertainments in London."

Only in a very narrow sense could his uncle's response be regarded as a reply to his words.

"You're an infernal young scoundrel!"

Rodney did not attempt to feign resentment he did not feel. His quickly-moving wits told him that he was at last brought face to face with a position which he had for some time foreseen, and that for him the best attitude would probably be one of modest humility—at least, to begin with.

"I don't think, sir, you are entitled to use such language to me on such slight grounds."

"Don't you? You—you—beauty!"

Obviously Mr. Patterson had substituted a different word for the one he had intended to use. Taking a slip of paper out of the drawer of the writing-table at which he was seated, he held it out towards Rodney.

"You see that?"

"I do, sir."

"You know what it is?"

"It appears to be a cheque."

"You know what cheque it is."

"If you will allow me to examine it more closely I shall perhaps be able to say."

"You can examine it as closely as you please so long as it is in my hands. I wouldn't trust it in your hands for a good deal."

"Why do you say that?"

"You impudent young blackguard!"

"And that, sir?"

"I say it, you brazen young hypocrite, because that cheque happens to be a forgery, and you are the man who forged it."

"Sir! I know that you are used to allow yourself a large license in the way of language, but this time, although you are my uncle, you go too far."

"I intend to go much farther before I've done—and don't you throw the fact that I'm your uncle in my face, the most decent men have blackguards for relatives. This cheque was originally made out for eight pounds. I told you to ask young Metcalf to get cash for it. Between this room and Metcalf's desk you altered it to eighty pounds. It was easily done—especially by an expert like you. He brought you eighty pounds; you gave me eight, and kept seventy-two. You were aware that Metcalf was leaving the office that day to join his brother in Canada; you calculated that probably before the thing was discovered he would be on the high seas, and that, therefore, since everyone knew how much he was in want of cash, I should lay the guilt at his door—you dirty cur! But I didn't, never for one instant; the instant I saw the cheque I recognised your hand."

"You recognised my hand? What do you mean by that, sir?"

Mr. Patterson took something else out of his writing-table drawer, which, this time, he handed to his nephew.

"Look at that."

It was a portrait—the photograph of a man in the early prime of life.

"Don't you think it might be yours?"

Rodney felt that, allowing for the changes made by a few superimposed years, the resemblance to himself was striking, so striking that it was startling. The eyes looked at him out of the portrait with an expression which he recognised as so like his own that it bewildered him.

"That's the portrait of your father. You don't remember him?"

"Not at all."

"I knew him all his life. You are so like what he was at your age that more than once when I have looked at you I have had an uncomfortable feeling that he had come back again to haunt me. Never was son more like his father, in all things."

Rodney winced, scarcely knowing why. His uncle went on.

"Your mother never spoke to you of him?"

"Never."

"She had what she supposed to be sufficient reasons for her reticence; she wished to hide from you, if possible, the knowledge of what manner of man your father was, thinking that the knowledge of the heritage of shame which he had left behind might drive you to walk in his footsteps. I was of a different opinion. I held that if you had in you any of the makings of a decent man, the knowledge of the sort of man your father was would serve you as a warning to keep off the path he'd followed. However, you were your mother's child, not mine, thank God; she had her way, though I warned her that the time would probably come when I should have to tell you the story she would rather have bitten off her tongue than tell."

Mr. Patterson paused, keeping his eyes fixed on the young man in front of him. There was a quality in his gaze which made Rodney conscious of a sense of discomfort to which he had been hitherto a stranger.

"You are so like your father that you even have his Christian name. Rodney Elmore the first was one of those creatures who sometimes come into the world, who could not run straight if they tried—and they never try. He was one of Nature's thieves; a born scamp; a lifelong blackguard. Your mother was my only sister; the only relative I had. I did not understand him so well before she married him as I did afterwards, but I understood him well enough to have kept her from marrying him if I could. But he was one of those hounds who, if they cannot get what they want by fair means, will not hesitate to get it by foul; he even won his wife by foul means, taking advantage of her girlish innocence so that she had to become his wife to save her good name. She lived for six years with him in hell. Then he was detected in a series of frauds which would probably have resulted in his being sent to penal servitude for life. Rather than face the music, he committed suicide."

Again Mr. Patterson paused, and his nephew, on his side, kept still. It seemed to him that his uncle's voice was the voice of doom; he was aware of a sensation of actual physical pain as he listened, as if sentence had not only been pronounced, but punishment also begun. He had wondered vaguely more than once what manner of man his father was, and, since she had volunteered no information, had put questions on the subject to his mother. But she had staved them off in a fashion which suggested—since even in the days of his boyhood his mental processes were sufficiently acute—that there was not much to be told about him which redounded to his credit. So, as years brought wisdom, his curiosity became less and less; a feeling grew up in his bosom that perhaps the less he knew about his father the better it might be. Never, however, had his most pessimistic imaginings come near the reality as portrayed by his uncle. He, the son of a lifelong rogue, who had only escaped the penalty of his misdeeds by self-destruction! He began to apprehend the meaning of the attitude his uncle had taken up towards him. His uncle did his best to assist him to a clearer comprehension.

"I never would have anything to do with you. I had suffered too much from your father to be willing by any overt act to acknowledge your existence, especially as a relative of mine. I resented your existence. I am not more superstitious than the average man, but I had a strong conviction that with you it would be a case of like father like son. The paternal qualities were too strong, too ingrained, too much the very essence of his being not to be transmitted. When your mother came and begged me to take you into my office I asked her point-blank if you were not your father's son. She denied it. I believed then that she lied; now I know it. I have no doubt that she had detected you over and over again in acts which recalled your father."

Rodney wondered if that really was the case. She had never hinted anything of the sort to him. He understood now why, with her dying breath, she had entreated him to be honest. Did she realise at the very portals of death what a broken reed his promise was? He shivered at the thought.

"So soon as you came into this office I knew that I had been right, and that you were every inch your father's son. You are clever; don't suppose that I don't appreciate the fact. I am not so clever, which fact you have taken rather too much for granted. You have overlooked one quality I have, and that is—a nose for a thief. I owe to it a good deal of such success as I have had—in a sense, I can smell a thief so soon as he comes near me. Of course, in your case I had your father's record to help me; but I think that, without it, I should have scented you, your odour was so pungent. You had not been in the place a month before you began to play your little tricks. I do not flatter myself that I found you out in all of them, but I did in a good many. I said nothing, but I made a note of each, and have the complete record in a certain volume which will possibly be produced one day in a court of assize. Then there came the incident of the cheque—the eight pounds which you turned into eighty. When I saw that cheque I realised that immunity had given you courage, and that you were beginning to fly at higher game. I am, as I believe you and other gentlemen in the office are aware, a regular old fogey, a dray-horse sort of man. I never, if I can help it, arrive at a hasty decision. I put that cheque aside and waited; you see, although you live to the age of Methuselah, a thing like this is always up against you—you can never get away from it. I was in no hurry."

Again Mr. Patterson paused. Leaning back in his chair, he smiled. Rodney told himself that he resembled an ogre who was enjoying, in anticipation, the meal he proposed to make of him.

"After all, my lad, although you are so clever, you're a fool—indeed, your cleverness is folly. If you had to be dishonest, hadn't you sense enough to gratify your instincts on less dangerous lines? You have made a serious mistake in underrating me; perhaps that's because your experience of men is small. I've been watching you; you've been living in a fool's paradise—your conscience has never pinched you because you have never feared discovery. Yet, if you had troubled yourself to think, you must have known that, sooner or later, discovery was bound to come, and that, when it did, I had you. You were a fool, my lad, a fool."

The speaker's smile grew more pronounced. To his nephew's thinking it became more and more like an ogre's grin. But when he went on it not only vanished, but its place was taken by something which was unpleasantly like a snarl.

"Then my daughter came on the scene. There, again, you were at fault, because it so happens that I understand my daughter almost as well as you do. She may think herself romantic, but she isn't—there's no more romance about her than there is about me. She's a healthy, vigorous female animal, with her father's blood in her veins, and her father's fondness for the good things of this life of all sorts and kinds. She's seen little of men, especially young men, and I quite appreciate the fact that you're just the sort of young man at whose head she would fling herself—with a little delicate encouragement from you. But she won't, don't you make any mistake, my lad. I haven't forgotten how your father won your mother; and I promise you you shan't win my daughter in the same way. On the day on which I suspected you of any such intention you'd be branded as a gaol bird, and for the whole remainder of your life you'd be passing in and out of prison gates. I'm asking for no promise, being aware that you're one of Nature's liars, I know that not the least reliance is to be placed on any word you utter, but I'm giving you a promise. You can make any excuse to her you like—I'm sure you're a whale at excuses; if you ever speak to her again, even to tell her that you're not to speak; if you ever write to her; if you ever hold any communication with her whatever, you'll pass into the hands of the police, and I'll tell her your story and your father's. My girl has another thing in common with her father—she's honest, she hates a rogue. And if she knew that you were a common kennel thief, as your father was before you, she'd have no more truck with you if you were twenty times her husband, and I don't believe she'd move a finger to save you from penal servitude. I'm not going to turn you away; you're going to continue to occupy your present position in my office, so that I can keep my eye on you, so don't you try to turn tail and run. Now we understand each other. I have my morning letters to attend to, but I thought I'd better have this little explanation with you first. Now you can go; take my advice—if you can—steal no more. If you keep along the same path you'll find at the end what your father found, he was no more anxious to find it than you are—suicide."

CHAPTER IV

THE THREE GIRLS AND THE THREE TELEGRAMS

His uncle's words were in Rodney's ears for days afterwards. Was it conceivable that he, to whom life was so sweet a thing, could under any circumstances seek refuge in a suicide's grave? It was horrid that his father should have been that sort of man; it was hard on him. His mother ought to have told him; at least he would have been on his guard. No wonder his uncle had been prejudiced against him; had his mother not been so unkindly silent, he might—well, he might have framed his conduct, so far as his uncle was concerned, on different lines. How could he have guessed that his uncle was observing him with almost unnatural keenness; while, all the time, he supposed him to be purblind? It was a most unfortunate position for a young fellow to be placed in; a word from his mother would have been of such assistance. He was always reluctant to blame anyone; yet he could not but feel that his parents had not used him well; with that moral colour-blindness, which was one of his most striking characteristics, he was already beginning to lump them together, though he knew perfectly well, of his own knowledge, that, in all things, his mother had been the soul of honour.

He was most awkwardly placed as regards his cousin; he had engagements with her which he was aware she would resent his breaking; and her father had even forbidden him to explain. Not that he could think of any explanation which would meet the case from her point of view; she was apt to be quick-tempered where he was concerned, and he was most anxious to keep in with her; one never knew what might happen. He had been cramming up the subject of apoplexy, both from books, and from the lips of medical acquaintances; and he felt sure, from certain little things he had noticed, that it was quite possible that his uncle might have a stroke at any second; and, of course, if he did, the situation would be entirely altered. But, at the same time, that could not be counted on; and, in the meanwhile, there was Gladys both to consider and conciliate. Still, he managed; his dexterity in such matters was remarkable. He contrived that a communication should reach his cousin to the effect that her father had forbidden him to meet her, on pain of instant dismissal, and that, to save her from the paternal anger, he had promised that he would not even write to her. He counselled her, however, to be patient, expressing his conviction that this state of things was not likely to continue, and that before long they would be more than compensated for the brief period during which they would be separated one from the other.

Then he went to his uncle in his room at the office, and telling him, what was quite true, that Gladys had written asking for an explanation of his sudden cessation of their intimacy, requested him, for everybody's sake, since he had ordered him not to write to her, to inform her himself of the prohibition he had laid upon his nephew. This, grimly enough, Mr. Patterson undertook to do, and doubtless did. And for more than a fortnight Rodney Elmore had quite a dull time. Then a sequence of events came crowding on him so rapidly that within a period of some eight-and-forty hours the whole course of his life was changed.

The sequence began on a certain Saturday morning. Before he was yet out of his bedroom he was informed that Mr. Austin had called; and, indeed, the words were hardly spoken before Tom showed himself in. Rodney was unfeignedly glad to see him. He had always liked Tom, who was the antipodes of himself; a red-headed, freckle-faced, simple-minded youth, who was not likely to set the Thames on fire, and who, in fact, had no desires in that direction. He had "cut" college for a few days, but had to hurry back by an early train; which explained the matutinal hour he had chosen for a call. He brought news that Stella was in town, staying with some people over Kensington way; and suggested, as he rather thought that Stella found it dullish, that he should look her up, if possible that very afternoon, and take her somewhere. Rodney declared that he would be only too glad to have the chance; he would get away early from the office, and go straight to her, and would let her have a wire at once to let her know that he was coming.

Then, when they adjourned to breakfast, a meal at which the visitor expressed his readiness to assist, Tom volunteered the information that he had been down to see Mary Carmichael, who was staying with an aunt at Hove. She was quite well, was Mary, and, if anything, prettier than ever; and he rather thought that, at last, he had fixed things up with her. As he said this he flushed a red which was not at all the same shade as his hair.

"You know," he observed, "how she's always refused to take me seriously, and what a job I've had to get her to do it, and how she's always ragged me, pretending that I was too young to know my own mind, and all that sort of rot. Well, this time I rather fancy that I've convinced her that I do know my own mind; and, what's more, I fancy that I've found out what's in hers too. You know, she's always stuck out that she'd have nothing to say to me about—you know what, till I'd taken my degree. Of course, I ought to have taken the beastly thing ages ago; there's no need for anyone to tell me that; but this time I am going to do the trick—you see. Everyone will tell you that I've been working like blazes, and even my tutor has hopes. Mary as good as told me last night that if I once got the thing the banns could go up inside three months—honestly, she did. Of course, she was only laughing; you know how she does laugh at a fellow; but I believe she meant it, all the same. I say, this ham of yours is top hole; I'll have another whack."

While Tom helped himself to the other "whack," his friend said with a sigh:

"You're a lucky beggar to be able to think of marriage at your time of life."

"Don't I know it? For that I've got the pater to thank; he's been making more piles. All he really wants is that I should settle down; nothing would please him better than to see me married; he'd be almost as glad as I should to have Mary as a member of the family. Isn't it queer that while I've liked Mary all her life I've liked her more and more as time went on, until—well, if I do get her I shall have got all I want."

"Then, with all my heart, I hope you get her."

"I've decided hopes, old man—decided. I say, you know, Stella's not a bad sort, although I am her brother."

"Do you think that I don't know it?"

"You're the best pal I have in the world, and—I don't think she objects to you."

"Tom, dear old chap, don't say another word—please. I'm never going to ask a girl to marry me until I'm in a position to keep her as my wife should be kept."

"That's sound enough in a general way; but as regards this particular case it's all tuppence. Stella has money, and the pater, if properly worked, would supply more; I happen to know that he's quite willing she should marry anyone she likes, so long as it's a decent chap—and he knows you're that. Why, if it comes to that, he could slip you, as easy as winking, into a much better berth than the one you have at your uncle's."

"Tom, I know you're the best chum a man ever had, and one day I'm going to prove it. I haven't your happy knack of baring my heart, even to myself; I'm a more secretive kind of brute; but, like you, I have my dreams, and before very long I hope to have good news for you. But now, please, don't say anything more about it."

And Tom said nothing; he changed the subject to Oxford gossip, chattering away light-heartedly while Rodney glanced at the letters which the morning post had brought. Among them was one in a bold, slashing hand, which he knew well.

"90, Russell Square.

"Friday.

"DEAR OLD BOY,—The dad's gone off weekending without notice, and I never found out what he was going to do till it was too late to get at you, or I would have got; so here am I in this great mausoleum of a house all on my lonesome. To-morrow, early, I've an engagement with Cissie Henderson, but in the evening—and no nonsense, sir!—you'll have to dine me in some quiet place, where there are no prying eyes; and afterwards you can amuse me as you like. No excuse will be accepted; I want to spend to-morrow evening in your society, and I'm going to—and the dad can go hang! So mind you send me a wire directly you get this to let me know where I'm to meet you—at seven, sir!—and don't let there be any mistake about it. Until we do meet,

"Yours, G."

As he read this characteristic note of an up-to-date young woman a chord was touched somewhere in Rodney's being which made him conscious of a pleasant little thrill. Even while Austin chattered he was telling himself that he also would let the lady's "dad go hang," and that she should spend the evening in his society, be the consequences what they might.

When the visitor departed it was understood that Rodney would send a wire on his way to the office to let Stella know at what time she might expect him. Scarcely had Austin left the house than there came a telegram for Elmore. He opened it, supposing it to be from the impatient lady in Russell Square; but he was wrong. The message ran:

"Do come down to-morrow and cheer me up. Aunt is going out. I shall be alone. I have had Tom as companion for three whole days, so am in need of a tonic. Wire train. Be sure and come.

"MARY."

Mary? For a moment he wondered who Mary was. Then he saw that the message had been handed in at a Brighton post-office, and he understood. Mary? Mary was Mary Carmichael. At the thought of her his eyes sparkled and his spirits rose. After a fashion Mary Carmichael was the feminine creature in all the world that he liked best. Not only was she pretty, and dainty, and bright, and smart and clever, but just as Gladys Patterson appealed to him in one direction so Mary Carmichael did in another. Her telegram suggested what that direction was; in a way they were birds of a feather. Tom Austin had been her life-long admirer, slave, her avowed wooer; quite probably one day she would become his wife; yet she was not averse to being "cheered up" by his bosom friend, after confessing, by telegram, that she had been bored by three days of his society. Rodney chuckled at the thought of it; the thing seemed to him to be so amusing. Just now Tom had been telling him, with boyish candour, in single-hearted confidence in his integrity, that he had come away from Brighton under the impression that he was shortly to be made the happiest of men; and here was the girl who was to make him happy so anxious for an antidote to his society, begging him to do what Tom clearly had not done—cheer her up—and adding, as a peculiar inducement, that she would be alone. Poor old Tom! what a fool he was—and what a little minx was pretty Miss Mary!

On his way to the office Rodney sent three telegrams. One to Stella Austin, at Kensington, to say that he would be with her as near to two o'clock as possible, and that he hoped she would come out with him; one to Gladys Patterson, in Russell Square, asking her to meet him at a restaurant in Jermyn Street at seven sharp; one to Mary Carmichael, at Hove, informing her that he would arrive in Brighton to-morrow morning by the train due at noon. It was a female clerk to whom he handed these three messages; when she had scanned them she glanced up at him, as he felt, with a species of curiosity; he had a suspicion that she smiled.

CHAPTER V

STELLA

On the whole, Rodney Elmore spent a pleasant afternoon with Stella Austin. He took her to the Zoological Gardens, which was a place she liked. Beyond doubt she enjoyed herself immensely. She was very fond of animals, even of the most savage kind. In the wild-beast house, confronting the lions and the tigers, with Rodney at her side, she wondered, with a little shudder, what would happen if the creatures all got out. Drawing her arm in his, he pressed it closely; she liked that, too.

From his point of view, the pleasure with which she greeted him on his arrival at the house in Kensington was almost pathetic. He reproached her gently for not having told him she was coming to town. She replied that it had only been decided at the last moment, and that she was just going to write to him when Tom, appearing on the scene, offered to take the news in person. The way in which she took it for granted that he was as glad to see her as she was to see him appealed to his sympathy so strongly that he was nearly moved to take her in his arms and kiss her there and then. But he refrained. He never had kissed Stella, even in the old days. He had always had a feeling that a kiss would mean so much more to her than it did to him; indeed, that was one of her faults in his eyes, that everything meant so much more to her than it did to him. Often he would have liked to kiss her; having brought matters so much to a point at which a kiss was the next thing which might have been expected, he felt sure that she had expected it. But he kept himself sufficiently in hand to stop on the very edge, having it in his mind that it might be as well for him to be able, some day, if need be, to assert with truth that he had never gone beyond it.

Ordinarily he would have had no scruples on such a point. Oddly enough, in a sense, he was afraid of Stella, recognising in her an essential purity with which he himself had nothing in common. Her standard of life was so infinitely above his own that he was always conscious of a sense of strain after being some time in her company; it came from his attempting to sustain himself in the rarefied atmosphere in which she moved with ease. He would have been willing to hold her in his arms; he would have loved to; but he would not have liked to know that she was his superior in all essentials; and he would have to know. Sooner or later she might discover what kind of creature he was; but, though he believed that in such a plight she would keep her own counsel, none the less he would resent the discovery she had made.

Then, again, his taste in women was fastidious; he was not sure that she filled all his requirements. She was pleasant enough to look at; had pretty eyes, a fresh complexion, a tender smile—sometimes when she smiled he loved her so that it was all he could do to keep from committing himself utterly. But she was short and broad for her height; to his thinking her figure lacked dignity. He had the modern young man's notion that if you look at the mother you will see what the daughter is going to be. Mrs. Austin was plump and matronly; he feared that before long Stella would be the same. He did not care for matronly women; he liked them tall and slim. Then he was particular about the way in which a woman dressed; he liked those whom he favoured with his society, as he put it, to do him credit. He had felt, only too often, that Stella was almost dowdy; she was never really smart. Her clothes were good of their kind, but they suggested the provinces; or she had not the knack of showing them off to advantage. He liked a girl's foot to be cased in what he called a pretty stocking, and a smart shoe with a Louis heel; Stella wore serviceable shoes with low heels, and the plainest of stockings. With these things in his mind he had ventured, once, to hint that he would like to have the dressing of her. She had been silent for some seconds, and had then replied, scarcely above a whisper, and with downcast eyes:

"Perhaps one day you will."

He was perfectly conscious that that "one day" was the day of which she was always dreaming. He was not sure that he was so willing it should come as she was.

But that afternoon he was not disposed to be critical. He was really glad to see her. It was some time since they had met; he was nearly surprised to find what a jolly girl she was; her smile was unusually tender. As they quitted the monkey-house she spoke of Tom and Mary.

"Did Tom tell you that he has nearly brought that hard-hearted Mary of his to the promising point?"

"He did seem to be sanguine."

"Poor old Tom! I believe if she'd promise quite he'd pass straight off; it's anxiety which causes him to be ploughed. I've written to Mary telling her just what I think, and informing her that she's to keep him no longer suspended between heaven and earth, but that she's to marry him at once. Mamma wants it, papa wants it, I want it, Tom wants it—everybody wants it. She's the dearest girl in the world; but she's a goose."

"Because she hesitates?"

"Why should she? Tom will make her the best husband in the world—you know he will."

"Perhaps every girl doesn't want 'the best husband in the world.'"

"Are you trying to say something clever? If she has a husband, of course she does. Do look at those two in front; I've been watching them. She keeps putting out her hand to feel for his, or he puts out his to feel for hers. Do you think they're newly married?"

"Is that how you mean to behave when you're newly married?"

"It depends."

"On what?"

"Oh, it depends."

"You said that before. On what does it depend?"

Suddenly a glimpse he caught of the smile which lighted up her face started him off at a tangent— without waiting for her answer.

"It seems ages since I saw you last; it's awfully nice to see you again—especially as you're looking prettier than ever."

"Do you like this frock that I've got on? You ought to, I had it made specially for you—you are so critical about my clothes."

"Oughtn't a man to be critical about the girl he—he cares for?"

"Do you care for me?"

"You know I do."

"How much?"

"More than I—dare tell you."

"Rodney."

"Stella."

"I hope one day, before very long, you'll find courage enough."

The challenge was a direct one. In such matters he was such a creature of impulse that it set his pulses galloping. They had reached a spot where they had for sole society some queer-looking birds who peered at them through the wires which confined them to their runs.

"Stella, you mustn't tempt me. If you only knew what I'd give to be able to take you in my arms."

"Rodney, it isn't fair of you to talk like that. You say that sort of thing, and make me feel as if the world were whirling round and round, and then you go no farther."

"You know why I go no farther."

"I don't! I don't!"

As she turned and looked at him he saw how her cheeks were flushed; that tears were in her pretty eyes; how her lips were twisted as by physical pain. He really was so fond of her that the sight of her suffering moved him almost beyond endurance. Careless of spectators who might come at any moment to look at the birds, he took both her hands in his.

"Stella!"

He paused; he was conscious how pregnant with meaning the pause was to her, how she waited for his words. He let them come.

"Stella, will you be my wife?"

"You know I will! How long have you known it, sir? How long have you been aware that you had only to ask to have? I go all over shame when I think of it. I don't—I really don't—think you've used me quite fairly, sir. Because, you know, you oughtn't to keep on telling a girl that you care for her, and—then say nothing more. I've even sometimes wondered if you were playing with me—I have! Were you?"

"Never. How could you think it?"

"I had to think something, hadn't I? And—what could I think? Then you do really and truly care for me?"

"With the whole force of my being."

She drew a long breath, as if it were a sigh of pleasure.

"And you really and truly want me to be your wife?"

"As Tom said of Mary—if I get you I get all that I want in the world."

"Then, why didn't you try to get me before?"

"Stella, every man has his own standard. You have money; perhaps one day you'll have more; I have no money; perhaps I never may have. Under those circumstances, though I worshipped the ground you stood on, I had, and have, no right to ask you to be my wife. I have held out against the temptation to do so over and over again, but—I could hold out no longer. You must forgive me."

"For what? For having what you call 'held out'? I am not sure that I do. You can't have wanted me so very, very much, or you wouldn't have held out so long. That's what I feel."

"Stella, if you only knew!"

"And if you only knew!"

"The days I've thought of you, and the nights I've dreamed!"

"And do you suppose that I can't think—and dream?"

"Sometimes, after I've left you with the words unuttered, and thought of what I should feel if I had you in my arms, it was pretty hard to bear."

"Rodney!—I wonder if anyone is coming? After all your holding out, you have—chosen a funny place."

Heedless of anyone coming, he put his arm about her waist and drew her quickly to the comparative shelter of a fairly grown tree.

When Rodney Elmore had started out with Stella Austin nothing had been farther from his mind than any intention of asking her to be his wife. He was amazed to find, now that the thing was done, how pleasant it had been. The whole episode had been delightful—so delightful that he was loth to bring it to a close. The rubicon being passed, another Stella was revealed. The simple question he had put to her might have been some magic formula, so great a change had it wrought in the maiden. He had never credited her with the capacity to be so delicious; for she was delicious in a dozen unsuspected ways. He had been fond of her before he asked her to be his wife; in less than half an hour! afterwards he was in love with her. The new Stella had bewitched him; to such a degree that he would have been willing to stay with her in the Zoological Gardens for an indefinite period of time, had he not had a previous engagement. It was with a feeling of distinct disgust that he realised that he would have to tear himself away. Nor was the parting rendered easier by the lady's attitude. She could not be brought to see that any engagement was of such importance that, on that day of all days, he was forced to leave her so summarily. Nor would he have left her, could he have helped it. He assured her, with perfect truth, that he would have only been too happy to spend the evening with her at the house of her friends in Kensington, had he dared, but he did not dare. She asked him why, being now entitled to ask such questions. He did not tell her that it was because he was conscious that it might be almost more dangerous to disappoint his cousin than to rob her father. He fabricated instead an ingenious lie, which convinced her against her will.

Then there arose the question of the morrow. Being Sunday, of course he would be able to spend the whole of it with her. There, again, a previous engagement blocked the way. He explained that, never having anticipated the delightful footing on which he stood with her, he had made the engagement long ago. Would she have him break his word? It depended, she said, to whom his word was pledged; she did think that he might spend that first Sunday with her. Then he spun a yarn about an old friend of his mother who had begged him again and again to visit her, to whom he had promised to go at last. He knew that she had made all sorts of preparations for his reception; now, if he were to throw her over she would feel, with justice, that he had treated her very badly. He could not bear that she should feel that. She was his mother's dearest friend. Her name was Staples. She lived in a little village the other side of Dorking. Stella supposed that, anyhow, he would not have to stay there late. As to that, he could not say. The Sunday trains to Dorking were very awkward. But this he promised, at the earliest moment at which with decency he could get away, he would; and if the hour of his return to town were not frightfully late he would rush over to Kensington, if it were only for half a dozen words. But of this she might be quite certain; he would spend the whole of Monday evening with her if she would let him; he would come straight to her from the office.

So, finally, on that understanding, they parted; that he would come to her on Sunday, if only for a minute or two, and that, anyhow, he would revel in her dear society for so much of Monday as was left after his office work was done. But, for him, between that and Monday, the world was to be turned upside down.

CHAPTER VI

GLADYS

Hurry as he might, it was nearly half-past seven before Rodney Elmore reached that restaurant in Jermyn Street at which he was due at seven. The fault was Stella's. Had she not spun out the parting to such an unconscionable length, he would have been able to be there in time. But he could not explain this to Gladys Patterson, who had never heard of the girl. She rose, as he came in, from a seat in the vestibule, with a face which mirrored the anxiety she had felt.

"Whatever is the matter? I thought that something had happened, and you weren't coming."

"My dearest child, I've been the victim of a series of accidents; I was beginning to wonder myself if I should ever get here."

Then he told another lie—invented on the spur of the moment. He had not troubled to prepare one on the way; he was not sure of the mood in which he might find her; one story might suit one mood another another. With him, to lie was as easy as to breathe; he himself was often hardly conscious he was lying, he lied so like truth.

"So you see, I've been half off my head, and in a deuce of a stew. Perhaps you'll tell me what you'd have done in my position. But, thank goodness, I'm here at last. The worst of it is, I haven't ordered dinner, or reserved a table; we shall have to take pot-luck; let's hope that the table d'hôte is worth eating."

It so chanced that there was a table, and that the menu of the set dinner read quite well. Presently they were fronting each other at a little table in a corner of the room, each in the best possible frame of mind. She had forgotten the strain of waiting in her delight that he had come, while he was charmed to find her in so good a temper. Indeed, he seemed to be in the very highest spirits, and when he was that no one could be better company. Then the food was good; that was a point on which they both were excellent judges. On the occasion of that first dinner in Russell Square each had played on the other a pleasant comedy; to make a good impression on the strange cousin, who might have views on such matters, Gladys had drunk nothing but water, and, for some similar reason, Rodney had done the same. It was only when, later, they were on more intimate terms, that they learned that neither was a teetotaller. It was rather funny. As a matter of fact, so far as the pleasures of the table were concerned, Gladys was in very truth her father's child; not only could she appreciate good food well cooked, but she was by way of being a connoisseur of certain wines; and in such respects Rodney was an excellent second.

Before the dinner was half way through she was looking at him with something in her eyes which spoke to a similar something which was in his. He had forgotten the episode of the afternoon as if it had never been. This was the sort of girl he loved to have in front of him on the other side of a table—one who would eat what he ate, drink what he drank, do as he did; to whom he could say whatever he pleased. They joked on the subject of the absent Mr. Patterson.

"I wonder," she said, "what would happen if he walked in here at this very moment."

Rodney also wondered, for a second, in silence.

"For one thing, he'd spoil our evening, because he'd start you straight away off home."

"Would he? I should take some starting. I never am particularly afraid of him, and I'm not in the least when I've had two glasses of Montebello—rattling good bottle, this is. Thank you; that's the third. What beats me is why you're afraid of him. You don't strike me as being a person who's afraid of much. What would it matter if he did give you the key of the street, so far as his office is concerned? You'd easily find a better one. There's a mystery somewhere. Don't imagine, my dear old man, that I don't know so much. Why has he such an objection to you? And why are you so much in awe of him? Now's your time—out with it. Make a clean breast of it—between this glass and the next."

"I can't tell you why he objects to me, but I can assure you that I don't stand in awe of him."

"Rubbish! If you don't, why have you kept away from me in the way you have done?—you exasperating boy! I console myself with the reflection that if I'm losing your society you're losing mine; because I'll bet a trifle that you're just as fond of seeing me every other day or so as I am of seeing you."

"You're right there. If I saw you all day and every day I shouldn't mind."

"I'm not so sure of that; there's a limit. It might be all right for a time; but, my hat! wouldn't you get bored after a month of nothing else but my society!"

"What price you—after a month of nothing else but me?"

She seemed to reflect before she answered.

"You see, it's like this; if you and I were alone together for a month, or longer—"

"I'd be willing to make it longer."

"Would you?"

She looked at him with shining eyes.

"Rodney, you're a dear. If we were to be alone together for so long as that, we should have to alter the pace. I fancy that where a man and a woman are concerned it's the pace that kills."

"What do you mean by that, oh, wise one?"

"If you had one pound of chocs to eat you might gobble them down as fast as you please, and no harm would be done."

"You've tried it?"

"Perhaps! But if you had a ton you would have to go, oh so carefully, or you would be so sick. But we meet so seldom that when we do we want to gobble; I know that, so far as I am concerned, I want to get as much of you as I possibly can during the short time we are together."

"Same here—only more so."

They smiled at each other across the little table. Then, glancing down, she transferred her attention to what was on her plate.

"But, of course, if we weren't to part for a month—or more—it would be different."

"True, oh, queen! And suppose we were to marry!"

"I don't think I'd mind."

"I'm pretty nearly sure I shouldn't."

"That's very sweet of you to say so. Only—there's dad!"

"There's very much dad!"

"He can forbid my seeing you, and that kind of thing, if he pleases; and if he finds out that I've been disobedient he'll make himself extremely disagreeable. Still, I fancy I could manage him. But if I were to marry you against his wishes, I don't believe I'd ever get another penny from him, living or dead; and as you have no immediate promise of becoming a millionaire, that would be awkward for both of us."

"It would. All the same, don't you think it would be comfy if we were secretly engaged—in the event of anything happening to him?"

"What's going to happen?"

"Anything—living the sort of life he does."

"Are you hinting that there's anything the matter with his health?"

"My dear girl, you've only to use your eyes to be aware that a doctor would tell him that he's the kind of man who ought to swear off everything. And does he?"

"You make me feel all shivery. You talk as if you expected him to die right off."

"We've all had sentence of capital punishment pronounced against us, and, though we don't know when it will be put into execution, in such a case as his it's possible to guess that it mayn't be very long postponed."

"Rodney! I don't like to hear you talk like that. He's fond of asking me questions about you; I hate telling lies; if we were engaged, and he were in one of his cross-examining moods, I might find myself in a fix."

He played with his knife while a waiter was bringing another course.

"Consider something else. Let me put a hypothetical case. Suppose a girl were to make a dead set at me, I might like to be able to tell her that I'm engaged already."

"Who's the girl?"

"The girl, like the case, is hypothetical; but I can conceive of circumstances in which I should like to feel that we were engaged."

"You've changed your mind. A short time ago you were all the other way."

"I've been considering matters. Say, for example, that your father puts his foot down, and that we don't see each other again for an indefinite period. Do you not think that then I should not like to feel that we were engaged?"

"You can feel that we're engaged all you want to, without our setting it down in black and white. Aren't you as sure of me as if I were your wife already? Don't you know that if circumstances permitted I would become your wife? Do you wish me to understand that I'm not as sure of you?"

"Gladys, you're a goose. So far as I'm concerned, I'm inclined to the opinion that I'd like you to be my wife to-night."

"It's you who are the goose. As if we didn't understand each other far too well to render it necessary to have things placed on a ceremonious footing. We can do without formulas."

CHAPTER VII

MARY

On the Sunday Rodney Elmore kept his engagement with the third young woman, with the punctiliousness on which, in such matters, he prided himself. He went down to Brighton on the Pullman, Limited, and was met at the station by Mary Carmichael. He exclaimed, at sight of her:

"You angel!—to come and meet me!"

"I'm not quite sure that I did come to meet you, in the strict sense. I'd nothing to do; I've always a feeling that the queerest lot of people come by this train, the oddest sort of week-enders—didn't you notice how the platform reeked of perfume?—so that its arrival's generally worth seeing. Besides, between ourselves, I'd a kind of notion that Tom might come by it. If he had I should have ignored you utterly, and should have explained that something within told me he was coming, and that was why I was here. Wouldn't he have been enraptured?"

As he listened—and, in his observant way, took in the details of her appearance—Rodney was conscious, not for the first time, of how beneficent Providence had been in making girls in such variety. Stella, emblematic of the domestic virtues; Gladys, for physical pleasure; Mary, suggestive of the arch in the sky, which, though a man may walk for many days, he shall never find the end of. To his thinking she was as many-tinted as a rainbow; as beautiful, as elusive. He doubted if the average man were her husband whether he would have any but the dimmest comprehension of her at the finish; she had a knack of surprising even him. He had known her a good long time, yet he admitted to himself that in many respects she was still wholly beyond his comprehension, and he prided himself, not without reason, on his gift for understanding persons of the opposite sex.

They went down towards the Hove lawns in a fly, and were still in Queen's Road when she said:

"So you've done it at last."

He turned towards her as if a trifle startled.

"Done what?"

"Asked Stella to be your wife."

"How on earth do you know that?"

"My simple-minded babe, aren't I the very dearest friend Stella has in the world? And didn't she, directly you left her yesterday afternoon, send me a telegram conveying the news? Do you think she would keep it a moment longer than she could help from me, especially as she is perfectly well aware that I've been on tip-toe for it for goodness alone knows how long? And aren't I expecting a letter of at least half a dozen pages to-morrow morning to tell me all about it? I wired my congratulations to her at once, and I almost wired them to you; then I thought I'd keep them till you came this morning. My congratulations, Rodney, dear."

He was more taken aback than he would have cared to own. What an idiot he had been! Had he had his senses about him he would have given Stella to understand that the new relationship between them must be kept private till it suited him to make it public. That she should have telegraphed to Mary the moment he had left her! Could anything be more awkward? If to Mary, why not to others? To her mother, her father, her brother, her cousins, and her aunts; and she had crowds of dearest friends. Possibly by now the news was known to fifty people; they would spread it over the face of the land. Had he foreseen such a state of things he would have torn his tongue out rather than have said what he did in Regent's Park. Imbecile that he was; he had forgotten altogether that that was just the tale a girl of a sort loves to tell. Had he had his wits about him he might have known that she would be all eagerness to proclaim her happiness to her friends. To have had a private understanding with Stella might have been fun. He might have lied to her; played the traitor; done as he pleased—it would not have mattered if her heart was broken so long as she suffered in silence. But the affair assumed quite a different complexion if her confounded relations were to have their parts in it. He would have to endure all kinds of talkee-talkee from her mother. That oaf Tom might want to thrust his blundering foot into what was no concern of his. Worst of all, there was her father. Rodney was quite certain that he would want to regularise the position at once; that he himself would be helpless in his hands. Mr. Austin would require a clear statement of his intentions; having got it, he would see that it was adhered to. Being opposed to long engagements, he would want to fix the wedding day—and he would fix it. Rodney was uncomfortably conscious that he had made such a conspicuous ass of himself that, being delivered into her father's strong hands, almost before he knew it he might find himself the husband of Stella Austin.

He shuddered at the thought—a fact which was observed by the young lady at his side.

"Whatever is the matter? You shook the fly! You haven't thanked me for my congratulations, nor do you seem so elated as I expected. You know I'm not sure that it was quite nice of you to propose to another girl on the very day before the one on which you knew you were coming down to me. For all you could tell, I was expecting you to propose to me."

"If I'd only thought there was the slightest chance, wouldn't I have loved to."

"I suppose for the sake of practice."

"Well—there are girls with whom one would like to practice love-making."

"That's a nice thing to say, and you an engaged man of less than four-and-twenty hours' standing. There's a taximeter—stop him! Pay the driver of this silly old cab and let's get into the taxi."

The transfer was effected, the driver of the "silly old cab" expressing himself on the subject with some frankness. When they were in the taxi the lady set forth the idea which had been in her mind.

"I don't want to go on to the horrid lawns and see the stupid people in their ugly dresses; I can't take you to aunt's house, because, as you know, she's away, and I don't want the servants to talk; I don't want to lunch at either of the hotels, because I hate them all; I do want to go where we can be all by ourselves, so I suggest the Devil's Dyke. This taxi will romp up; it's the most vulgar place I know, so we go where we please and do as we choose—everybody does up there."

So it was the Devil's Dyke. The taxi did "romp up." They had lunch at the hotel, and afterwards went out on to the downs, Rodney carrying a rug which he had borrowed from the hotel over his arm. They had not to go far over the slopes before they had left the few people who were up there behind, and were as much alone as if they had the world to themselves. Rodney spread the rug on the grass at the bottom of one of those little hollows shaped like cups which are to be found thereabouts by those who seek. On it they reclined; the gentleman lit a cigar, the lady a cigarette. They were as much at home with each other as either could desire. Their conversation was frankness itself.

"When I feel like liking it," observed the lady, "this is just the sort of thing I do like. You're engaged, and I'm engaged, so we ought to be nice to each other. Do you mind my kissing you?"

"Not a bit."

She leaned over and kissed him on the lips, he removing his cigar to enable her to do it. Then she blew her cigarette smoke in his face and laughed. He said nothing; he was thinking that there was a good deal to be said for being on such terms with three nice girls. After all, there might be something in the Mohammedan's idea of paradise. She was silent for a moment; then inquired:

"Why did you ask Stella after all? Because you knew she'd like you to?"

He considered his reply.

"No; not altogether. Of course, at the beginning I never meant to, then all of a sudden I felt as if I had to. I had a sort of feeling that it would be such fun."

"And was it fun?"

"Distinctly; I wouldn't mind going through it all over again."

"Wouldn't you? Now you'll have to marry her."

"Shall I?"

"Don't you want to marry her?"

"I do not."

"That's unfortunate, because you certainly will have to."

"We'll see."

"Stella'll see—or, rather, her family will. If it were any other but the Austin family I should have said that a person of your eel-like slipperiness—"

"Thank you."

"Might have wriggled away; but if you wriggle away it will be out of the frying-pan into the fire. For ever so long the family has been expecting you to ask Stella to marry you; you've fostered the expectation, and now that you have asked her, if you try to sneak out of your engagement, Mr. Austin will make things so uncomfortable that you'll find it easier to make Stella Mrs. E."

"And do you want to marry Tom?"

"I do not. All the same, I expect I shall."

"Why? If you don't want to?"

Miss Carmichael sent a cloud of smoke up into the air.

"A girl's position is so different from a man's. I must marry someone, and, so far as I can see, it may as well be Tom."

"Why must you marry someone?"

"Don't be absurd! Can you conceive me as a spinster? Rather than be an old maid I'd—marry you; I can't say anything stronger."

"You've a friendly way of paying compliments."

"My dear young fellow; as a—chum, when I'm in the mood, you're ripping, simply ripping; but as a husband—good Lord, deliver us! If Stella understood you only a quarter as well as I do she'd be only too glad to let you go the very first moment you showed the faintest inclination to bolt."

"And, pray, what sort of wife do you think you'll make?"

Again a pause, while more cigarette smoke went into the air.

"Depends on the man."

"I presume to what extent you can fool him."

"I can imagine a man to whom I would be all that a wife could be, the whole happiness of his whole life."

"I can't."

"That's because you don't understand me as well as I do you."

"What sort of wife do you think that you'll make Tom?"

"Oh, he'll be content."

"Poor devil!"

"I'm not so sure; it's a good thing to be content. Each time I put my arms about his neck he'll forgive me everything."

"So far as I gather, the difference between me as a husband and you as a wife consists in this: that while I'm going to be found out, you're not. I don't see why you should be so sure of the immunity you refuse to me."

"I admit that in this world one never can be sure of anything. I quite credit you with as much capacity to throw dust in a woman's eyes as I have to throw dust in a man's. Still, there is a difference between us of which I'm conscious, though just now I'm too lazy to attempt an exact definition. I really can't see why you object to Stella; she'll make you a good wife."

"Hang your good wives!"

"My child! Do you want a bad one? You should have no difficulty in being suited."

"Is a sinner likely to be happy if mated to a saint?"

"Would he be happier if mated to another sinner? In that case you might do well to marry me—which I doubt."

"I don't. I'm disposed to think that ours would be an ideal union."

"I wonder."

"Neither would expect the other to be perfect; each would allow the other a wider range of liberty for purely selfish reasons."

"I say, wouldn't it be rather a joke if you were to throw over Stella and I were to throw over Tom and we were to marry each other?"

"I'd do it like a shot if it weren't for one drawback—that we both of us are penniless."

"That is a nuisance, since we are both of us so fond of what money stands for. If you had five thousand a year perhaps I might marry you after all."

"I'm sure you would."

"Pray why are you sure? You've a conceit!"

"I am sure."

"If—I say if—I were to marry you, would you give me a good time?"

"The very best—a time after your own heart."

"Would you? Lots of frocks?"

"All the frocks your soul desired."

"Everything I wanted?"

"That's a tall order. I'm only human."

"That certainly is true. I shouldn't be surprised if you were more generous even than Tom."

"I don't call that sort of thing generosity. A man gives things to a woman he cares for because he has a lively sense of favours to come."

"That's candid. You've given me one or two trifles already. Has that been with a lively sense of favours to come?"

"Perhaps."

"You wretch! Would you care for me a little?"

"I care for you more than a little now, as you are perfectly well aware."

She turned and whispered something in his ear. He smiled, but kept silent. Presently she said aloud:

"It would be rather a joke if we were to marry. Now that the idea's got into my head I can't get it out again. It makes little thrills go all over me—dear little thrills. I hope that if ever you do marry me it will be before I have had to resort to any of women's aids to beauty. I should like you to have me just as I am, while I am really at my best and while I can still bear the most searching investigation. My complexion's my own; I use no powder, rouge, or pencil. I haven't a false tooth in my head or even a stopped one. I've only a weeny pad on the top of my head, which is rendered absolutely necessary by the present style of hairdressing—everything about me's true."

"Outside."

"Sir! I dare say we shouldn't make such a very bad pair. Would you—like to marry me?"

"Given an assured position, I would marry you."

"Well, then, I'll tell you what we might do. You might marry Stella, and—dispose of her with some nice painless thing like chloral; and I might marry Tom, and—delicately dispose of him. Then we should both of us have an assured position, and—we could marry."

"There's more in the idea than meets the eye."

She threw the fag-end of her cigarette away from her and laughed.

"You're simply ripping!" she exclaimed.

Rodney Elmore returned by the 9.10 to town. He had meant to travel by the Pullman, but as he entered the station the train was drawing clear of the platform. Being informed that another express was starting in ten minutes, he had to be content with that. Beyond doubt the Pullman had been crowded; as he found himself the sole occupant of a first-class carriage, he was inclined to think that he had not lost by the exchange. He was in a mood for privacy. Events had followed each other so quickly; he had so many things to consider that he was glad of an opportunity for a little solitary self-communion. He was not pleased, therefore, when, just as the signal had been given to start, someone came rushing along the platform, the door was thrown open by an officious guard, and a passenger was hoisted into his compartment while the train was already in motion; nor was his pleasure enhanced by the discovery that the intruder was his uncle, Graham Patterson. In such disorder had Mr. Patterson been thrown that it was some seconds before he even realised that he had a companion. Uncovering, he wiped first his brow, then the lining of his hat. He panted so for breath that his critical nephew said to himself that if he had run a little further, or even a little faster, he might have panted in vain; he had never seen a man in such difficulty with his breathing apparatus. His face was purple, his eyes seemed to be bulging out of their sockets.

The train had passed Preston Park station before Mr. Patterson had sufficiently recovered himself to become alive to the fact that he was not alone. But that he still did not recognise his companion his words showed.

"I'm not exactly—of the build—to—run after trains."

The moment he spoke Rodney became aware that Mr. Patterson had been drinking. Not enough, perhaps, to affect his speech—the hyphenated form of the remark he had just made was owing to the trouble he still had to breathe—but sufficient to place him at the point which divides the drunk from the sober. Elmore was still; possibly because he was unwilling to spoil what he felt was the grim humour of the situation. His silence apparently struck the other as odd. Presently Mr. Patterson glanced round as if to learn what manner of person this was who offered no comment on his observation. Then he perceived who his companion was.

The discovery seemed to fill him with amazement which approached to stupefaction. His jaw dropped, his eyes bulged still farther out of his head, his face assumed a darker shade of purple; he looked like a man who was on the verge of a fit. His nephew felt that he had never seen him present so unprepossessing a spectacle. His surprise was so great that an appreciable space of time passed before he could find words to give it expression. Then they were of a lurid kind.

"By gad!—it's you! Well, I'm damned!"

"I'm sorry, sir, to hear it."

The retort was so obvious that it had slipped from Rodney's lips almost before he was aware. Its effect on Mr. Patterson was so great that for some moments his nephew was convinced that that apoplectic fit which he had so often seen threatening was hideously close. Mr. Patterson himself seemed conscious of the risk he ran. He made a perceptible effort to regain self-control—a painful one it evidently was. He put his finger to his collar as if to loosen it; one could see that his hand shook, his lips trembled, beads of sweat stood on his brow. Probably more than a minute had passed before he felt himself in a condition to speak again. Still his voice was a little hoarse, his utterance not quite clear.

"My lad, if I could have got at you this morning I should have killed you."

"Should you, indeed, sir. Pray why?"

The young man had been observing his senior's plight with a sense, not only of amusement, but of positive relish. He was conscious that a spirit of malice had entered into him. He was prepared to return insolence with insolence. This bloated relative of his should this time not find him disposed to cringe.

Still with his finger to his neck, as if he would have liked to loosen his collar, Mr. Patterson went on, yet a little huskily:

"Luckily I didn't get at you, because I'll do worse than kill you, now."

"I thank you for your kind intentions, sir. You have not yet told me what I have done to deserve them."

"You've been getting at that girl of mine again."

"You use unpleasant phrases, sir. I'm afraid you have been drinking."

"You young swine! In spite of what I told you, last night you took her out with you again to dinner."

"Premising that I don't see why you should so resent my showing little courtesies to members of your family, may I ask on what grounds your statement is based?"

"You young word-twister! You've your father's tongue. Do you deny it?"

"That I've my father's tongue?"

"That you took my girl to dinner?"

"It's for you to prove; not for me to disprove."

"A man came to me on the front this morning and said that he saw my daughter dining last night in Jermyn Street with a young man. He described the fellow; from his description I knew that it was you. If I could have got at you then and there I'd have broken my stick across your back! I'd have—I'd have— Are you going to tell a lie, and say it wasn't you?"

"It was."

"It was?"

"It was. Why not? We had a most agreeable evening, much more agreeable, perhaps, than you have any notion of. Possibly, if you ask Gladys, she herself will tell you so."

"You—you—!"

"Steady—go slow! If you don't take care you'll have a fit—you know you have been drinking."

Possibly because he had given way to such a sudden access of rage, Mr. Patterson again went through all his former disagreeable physical experiences, while his nephew smiled. He sat inarticulate and gasping, incapable alike of speech or movement. When, after a prolonged interval, the faculty of speech returned, his voice had grown huskier than ever; he spoke slowly, with a pause between each word.

"All right, my lad—laugh, but you won't laugh last. You're not going to put me in the cart, as your swindler of a father did; I'm going to put you there. I warned you what would be the result of your attempting to have any more traffic with my girl, so you've yourself to thank for whatever happens."

He stopped, as if he found a difficulty in saying much at once. When he continued, while his tones were a little clearer, they were more bitter.

"Directly I get home I'm going to tell my girl what kind of man you are, and what kind of man your delectable father was. When she knows, I'll wager you a trifle that she never willingly speaks to you again; she'll despise herself for ever having spoken to you at all; she'll treat you in the future as if you had never been. She has her faults, but she resembles her father on one point—she has no use for a thief, and especially for a thief who is the son of a thief."

Another pause; this time, apparently, not so much for the sake of gaining breath as to enable his words to have their full effect on the smiling young man at the other end of the carriage. If he looked for some sign of their having touched him on a sensitive spot, he found none; the young man continued to smile. Possibly because he suspected that it might be the other's intention to irritate, he kept himself the more in hand. Leaning back in his seat, laying his parti-coloured silk handkerchief across his knee, for the first time he wore an appearance of ease, and he also began to smile.

"However, since I'm a cautious man, and you never can be certain what trick a blackguard will play upon a girl, I'll make assurance doubly sure; I'll take steps which will render it impossible for you to play a trick on my girl. The first thing to-morrow morning I'll take out a warrant for your arrest as a forger and a thief, and I'll give instructions to have it executed at once; so, you see, I'm better than my word, as I generally am. I warned you that if you dared to force yourself upon my girl again I'd have you gaoled, and I will. But I didn't undertake to give you a chance to show the police a clean pair of heels; yet I'm giving you one. If, between this and to-morrow morning—say, at ten—you can make yourself scarce, you can. But you'll have to be spry, because I give you my word that if the police do let the scent go cold it won't be for want of my urging them after you. You may run to earth if you like, but they'll dig you out. Don't you flatter yourself on your dodging powers; they'll get the handcuffs on your wrists."

Picking up his handkerchief with his finger-tips, Mr. Patterson let it fall again across his knee, smiling broadly as if in the enjoyment of a joke.

"And don't you flatter yourself that you'll come under the First Offenders Act—you won't, I'll take care of that. I've a list locked up in a drawer at the office the details of which, when they are produced in court, will surprise you. No jury will recommend you to mercy after hearing that, and no judge will listen to them if they do. You'll be sentenced to a long term of imprisonment as sure as you are sitting there. You'll be branded as a felon for the rest of your life. I'll teach you, you thief, to try to associate as an equal with that girl of mine."

Again he picked up his handkerchief; on this occasion to wipe his lips. But this time he did not return it to his knee; he continued to hold it in his hand—indeed, he waved it affably towards Elmore.

"I owed your father one—such a one! But he never gave me a chance of paying him. Now I owe you one—also such a one—and I'll pay you both together—by gad, I will! Oh, you may keep on smiling, you brassbound blackguard; I hope you'll find the reality as amusing as you seem to find the prospect. When you feel a policeman's hand upon your shoulder and handcuffs on your wrists, then you'll stop smiling. Make no mistake; for you there's only one way of escape, and that's your father's—suicide."

Stopping, Mr. Patterson thrust his handkerchief into the outer breast-pocket of his coat in such a fashion that the hem protruded. There was silence, broken only by the rushing noise made by the train. All at once Rodney Elmore, rising, moved along the carriage and placed himself on the seat immediately in front of his uncle.

CHAPTER IX

THE SECOND

Mr. Patterson glared at his nephew as if he had been guilty of a gross liberty in placing himself where he had done—indeed, he said as much.

"Go back to your own end of the carriage at once, you young scoundrel. How dare you come so close to me? Isn't it sufficient contamination to have to breathe the air of the same compartment, without being polluted by your immediate neighbourhood?"

Rodney was not at all abashed, nor did he show any sign of an intention to return whence he came. On the contrary, leaning a little forward, he smiled at his uncle blandly.

"Softly, sir, softly! If you allow yourself to become excited you may do yourself a mischief—excitement is the worst possible thing for you."

"None of your insolence, you young hound; don't you think I'll allow you to be insolent to me! Are you going back to the other end of the carriage?"

"No, sir; I am not."

"Then—"

Mr. Patterson made as if to move, then checked himself. Rodney asked:

"What were you going to do?"

"If you don't go back to the other end of the carriage at once I'll pull the communication cord and stop the train."

"And then?"

"I'll give you into custody before the whole trainful of passengers."

"Into whose custody?"

"The guard will take charge of you till we get to a station; he won't let you go till he has seen you safe in the hands of a policeman. You won't have a chance of running; you'll sleep in gaol tonight. Are you going back to your own seat?"

"I propose to remain where I am."

"Then I'll stop the train!"

He made as if to do as he said, but Rodney, rising first, laid his hand upon his shoulder to such effect that he found himself unable to move. Indignation brought back the purple to Mr. Patterson's face.

"You dare to touch me? You infernal young villain—take away your hand!"

"I don't intend to allow you to touch the communication cord."

"You don't intend! We'll see about that."

They did see, on the instant. The black knob of the alarm bell was over the centre seat in front of Mr. Patterson. Putting out his strength, evading Rodney's grip, he gained his feet. Elmore took him by the shoulders with both his hands. There was a scuffle—sharp, but brief. For a moment it looked as if the elder man might be a match for the younger, but for a moment only. On a sudden Mr. Patterson collapsed on to his seat as if the stiffening had gone all out of him and left him but a mass of boneless pulp. He could only gasp out words.

"You shall smart for this!"

"If you're not very careful, sir, you'll smart first—my dear uncle."

"Don't you call me your dear uncle."

"My dear uncle."

"Damn you, you—"

A flood of vituperation poured from the elder man's lips, which, when he had finished, left him an even darker shade of purple. Rodney never ceased to smile. So soon as the flood had stopped he repeated the endearing form of address.

"My dear uncle"—Mr. Patterson was panting, for the moment he was speechless—"turn and turn about's fair play, and fair play's a jewel. You've had your say, now I'm going to have mine—you'll find mine as interesting as I found yours. To begin with, I'm going to ask you one or two questions."

"I'll answer no questions of yours."

"Oh, yes, you will, when you find what they are. In the first place, am I to understand that you are really serious—weigh your words, my dear uncle!—in saying that you'd tell Gladys—what you said you'd tell her?"

"So soon as I get home I'll tell her everything—everything—about you, and your rascally father, too."

"Will you?"

"I will—as sure as you are living!"

"So surely as that? And are you prepared to take your oath that you'll take out that warrant you were speaking of, or—was that intended for a jest?"

"Oath! I'll take no oath to you—you Nature's gaol-bird! But of this I assure you, you'll sleep in a prison cell to-night, and many and many another night to come."

Mr. Patterson, dragging the silk handkerchief from his breast pocket, used it to wipe away the perspiration which again bedewed his brow.

"Shall I?"

"You will."

"Oh, no, I won't; nor will you tell Gladys those unkind things about me and my father."

"Who the devil's going to stop me?"

"I'm the devil who's going to stop you."

Rodney was leaning a little forward. His uncle stopped in the process of wiping his brow to stare at him, as if there were something in his manner which struck him as peculiar. About the young gentleman's lips was the same easy, unconcerned smile which had been there all the time; there was a smile also in his eyes—it was, apparently, this latter which gave him the odd expression which had struck his uncle. Mr. Patterson glanced about him as if in search of something he would have liked to find. Rodney sat perfectly still. As he put a query to him his uncle's pursy lips showed a tendency to twitch.

"How are you going to stop me?"

"Can't you guess how I am going to stop you?"

"I can do nothing of the kind. You can't stop me, or anyone. I am going to do my duty to my daughter and to society, and nothing can stop me."

"You know better than that. From something which has just come upon your face I can see that already you know better."

Mr. Patterson gave what he doubtless meant to be a spring towards the alarm bell opposite; but, for reasons which were beyond his control, his movements were slower than they should have been—the younger man was much too quick for him. Gripping him again by both his shoulders, exerting greater strength than on the first occasion, he forced him back upon his seat with a degree of violence which seemed to drive the sense half out of him. As Rodney, remaining on his feet, stood towering above him, one perceived more clearly that his was the build of the athlete, and how great were the probabilities, if they came to grips, that the big man would be helpless in his hands. He addressed his uncle as an elder person might have spoken to a mutinous child.

"My dearest uncle—you really must permit me to lay stress upon your avuncular relationship on what will probably be my last chance of doing so—you are not going to pull the alarm bell, you are not going to stop the train. You have no more chance of doing either than you have of flying to the moon, so get that into your drink-sodden brain. Nor are you going to libel me to Gladys, nor commit me to the mercy of a ruthless police. Presently you will see that as clearly as I do now."

Rodney resumed his seat, still keeping his glance fixed on his uncle, in whose demeanour a change seemed to have taken place which was both mental and physical. Possibly his nephew had used more violence than he supposed. The vigour had gone all out of him; inert, he stared at Rodney with bloodshot eyes, as if drink had taken sudden effect and bemused his brain. The young man's smile became more pronounced, as if he found the singularity of the other's appearance amusing. The tone of his voice, when he spoke, was genial and pleasant.

"My dear uncle, if you, the only relative I have in the world, had treated me, when first I entered your office, as you might have been expected to do, I might have become an affectionate and worthy nephew."

"Not you. You started robbing me before you'd been in the place a week."

"Is that so? So soon as that? Perhaps you have never known what it is to be in want of ready cash."

"When I was eighteen I was keeping myself on fifty pounds a year, for which I was working anything up to sixteen hours a day."

"Indeed! It might have been better if that period of your life had lasted longer. You wouldn't have been in the rotten condition you are."

"What's the matter with my condition? I never had a day's illness in my life."

"My dear uncle, if you weren't in a rotten condition you'd have rung that alarm bell before this, wouldn't you? But, although it's only within a foot or two, you'll never ring it—never, because you are rotten."

Mr. Patterson glanced towards the black knob. Rodney shook his head.

"It's no good, uncle. You won't be able to get at it—you know that. What an illustration you are of the desirability of keeping oneself fit! It seems that from the first you kept a sharper eye on me than I suspected."

"I'm not the fool you took me for."

"Aren't you? That remains to be seen. Do you think that it was the part of wisdom to threaten me as you have been doing when you and I were alone together in a compartment of a railway train which doesn't stop, at least, till it gets to Croydon?"

"I've not been threatening you; I wouldn't condescend. I've only been telling you what you may expect."

"That's all; and by doing so you've made the issue a simple one. If you reach town alive, to all intents I shall be dead; whereas, if you reach town dead, I—shall be on velvet, because you see, my dear uncle, I'm Gladys' lover; and she loves me, if possible, even more than I do her. I've proofs of it. Since she is your only child, when you are dead everything you have will be hers, which is tantamount to saying that it will be mine, which is just what I should like. So you will at once perceive how—from every point of view—very much to my advantage it would be that you should be dead."

"You young hell-hound! Unfortunately for you, I'm not dead, and I'm not likely to die."

"Oh, yes, you are, very likely—unfortunately for you. You told me that my father only found one way to escape trouble—suicide. You hinted in your most affectionate manner that some time, in my turn, I might only find one way. Your kindly hint made such an impression on me that I actually made preparations, so that I might never be at a loss if ever that time should come. Those preparations are contained in this dainty little box."

Rodney took from his waistcoat pocket what might have passed as a silver needle-case or receptacle for pins. He held it out in front of his uncle, who was as much moved by the sight of it as if it had been some object of horror.

"You—you're not going to make away with yourself before my eyes? You—you don't suppose I'll let you do it?"

"How would you propose to stop me?"

Again Mr. Patterson mopped his brow with his silk handkerchief of many colours. He presented a pitiable spectacle. His lips twitched, his hand trembled, and his whole huge frame seemed to shiver like a mass of jelly. His voice was broken and husky, he stammered in his speech.

"Elmore, you—you're quite right; I'm—I'm not very well. I—I've had a great deal to put up with lately, and it's unhinged me. Give me that infernal thing you've got there—I don't know what is in it, or if you're playing a trick with me, but—you give it me."

"I'm going to—shortly."

The young man's airy self-possession was in almost painful contrast to the elder's agitation. He glanced at his watch, holding the slender, round case between the finger and thumb of his other hand.

"Nearly half-past nine. What was that station we passed? Was it Hayward's Heath? I fancy we do stop at Croydon, so that there's not much time to spare. I'm going to act on your suggestion, uncle—with a difference. I am not going to commit suicide, but you are!"

"I am?—you young fool!—what do you mean?"

"In fact, you practically have committed suicide already."

"The man's mad."

"Possibly—but not on this particular point. When you told me in such very coarse language what I might expect, you practically committed suicide, as—I'm about to prove. You remember the case of the eminent financier who, within five minutes of being sentenced to a long term of penal servitude, was in a room which was immediately outside the court in which he had received his sentence, from which he was instantly to be haled to gaol, under the very noses of his warders slipped something between his lips and—escaped. You will probably remember the case better than I do, since at the time I was only a boy; yet I have studied it to such purpose that within this pretty little box are—shall we call them tabloids?—which are in all essentials identical with the one he swallowed. They kill as by a flash of lightning. Whoever has one of these within his reach no man shall stay him from—escaping. You are going to swallow one of these tabloids, uncle—this one."

Unscrewing the top of his silver box, Rodney removed the cap, and took from it what looked like a small peppermint lozenge, holding it up between his finger and thumb.

"You see, uncle—this one; as it were, death reduced to its lowest possible denomination."

At that moment Rodney seemed to be exercising over his uncle some of the fabulous qualities attributed to the serpent. Beyond doubt Mr. Patterson recognised with sufficient vividness that this young man in front of him was much more dangerous than he had supposed; that he had underrated his capacity for evil; that he might as well have shut himself in with a tiger as with his sister's son. But the recognition came too late. The very force of it had the effect of destroying his few remaining powers of volition. In face of the deadly purpose with which he perceived that his nephew was filled, he was as one paralysed. He could only grow purpler and purpler, and splutter.

"Don't—don't you play any of your infernal tricks on me, you—you villain! Curse it, why can't I get at that bell!" He made as if to rise, but, seemingly, was as incapable of movement as if he had been glued to his seat. As if conscious that his peril was imminent, he raised his voice to a raucous scream.

"Don't—don't you dare to lay your hands on me! Don't—don't you dare to touch me! Help!"

As the uncle opened his mouth to cry for aid the nephew caught him by the throat and slipped between his lips the tiny white lozenge which he had taken from the silver box. Then he struck up his jaw with a click and held it shut, so that he could not put it out again. Forcing back his head, he gripped him tight. His uncle was seized with a convulsion which seemed to Rodney as if it must have shaken the carriage.

Almost at the same instant it was as if all vitality had gone clean out of him. The nephew was gripping a limp corpse.

CHAPTER X

IN THE CARRIAGE—ALONE

Graham Patterson, in the agony of that last convulsion, had nearly slipped off the seat, so that, with a very little, he would be on the floor. His nephew, who hitherto had not for a moment lost his presence of mind, and who kept it then, was at a loss. Would such an attitude be recognised as proper for a suicide? Would, that is, a doctor—any doctor—be prepared to assert that a man who had killed himself with potassium cyanide might, under the circumstances, quite conceivably die in such an attitude, or assume it after death? To Rodney's supernaturally keen vision there were trifles about his uncle's appearance which scarcely marked this as inevitably a case of suicide. The collar was a little crumpled; the tie a little disarranged; he even fancied that there were prints of his fingers on the skin of the throat. He was conscious that he had gripped him with great force—perhaps a little clumsily; he certainly ought to have avoided contact with the collar and the tie, but no doubt the prints would wear off. Indeed, as he bent closer he was not sure that they did not exist only in his imagination; the light was not good; he could not be certain. With dexterous fingers he smoothed the collar, he rearranged the tie—so deftly that he felt convinced that no one would notice that anything had been wrong with him. He raised the body a little, so that it was in what seemed to him to be a more natural position, on the edge of the seat; he felt that it would look better. He was surprised to find how heavy his uncle was—it required quite an effort on his part to lift him.

He turned the contents of the silver box on to his hand. There were seven tiny lozenges. He returned three to the box, and laid it on the seat; the other four he placed beside it. Taking an envelope out of an inner pocket of his jacket, he tore off a corner. In it he placed the four tabloids, carefully folded it, and put it in his waistcoat pocket. Then he balanced the cap of the box on the arm of the seat beside his uncle; the box itself he placed between the fingers of his uncle's left hand, with—in it—the other three tabloids. So tightly were the fingers clenched that Rodney had to use force to open them sufficiently to enable him to insert the box. Then, seating himself opposite, he looked his uncle carefully over with an artist's eye for detail. In his present attitude, with that open box with its tell-tale contents held tightly between his stiffened fingers, it seemed to Rodney that a coroner would be bound to instruct his jury that suicide was the only possible explanation of Graham Patterson's death. Having satisfied himself on which point, he withdrew to the opposite end of the carriage, being, in spite of himself, conscious of a feeling that the dead man's too immediate neighbourhood was not a thing to be desired.

Seated in his original place, he took out his white cambric handkerchief, and with it delicately wiped his fingers, having an uncomfortable notion that something disagreeable had adhered to them which it would be better to remove. Then he set himself to consider the position. A great smoker of cigarettes, absent-mindedly and as a matter of course he took out his case, and was about to light one when it occurred to him that it might be a dangerous thing to do. It was not a smoking carriage; if, when the discovery was made, it smelt strongly of smoke—and nothing lingers like a cigarette—it might be shown that his uncle had not been smoking, and the question might arise—who had? He returned the case to his pocket. As he did so the train rushed past a signal-box. He remembered reading of the strange things which signalmen see in trains as they rushed past them. When his uncle was found, exhaustive inquiries would be set on foot. Quite conceivably some signalman had seen them struggling, or something which had piqued his curiosity as it had caught his eye. His uncle would be found alone. The signalman's story might suggest that at one period of the journey someone had been in the carriage with him. What had become of that someone? The mere question might start a hue and cry. Rodney recalled, with quite a little sense of shock, that his uncle had been partly pushed into the carriage by an official on the Brighton platform. Graham Patterson was a noticeable-looking person; he must have presented a striking spectacle as he had come hurrying along the platform. When discovery came about, the official would recollect the incident and recognise him beyond a doubt.

Had he noticed that somebody was already in the carriage when he was thrusting the fat man in? Rodney was compelled to admit that the probabilities were that he had. So far as he himself was concerned, Rodney recalled the whole sequence of events. How he had rushed up to the ticket inspector just as the Pullman was moving; how the man, slamming the gate in his face, had informed him that another train was due to start in ten minutes. The young gentleman had a suspicion that the fellow had looked him up and down as he was explaining. There were others about who might also have looked him up and down. Rodney had an uneasy feeling that, in his way, he was perhaps as noticeable a figure as his uncle—so tall, so upright, so well groomed, so handsome, with something about his appearance which almost amounted to an air of distinction. He had walked a few paces to another platform, as directed; the man at the gate, in his turn, had looked him up and down as he clipped his ticket; he had strolled leisurely along the platform, which he had had almost entirely to himself; when he reached a carriage which he thought would suit him, he stood for a second or two at the open door— as he remembered, right in front of the official who, later, had helped his uncle in.

He sat up very straight as that little fact came back to him. He remembered very well eyeing the man, whom, certainly, he would know again anywhere. No doubt the man had eyed him, and had his likeness in his mind's eye. The fellow had seen him enter the compartment and shut the door; a few minutes later he had opened the door again to admit his uncle, well knowing that he was already within. The accident might prove very awkward for the nephew later on; no one could have appreciated the possibilities of the position more clearly than he did.

As he pondered the matter he was inclined to think that he had made a mistake in doing what he had done. Such a fuss is made about a thing of that sort that, in any event, one runs a risk. Had he had more time to appreciate exactly what would be the nature of the risk in his own case he might have— hesitated. If he had he would have been deposed from his cousin's good graces, and—to adopt her sire's rather melodramatic language—have been "branded as a felon," so that he would not have been much better off. Looking at it philosophically the result of what he had done was this: that whereas, if he had let his uncle have his own way, ruin was certain, as things were he had at least a fighting chance of postponing the evil day—perhaps to an indefinite period. More; in the meanwhile he could have a rattling good time. And he would have it. He smiled as he made himself that promise.

All the same, though he smiled, he realised that if he proposed to have a good time he must not continue to take his ease where he was—with his uncle on the seat at the other end. If he seriously wished the world to take it for granted that Graham Patterson had committed suicide, he must not be found in the same compartment. That was sure. He had been told by someone, or had read somewhere, that every express train, though assumed to be "non-stopping," stopped at least once, because a signal was against it, or at least slowed down sufficiently to enable an agile passenger, with safety, to alight. So far that train had neither stopped nor slowed. His watch told him that it was about twenty to ten—ten minutes ago his uncle had been alive. It seemed longer ago than that. He had a fair knowledge of the line by daylight; it was different at night. Objects—even stations—were difficult to distinguish. He peered through the open window without thrusting out his head. They seemed to be running through open country, possibly on the top of the ballast. He could make out lights, though they were few and far between; they seemed to be passing a number of trees, with a big building beyond. They crashed through a station—it was Earlswood; they had just passed Earlswood Asylum. Immediately they would be on the new part of the line, which avoids the South-Eastern station at Redhill. There was no station between this and Purley. He might leave the train anywhere with comparative safety if it would only slow a little. To attempt to alight while it was moving at that rate through the darkness would be equivalent to committing suicide. At the best he could not hope to avoid serious injury. He must wait— till it slowed.

The whistle on the engine sounded; the train began to slow. Instantly he was leaning forward, his fingers on the handle, which was inside the door. The train slowed still more; it entered a tunnel, slowing all the while; in the heart of the tunnel it stopped—dead. The gods were on his side. Yet not for an instant did he lose his presence of mind. The signal was against them—that was why they had stopped. Was it on the left or the right? On the signal side the guard would possibly have his head out of the carriage with an eye for it; possibly some of the passengers might be observing it also. It would be fatal to get out on that side; his door would be seen opening; he might be seen to alight; he would be jumping out of the frying-pan into the fire; all sorts of consequences might accrue. He looked out of his own window; there was no signal in front or behind. Then it was on the other side, on the left, against the wall of the tunnel. He looked on to the six-foot way. He could see the whole length of the train; not a sign of a head at any of the windows. He had already turned the handle, opening the door just wide enough he stepped on to the footboard, closed the door, and dropped on to the permanent way. He had left his uncle to continue his journey alone. Lest his upstanding figure might be visible to someone, he crouched as close as he could to the ground. The train began to move very slowly. The door of the compartment next to that which he had just left was opened, a figure came on to the footboard, closed the door, sprang on to the ballast while the train was already in motion. For a moment Rodney was the victim of a gruesome delusion; to him it was as if the door of his own compartment had been opened; as if Graham Patterson had alighted at his side. He pressed the tips of his fingers into his palms to keep himself from exclaiming.

CHAPTER XI

THE STRANGER

The train went slowly rumbling by; who looked out of the windows Rodney neither knew nor cared. He was conscious of the guard's van passing, then the train had gone. He could see the tail lights moving quicker and quicker through the darkness. He himself continued motionless. He had realised by now that it was not his uncle who had alighted; that it was the door of the next compartment which had been opened. He could not believe that his own movements had been observed. He doubted if they could have been seen by a person who had not actually got his head out at the moment—even by his next door neighbour. He was certain that no head had been out. The thing had been a coincidence—a strange one, but nothing more. Someone also had reasons for wishing to quit the train in an unusual manner; someone who was unaware that he was out already. The chances were that he had not been noticed; that, if he kept quite still, he would not be noticed. The stranger would blunder along without ever becoming cognisant of his near neighbourhood; whichever way the stranger went, he would go the other.

Now that the train had left, it was very still in the tunnel; the air was close, full of smoke, which was bad both for the throat and the eyes. Something had dropped once or twice on Rodney's shoulder. He had heard that it was sometimes damp in tunnels; possibly it was moisture dropping from the brickwork overhead. He would have liked to move so as to avoid it, but was reluctant to make a sound—till the stranger had moved. He wondered what the stranger was doing; silence continued for what seemed to him to be a preternatural length of time. Possibly, less fortunate than himself, the stranger had been hurt in alighting, which explained the stillness. If that were so, his own position might be difficult. If he moved first the stranger might claim his help, might make a fuss if he refused it—such a fuss that the fact that he had left the train would be discovered.

Still not a sound. Momentarily the situation was becoming more delicate. He could not remain crouched down like that for ever, with big drops of something falling on to his shoulder. What should he do? The question was answered for him.

"Caught you!"

The words were whispered close to his ear. He stood straight up suddenly, startled half out of his wits. His impulse was to fly—anywhere, anyhow. Then that wonderful presence of mind of his, which never left him long, came back; he realised that haste on his part might involve disaster. He stood bolt upright, quite still, with fists clenched, prepared for anything.

Something came; fingers were laid upon his coat-sleeve. He showed no sign of resenting their coming, their touch was so soft that it hardly suggested danger. A voice came to him through the darkness, the one which had so startled him by whispering in his ear.

"That was a capital idea of yours—capital."

To Rodney's acute sense of hearing there seemed to be a curious quality in the voice; he was not sure if it belonged to a man or a woman. It came again.

"Have you ever been in a tunnel before? I haven't."

The last two words were spoken with a snigger which was certainly a man's, though he still felt that the voice itself might be either masculine or feminine. He had a fastidious taste in voices; apart from the circumstances under which he heard it, that one affected him unpleasantly. It continued, and his distaste grew.

"Do you know that our getting out here in the tunnel has proved something which I have always held as an article of faith; that I have cat's eyes—positively? Isn't it droll? I can see you—not plainly, but sufficiently well. Now I dare say you can't see me at all!"

Rodney could not; he did not believe that the stranger could see him. Darkness was about them like a wall.

"Come!"

He felt the fingers which had rested on his sleeve slipped under his arm.

"I will guide you; let me turn you round. We will go this way, towards the signal. You see?—it is set at danger. Some people would say that we are in rather a dangerous position."

Again that unpleasantly sounding snigger.

"I hope you're not feeling nervous; you needn't. That signal is not far off, and when we reach it we are out in the open. I know exactly where we are; this is Redhill tunnel. Not only can I see in the dark, dimly, but still see, but I also have, in a curious degree, the bump of locality. With me it amounts almost to an additional sense. I always know where I am, even when I am in a strange place; in a place in which I have been before I have an incredible perception of my surroundings. For three years I lived quite close to this—in Earlswood Asylum, as a patient."

Earlswood Asylum! Then the creature was a lunatic. That explained the singularity of his voice, of his manner, his proceedings. An idea came into Rodney's head. The creature was small; he felt, as he moved beside him with his hand under his arm, that he probably did not reach to his shoulder. It would be easy to leave him in the tunnel. Who cares what happens to a lunatic?

"I shouldn't if I were you; it wouldn't pay."

The words were so apposite that, despite himself, Rodney started. He had not spoken. Could the creature read what was passing through his brain?

"There are times when I can read people's thoughts just as plainly as if they had spoken them out loud, even when I can't see their faces—really! Isn't it odd? Oh, I am quite gifted. My argument always has been that, in a general way, a lunatic is merely abnormal, nothing more. At intervals a cloud settles on my brain; I can see, I can feel it coming; then, for an indefinite period, I am on the lap of the gods. When it passes my senses are more acute than other people's—abnormally acute, I know it as a fact. Now you see, as I told you, we are out in the open—look! the stars are shining. Look back at the tunnel; isn't it a horror of blackness? Like the horror I know. If we scramble up that bank we shall probably find a gap in the hedge at the top; platelayers often do leave a gap in a hedge close to the wall of a tunnel that they may descend to the line. As I told you, here's our gap; now, over the fence, and the rest is easy sailing."

It seemed to Rodney that since he had quitted the train something must have happened to him mentally; it was as if, all at once, he were playing a part in a dream. In silence, without offering the least remonstrance, he had suffered the stranger to pilot him out of the tunnel, up the steep bank beyond— to dominate him wholly. Now, except that they seemed to be standing in an open space of considerable size, he had not the dimmest notion of their whereabouts; but to the stranger it all seemed plain.

"That big building on our right's an orphanage—St. Anne's; I believe we're on their ground. If we keep straight on to our left we shall come to the high road, from which it is only a few minutes to Redhill station, whence we shall continue our journey to town. Quite an interesting episode this has been, has it not? I am indebted to you for much entertainment. I have seldom had so much enjoyment in a train, Mr. Elmore."

The creature knew his name! How? Who was he? What did it mean? Again he was conscious of an impulse to take him by the throat and—resolve the question in his own fashion. How came the creature to know his name? Although he had uttered no articulate sound, he had his answer.

"The explanation is simple, explanations often are. I heard your uncle address you by your name in a most audible tone of voice just towards the close. Most people have no idea how thin the partition really is which divides one compartment from another. Do you know I have heard that in some instances it is made of papier-mâché—fancy! You can always hear if a conversation is taking place in an adjoining compartment—it is surprising how much you can hear if you try, especially if your hearing is as good as mine is—that's another of my gifts. I had my ear glued to the partition most of the time. Of course, I could not hear everything—and I should very much have liked to see, but I gathered enough to enable me to form a general idea, particularly when you began to use violence towards your uncle and to hurl him back into his seat—it amounted to hurling. You see, I was his side. And, of course, when you both raised your voices I could hear a very great deal. I was not in the least surprised at the silence which followed. I understood—oh, I understood! At least, I think I understood. It was perfectly plain that only one person was left in the compartment who counted, and, of course, I knew that was you. I said to myself: 'Now, I wonder how long he'll stay there all alone? He's sure to take advantage of the first opportunity of getting out if the train stops or slows, and if he gets out I'll get out too.' Wasn't it lucky that it stopped in a tunnel, and that, therefore, we were both of us able to get out without being observed? Quite a stroke of fortune! Here we are, right on the high road, with the station a little more than a stone's throw in front of us."

Rodney listened to what the stranger had to say as, side by side, they tramped across the uneven ground with feelings which he would not have found it easy to clothe with words. Beyond all doubt this was a lunatic; but of what an uncomfortable kind! He had been wiser to have acted on his first impulse and to have left him in the tunnel. Now it was too late; it would not be the same thing to—leave him there. Yet, if he continued in his company, how should he muzzle him? With what would he make him dumb? By what means could he keep him from blurting out the whole story to the first person they might meet? Once more, though he had uttered not a syllable, there came an answer.

"You run no risk of my blabbing, I am not that kind of person—at least, while the cloud is yet afar off. Afterwards, believe me, no one pays any heed to what I say. I play the part of audience only. I am not, like you, one of Nature's criminals; but I am indifferent, which is about the same. What A does to B is A's business and B's, not mine; that I always shall maintain. Here we are at the station. It's been altered since my time; they've given it a new front. When is the next train to town?"

He put the question quite naturally to a porter who was standing about.

"Ten-forty; nearly half an hour to wait—that is if she is punctual, which she's not always of a Sunday night."

The stranger addressed himself to Elmore.

"That, perhaps, is fortunate, since that will enable me to offer you a little refreshment, of which I dare say both of us stand in need."

Rodney, always speechless, walked beside the stranger to the refreshment bar. Now he could see him plainly. A notion which had been fluttering at the back of his head took flight; there was no suggestion of a detective police official about him. He was shorter even than he had imagined, probably scarcely over five feet high; a mean-looking, ill-shapen fellow, with one shoulder higher than the other, which gave him an appearance of being one-sided. Badly dressed in an ill-fitting suit of rusty dark-grey tweed, clumsily shod, tie disarranged, doubtful collar, old tweed hat shaped like a billycock, about him the air of one who was not over fond of soap and water. Probably between fifty and sixty, a round, hairless, wizened face, all wrinkles, flat, snub nose, curiously small mouth—Rodney wondered if the peculiarity of his voice was owing to its coming through so small an aperture; queer, big, oval, ugly eyes—small pupils floating in a sea of yellow. The young gentleman was conscious of what an ill-assorted couple they must appear. He would have liked very much to put a termination to the association then and there, but—he could not, it was too late.

The stranger on his part seemed sublimely unaware of there being anything odd in their companionship. He gave his order to the young lady on the other side of the counter.

"One brandy, two Scotch whiskies, and a small soda divided."

The young lady looked as if she was not quite sure that she had caught what he said.

"I beg your pardon."

"I said one brandy, two Scotch whiskies, and a small soda divided. You've quite right, there are only two of us; I take brandy and whisky together—I'm a lunatic."

Two young men at the other end, with whom the young lady had been talking, looked at each other and smiled. The young lady also smiled, under the apparent impression that, somewhere, there was a joke.

"It is rather unusual, isn't it?"

"Not at all—with lunatics."

It was not easy for standers-by to decide whether or not he was in earnest. Rodney was in doubt; indeed, the man's words and manner started him wondering to what extent, in all he had been saying, the fellow had been "pulling his leg."

The young lady passed three glasses to their side of the counter. The stranger, taking two, emptied one into the other. He held it up towards Rodney.

"Your very good health, and the next time we meet may you afford me as much entertainment."

Swallowing the contents of the glass at a single gulp, he replaced it on the counter.

"The same again, miss; one brandy, one Scotch whisky; lunatics don't take long over a drop like that."

She looked at him doubtfully for a moment; then gave him what he ordered, saying, as she passed him the glasses:

"Two shillings, please."

As again he emptied one into the other he nodded to Rodney.

"Pay her; I've no money—lunatics never have."

Rodney drank what was in his glass, placed a florin on the counter, and left the place without a word. Hardly had he reached the door when he found the little man again at his side. He commenced pacing up and down the dimly lit platform; the little man paced also, two of his short steps being the equivalent of one of Rodney's strides. He asked himself if he could do nothing to shake the fellow off; with his usual singular intuition the other replied to his unspoken thought.

"Not nice, being in the company of one who knows as much as I do? Perhaps not; yet I don't see why. I'm incapable of giving evidence; if I weren't I wouldn't say a word to spoil the fun; I am as good as a dead man. You'll have a dead man for constant companion—why not me?"

Again he gave vent to the snigger which so jarred on the young man's nerves. When the train entered the station they were still pacing to and fro; Rodney not having yet uttered a single word. The little man followed him into the empty first-class compartment which he had selected, saying as he drew the door to behind him:

"Isn't it confiding of me to trust myself alone in a carriage with you—after what has happened? But I am not in the least afraid. I am sure you won't care to repeat your experiment to-night. And I shall find it so amusing to sit and watch you, and see what is passing through your mind; because, do you know, it will all be just as plain to me as if you said everything aloud."

While crediting the stranger with unusual perceptive powers, Rodney doubted if in his assertion he did not go too far. If he had the dimmest insight into the tangled network of thought with which the young man's brain was filled, then he was a marvel indeed. Elmore, leaning back in his seat, remained perfectly still, with his face towards the window, to all outward seeming as oblivious of the other's presence and occasional remarks as if he were not there. When they reached Croydon a person approached the carriage window whom the stranger plainly recognised; a pleasant-faced, brown-skinned and brown-haired young man with a slight moustache, with something in his bearing and expression which suggested reserve. Coming into the carriage, he said to the stranger, as he sat beside him, half smilingly, half chidingly:

"So it is you, is it? I hope you've enjoyed your little trip."

The stranger seemed to regard his coming with an air of not altogether pleased surprise.

"You're a most extraordinary man."

The other replied:

"One has to be a little that way if one is responsible for you."

The new-comer's good-humoured curtness seemed to disturb the stranger's equilibrium.

"Responsible for me, indeed! Upon my word, you are the most extraordinary man."

In his own fashion the stranger introduced the new-comer to Rodney.

"This is Dr. Emmett, my medical attendant. I left him behind me in Brighton because I am sick and tired of his society; yet here he is at Croydon before I am. How he does these things I do not understand. He's a most extraordinary man."

Then, also after his own fashion, he made Rodney known to the new-comer.

"Emmett, this is a valued friend of mine, whom I have met for the first time to-night. I know all about him, except his voice; and, do you know, he's never spoken once."

Rodney, observing the new-comer, perceived, from something which was in the glance he gave him in exchange for his, that the position had altered. Rising, he moved out of the carriage, still without a word. The stranger made as if to follow him, but the doctor put out a detaining hand. The train started just as Rodney, having gained the platform, was closing the door. The last he saw of the interior of the compartment was that the stranger seemed to be warmly expostulating with his medical attendant. At Redhill Rodney had got into the front part of the train—which was for London Bridge—because he felt that between the City and Notting Hill he might have an opportunity of shaking the stranger off. Now, as the London Bridge coaches glided out of the station, he passed to the Victoria half of the train, which awaited an engine, lower down the platform. The doctor's fortuitous arrival on the scene had saved him, at least temporarily, from what might have been a serious predicament.

CHAPTER XII

MARKING TIME

Rodney Elmore's rooms were within a short distance of Paddington Station. As his cab drew up at the house he saw that another hansom was already at the door. Since it was past midnight, its presence was suggestive; it betokened a visitor. The house being a small one, there was only one other lodger besides himself, and he occupied a modest "bed-sitting-room" on the upper floor. His instinct told him that the visitor was for himself. At that hour on Sunday night the fact was portentous. Opening the door with his latch-key, as he stepped inside a girl came hastening towards him from a room at the back, noiselessly, as if she did not wish to be overheard, rather a pretty girl, with fluffy, fair hair. She spoke in a whisper:

"There's someone to see you—a lady. She would wait, although I told her I didn't know when you would be in."

"What's her name?"

"She said Miss Patterson."

He understood—he had been making certain mental calculations as he came along. No doubt his uncle would have his name and address upon him; his identity would be discovered so soon as they searched the body. There had been time to carry the news to Russell Square; this was the result. Nodding to the fluffy-haired girl, he passed quickly into his sitting-room, which was on the left, in the front of the house. Gladys was standing by the table. As she came towards him he knew by the look which was on her face that his guess had been right—that already she knew at least part of the story.

"Where have you been?" she exclaimed. "I thought you were never coming."

Taking both her hands in his, he drew her to him.

"My dear child! how could I guess that you were here? What does it mean?"

She looked at him with a curious sombre something in her big dark eyes, which reminded him of a child who is about to cry. Her lips trembled.

"Rodney, dad's dead."

His tone was eager, gentle, sympathetic; instinct with surprise.

"Dead! You—you don't mean it!"

"In the train."

"In the train! What train?"

She told her tale, he listening with interest, anxiety, tenderness, which were sufficiently real.

"I was just going to bed."

"Dear, you're shivering. You'd better sit down."

"I'd rather stand—close to you."

He put his arms about her and held her tight. He kissed her. "Sweetheart," he whispered. He could feel her trembling; tears were beginning to shine in her eyes.

"I was in my bedroom, and—and—I was thinking about you"—about the corners of her lips was the queerest little smile—"when there was a ringing at the front door. I thought it was dad, who had forgotten his key; but they came and told me that there was a gentleman downstairs who wished to see me very particularly about my father, and that it was most important. So I slipped on a dressing-jacket and went down to him. It was someone from the railway company. They had found dad in the carriage of a train which had come from Brighton. He was dead—now he was at Victoria Station—he had committed suicide."

"Suicide!"

Rodney started; it could not have been better done if his surprise had been genuine.

"It's—it's incredible!"

"I can only tell you what the man told me. He said of course there would have to be an inquiry, but all the indications pointed at that. He had poisoned himself; in his hand they had found a box in which were some more of the things with which he had done it."

"I can only say that to me it seems—it does seem impossible. I should have said he was the last person to do anything like that."

"You never can tell what sort of person will do a thing like that. I once knew a girl who went straight up after dinner to her bedroom and—did it; no one ever knew why. I went with the man to Victoria, and—saw dad; I've come right on from there. I felt that I couldn't go home till I had seen you. I believe I should have stayed here all night if you hadn't come."

"You poor little thing!—sweetheart mine!—you only woman in the world!"

"You—you will be good to me, Rodney?"

"Never was man better to a woman than I will try to be to you."

"Suppose—suppose dad did it because he was ruined?"

"My dear girl, as you are aware, I was not in your father's confidence—still, I am pretty nearly certain that, commercially, it will be found that he was all right. Yet, should it turn out that he was even worse than penniless, it will not make a mite of difference in my love for you."

"You are sure?"

"Absolutely. Aren't you?"

"I do believe you care for me a little, or—I shouldn't be here."

"A little! You—you bad girl; you dearest, sweetest of darlings! Between ourselves, if it does turn out that you're no richer than I am, I shan't be sorry. He never did want you to have anything to do with me. I might have won him over if he had lived; you know, I believe he was commencing to like me a little better. I'm not sure that I wouldn't sooner have you without his money; I should feel as if I were playing the game."

"It will be horrid if he has left nothing; it will perhaps mean a scandal, and things are bad enough as they are."

"I see what you have in your mind, but I assure you you need not have the slightest fear. I'll stake my own integrity that in all matters of business your father had the highest sense of honour. I'll be willing to write myself down a rogue if it can be shown that he ever deviated in any particular from the highest standard of commercial rectitude."

"I hope you're right."

"I am right, on that point you may rest assured."

"You know, Rodney, you're all I have in the world—now."

The use of the adverb, in that connection, tickled him. The idea that, so far as she was concerned, her father ever had been much of a personal asset was distinctly funny. However, he allowed no hint of how her words struck him to peep out; never a more ardent lover, a more present help in the time of a girl's trouble. He escorted her to what bade henceforward to be her lonely home in the cab which still waited at the door. When he returned to Paddington it was very late. As he moved to his bedroom up the darkened staircase a door opened on the landing. The fluffy-haired girl looked out. She was in a state of considerable déshabillé.

"You are late," she whispered. "I thought you never were coming back."

"You goose."

He put his arms about her and kissed her with the calmest proprietary air.

"To think that you should be still awake."

"You knew I should sit up; you knew mother wasn't coming back to-night, and you said you'd be in early."

She spoke with an air of grievance. He smiled.

"It's been a case of man proposes. I have had many things to contend with—all sorts of worries. Now, as I want breakfast early, I'm going to bed, and, I hope, to sleep, if you aren't."

"You don't care for me a bit."

He kissed her again.

She waited on him at breakfast, which, as he had forewarned her, he had unusually early. She was his landlady's daughter; her name was Mabel Joyce. Among his letters was one from Stella Austin. He opened it as she placed before him his bacon and eggs; as he glanced at Stella's opening lines Miss Joyce talked.

"So you went to Brighton yesterday—by the Pullman, too."

He looked up at her as if surprised.

"Did I? Who told you that?"

"Didn't you?"

"You say I did. Pray, from what quarter did you get your information?"

"Oh, there are plenty of quarters from which I can get information—when I like. And your uncle was in Brighton. It doesn't look as if he had a very pleasant day there, as he committed suicide in the train on the way back to town. I dare say you had a pleasanter day than he did."

"I presume you got that information either from this morning's paper or else from listening last night outside the door."

"As it happens, I haven't seen a paper, and, as for listening, if you don't know I wouldn't do a thing like that it's no use my saying so."

"Then who was your informant?"

"That's my business. There is a little bird which sometimes whispers in my ear. Did you come back in the Pullman?"

He replied to her question with another.

"What's the matter with you, Mabel?"

"What should be? Nothing's the matter; I was only thinking that if you did, your uncle must have been in the train just behind you. If you'd have known what he was doing you'd have felt funny. Still, if you did come by the Pullman, considering that it's due at Victoria at ten, and yesterday was quite punctual, since you had promised to be in early, and knew that I was all alone in the house, I think you might have been back before midnight."

He eyed the girl. She was pretty, in a pink-and-white sort of way; fonder of him than was good for her. He had never seen her in this shrewish mood before.

"My dear Mabel, if I could have got back earlier I would have done so; but I couldn't. I was the sufferer, not you."

"I dare say! I suppose that Miss Patterson was your cousin. Are you going to marry her?"

"Really! you jump about! How do you suppose a fellow in my position can tell whom he's going to marry—on twopence a year?"

"I dare say she's got money, especially now. Since directly she heard of her father's death she came tearing round to you, at that time of night, it looks as if you ought to marry her if you don't!"

Miss Joyce flounced out of the room. For some moments he sat considering her words. Who told her that he went to Brighton, on the Pullman? Was it a lucky guess? Hardly; probably someone had seen him. People's eyes were everywhere. He would have to be careful what tale he told. It was odd how gingerly one had to walk when one was in a delicate position; there were so many unseen strings over which one might stumble.

As he ate his breakfast he read Stella's letter. It was a girl's first letter to her lover; which is apt to be a wonderful production, as in this case. He had not supposed that a letter from Stella could have stirred him as that one did. It suggested the perfect love which casteth out fear. She bared her simple heart to him in perfect trust and confidence, showing in every line that, to her, he was both hero and king, that man of men,—her husband that was to be. Tears actually stood in his eyes as he realised the pathos of it all; how sweet to hold such innocence in his arms. He was not sure that he had not been over-hasty in concluding that here was no wife for him. The picture which, as he read on, quite unwittingly she presented to his mind's eye, of the two wandering hand in hand down the vale of years, to the goal of venerable old age at the end, moved him to the depths. It was sweet to be so trusted; he would have loved to have her with him at the breakfast-table then. It was so dear a letter that he kissed it as he folded it, and slipped it into the inside pocket of his coat.

Then he set himself to thinking. Part of the point of Stella's letter lay in the fact that she expected him to go to her that night, and wished him to know all the things she set down in black and white, so that they might be able to talk about them when he came. The misfortune was that he was not going. He would have liked to go—truly. He felt that after what had happened lately an evening spent with Stella would be delicious. So strongly did he feel this that he cast about in his mind for some means of ensuring himself even a few fleeting minutes in her society; but could hit on none. Accident might befriend him, but he doubted if Gladys would give accident much chance. He had promised that he would go from the office straight to her; it might go ill with him if he did not. Once with her, she was not likely to let him go again till it was too late to think of Stella.

How appease the maiden for her disappointment? He could think of nothing but laying stress on the dreadful thing which had happened to his uncle, and putting all the blame on that. He had never mentioned his cousin to Stella, or to Mary, or to anyone, being of those who, if they can help it, do not like their first finger to know what their thumb is doing. Stella did not know he had a feminine relative; it might be inconvenient to acquaint her with the fact just now; quite possibly her soft heart might move her to go and offer the orphaned Gladys consolation. He smiled as the droll side of such a possibility tickled his sense of humour. Possibly the time might come when the two young women would have to know of each other's existence, but—perhaps it might be as well to put it off for awhile.

He scribbled a hasty note to Stella, speaking of the rapture her letter had given him, and dwelling, in lurid hues, on the tragedy of his uncle's end; then suddenly remembered that, from her point of view, he ought not to have heard of it. What a number of trifles one did have to think of. He had not seen a paper; he did not propose to tell her of his trip to Brighton; she had heard nothing of Gladys; she might ask some awkward questions as to how he came to know about it so early in the day. He tore the note up and made a bonfire of the pieces. Then he scribbled another, in which he only spoke of his rapture and of the ecstatic longing with which he looked forward to seeing her after his office work was done, and of how the intervening seconds would go by like leaden hours—he felt that a poetic touch of that sort was the least that was required. Then, when he reached the office, he might wire her the dreadful tidings in an agitated telegram, and, later, in a still more agitated telegram, inform her that one awful consequence of the upheaval which had followed the hideous tragedy was that he would be unable to come to her to-night. The tale would be much more effective told like that. Whatever her feelings were, he did not see how a loophole would be left to her to lay blame on him.

CHAPTER XIII

SPREADING HIS WINGS

A disagreeable surprise awaited him when he reached St. Paul's Churchyard. Taking it for granted that everything would now belong to Gladys, he was prepared to act as her representative and sole relative, and, if needs be, carry things off with a high hand—above and beyond all else, he was desirous of gaining access to certain documents whose existence constituted a peril to him. To that end he arrived before his usual time, being conscious that this was an occasion on which it might be an advantage to be first on the field. To his disgust he found that at least two persons were in front of him, and that they were both in what had been his uncle's private room. One was Mr. Andrews, the managing man, the other was a square-jawed individual, whose blue cheeks pointed to a life-long struggle with a refractory beard. He was seated, as one in authority, in his uncle's own chair behind his uncle's own table. They were busily conversing as Rodney came unannounced into the room, but paused to stare at him.

"This," explained Mr. Andrews to the man in the chair, "is Mr. Rodney Elmore—the nephew I was telling you about."

There was a lack of deference in the speaker's tone which the young gentleman resented, and had resented in silence more than once in the days which were past; but the time for silence was gone. He had been making up his mind on that point on his way to the City. Recognising, from the bearing of the two men in front of him, that a new and, as yet, unknown factor bade fair to figure on the scene, with characteristic readiness he arrived at an instant resolution. Ignoring Andrews, he addressed himself to the man in the chair.

"May I ask, sir, who you are?"

The stranger's penetrating eyes were set deep in his head; he fixed them on the young gentleman's face with a steady stare of evident surprise. Rodney returned him stare for stare.

"You may ask, young gentleman, and, though I seriously doubt if you are entitled to ask, I don't mind telling you. My name is Wilkes—Stephen Wilkes; I am your late uncle's legal adviser, and am here to safeguard the interests he has left behind."

"Then, Mr. Wilkes, be so good as to get out of that chair."

Mr. Andrews looked at the speaker in shocked amazement.

"Mr. Elmore! You forget yourself! How dare you speak like that to a gentleman in Mr. Wilkes's position."

For answer, Rodney turned to the managing man, addressing him as curtly and peremptorily as if he had been some menial servant.

"Andrews, leave the room!"

The other's eyes opened still wider; probably he had never been so spoken to before, even by his late master in his most irascible moods. He drew up his spare and rather bowed figure with what he perhaps meant to be a touch of dignity.

"Mr. Elmore, the consequences will be very serious if you talk to me like that."

"The consequences will be very serious if you don't obey my orders."

"Your orders?"

"My orders. Are you going to leave the room, or am I to put you out?"

"Steady, young gentleman, steady. I have been your uncle's legal adviser for perhaps more years than you have been in the world, and am, therefore, intimately acquainted with his wishes. I am here to see those wishes carried out. I understand that you occupied a very humble position in this office, and, though accident made you his relative, you were not in possession of your uncle's confidence. Your position is in no way altered by his death, and you have no right to issue what you call orders here— emphatically not to Mr. Andrews. If there is any question as to who is to leave the room, it is certainly not Mr. Andrews who must go, but you."

"Mr. Wilkes, I do not propose to bandy words, and when I have once pointed out that you entirely misapprehend the situation on that subject I have done. All that Mr. Patterson had is now his daughter's, including this business and all that it implies. I am here as Miss Patterson's representative."

"Indeed! By whom appointed?"

"By Miss Patterson. I may inform you that Miss Patterson will shortly be my wife."

"Is that so? This is news. Since when has that arrangement been made?"

"Your words imply a sneer and an impertinence. That being so, I decline to enter into any further details with you beyond a bare statement of the fact."

"Are you not taking too much for granted in asserting that everything is left to Miss Patterson?"

"I have not a doubt of it; with the exception, possibly, of some small legacies. He left a will?"

"He did."

"Is it in your possession?"

"It is."

"Then I must ask you to produce it at once."

"Produce it? To whom?"

"To me. Miss Patterson has instructed me to request you to hand it over at once to my keeping."

"Then, if that is so, I am afraid that, for the moment, I have no choice but to ignore the young lady's request. I will see Miss Patterson."

"Miss Patterson will decline to see you."

"She will decline to see me? On what grounds?"

"It is not necessary that she should state any grounds. Any communication you wish to have with Miss Patterson must be through me or her solicitor. Do I understand that you finally refuse to do as she requests, and hand me her father's will?"

"If you were not a very young man, Mr. Elmore, I should say that you were a foolish one; but possibly youth is your extenuation. The will will be produced at the proper time, in the proper place, to the proper person; it will certainly not be handed to you."

"Then Miss Patterson's solicitor will at once take steps which will compel its instant production."

"Miss Patterson's solicitor? You really are a remarkable young man! I am Miss Patterson's solicitor. It was her father's wish that I should continue to act for her, as I acted for him."

"You will do nothing of the kind. If Mr. Patterson has left any legal powers to that effect, his daughter will resort to every process of law to effect your removal; your refusal to withdraw will not redound to your credit. You say you have been his legal adviser for more years than I am old. Mr. Patterson was a bad husband and a bad father. He utterly neglected his daughter; he did nothing to show that he had any of a parent's natural feelings; although she respected his every wish and he had no complaint to make of her, he was wholly indifferent to both her welfare and her happiness; he saw as little of her and did as little for her as he could. In many respects he was to her both a reproach and a shame, the sole object of his existence being his own gross physical enjoyment. Without being, perhaps, what is called an habitual drunkard, he habitually drank too much, and was frequently intoxicated in her presence. He was an evil-liver—with his relations with notorious women you are probably better acquainted than I am; she, unfortunately, has good reason to know that they were of a discreditable kind. To crown an ill-spent career he has taken his own life, under circumstances which can hardly fail to be the cause of scandal, which may leave a brand on her for the remainder of her life, though she is still only a girl. You apparently pride yourself on having been confidential adviser to such a man through a great number of years. Is it strange, therefore, that she would rather that somebody else should advise her? Think it over; you will yourself perceive that it is not strange; I am sure that will be the feeling of a court of law. Now, Mr. Wilkes, I must again ask you to get out of that chair."

"And if I refuse?"

Rodney moved to the other side of the table, took Mr. Wilkes—who was not a big man—by either elbow, lifted him as if he were a child, and deposited himself on the chair in his place. The solicitor, who had made not the slightest show of resistance, stood ruefully rubbing his arms.

"I believe you have put both my elbows out of joint, you young ruffian."

Rodney was placidity itself.

"Have you never heard of Jiu-jitsu, Mr. Wilkes? You know even better than I do that you are a trespasser on these premises, and that a trespasser is a person towards whom one is entitled to use all necessary force."

Taking a bunch of keys out of his jacket pocket, he inserted one in the lock of the drawer which was in front of him. Mr. Wilkes surveyed the proceeding with obvious surprise.

"What keys are those?"

"These are my uncle's keys. They were handed to me by Miss Patterson, with instructions to go through her father's private papers and documents, and so ensure their not being tampered with by persons who certainly have not her interest at heart."

"If you take my earnest advice, young gentleman, you will not touch anything which is in those drawers. If you are not careful you will go too far."

"I will not take your advice, Mr. Wilkes—whether earnest or otherwise. I observe, Andrews, that you are still there. There are one or two remarks which I wish to make to Mr. Wilkes in private. Once more, are you going to leave this room?"

The managing man looked at the lawyer as if for advice and help in the moment of his hesitation.

"Perhaps," said Mr. Wilkes, replying to his unspoken question, "you had better go. You will commit yourself to nothing by going."

"Whereas," observed Elmore, with his smiling glance fixed on the managing man, "you will commit yourself to a good deal by not going, because I shall not only put you out of this door, but into the street. So far as this office is concerned, that will be the end of you. I will take steps which will ensure your never entering it again."

After another brief moment of hesitation, with a glance of what was very like reproach towards the lawyer, Andrews quitted the room, with the air of one who was both bewildered and hurt. So soon as he had gone Mr. Wilkes observed:

"Mr. Elmore, you are taking a very great deal upon yourself; you certainly have the courage of youth, but be warned by me, don't take too much. If it is shown that your uncle's depositions are not what you are taking it for granted they are, your position will be rendered more difficult by the attitude you are now taking up."

"I care nothing for any warning which comes from you, Mr. Wilkes. Why did my uncle commit suicide?"

"What do you mean by asking me such a question? Do you imagine that if I knew I should tell you?"

"Does that mean that you know?"

"It means nothing of the sort; but it does mean that if I had any such secret knowledge, the only person to whom I should breathe a word of it would be his daughter."

"That you certainly would not do. Miss Patterson's heartfelt prayer is that she may never know. That he had some shameful reason is plain; if it can be kept from her it shall be; if it reaches her through you, you will deserve to be whipped."

"Mr. Elmore, I knew your father."

"That's more, Mr. Wilkes, than I ever did."

"His end was like your uncle's."

"So I learned from my uncle before—he ended. And it is because the shame of what he did seems to rest on me, in the mouths of such as you, that I am resolved to shield my cousin—if I can. I imagine that, in a strictly scientific sense, you are, in part, responsible for my uncle's fate."

"How do you arrive at that—somewhat startling conclusion?"

"You aided and abetted him in what he did."

"Indeed! As how?"

"I happen to know that you were more than once his companion when he was in the society of certain notorious women, with whose character you were undoubtedly as well acquainted as he was."

"And if I was—what then?"

"If, on more than one occasion, A is in the company of B when B is in the act of committing a crime, what is the inference we draw as regards A?"

"You really are a remarkable young man!"

"More. On more than one occasion you have borrowed money from Mr. Patterson."

"We have had business relations for many years."

"Did he ever borrow money from you?"

"No; because he did not do the class of business I did."

"Exactly. At this moment you are his debtor in a considerable sum."

"I don't know from whom you get your information, but if it is from your uncle you must be perfectly well aware that the whole matter is on a proper footing, and that there can be no reasonable doubt as to my fulfilling my engagements both in the letter and the spirit."

"Still, you have been in the habit of borrowing money from your client, sometimes, I believe, to save yourself from a difficult position. Possibly his will contains a clause relieving you of your indebtedness; possibly, also, a court of law will see its way to relieve Miss Patterson from any obligation to accept your services. I will not detain you any longer, Mr. Wilkes. Good morning. Please don't gossip with the employés as you go out."

Mr. Wilkes looked as if he would have said a good deal; but Mr. Elmore had already begun to write a letter—there was an air of complete indifference about him which apparently brought him to the conclusion that it might perhaps be as well to say nothing. He took his hat off the table and went out in silence. Presently Rodney, ringing the bell, said to the lad who answered:

"Take that letter to the address which is on the envelope at once, and bring me an answer; also tell Mr. Andrews that I wish to speak to him."

Shortly the managing man appeared in the doorway. One felt that he had hesitated whether or not to come, and that he was oppressed by something like a sense of shame at the thought of having yielded. The young gentleman, leaning back, regarded him with the pleasant little smile which, so far, had not left him—it was odd of what a number of subtle inflections his manner was capable without once disturbing the smile.

"Sit down, Andrews; take this chair."

The other did as he was told, sitting on the extreme edge, leaning slightly forward, his long legs crooked in front of him, his hands resting on his knees.

"How old are you, Andrews?"

Instead of replying to the question, the managing man started off on a line of his own.

"Mr. Elmore, you must excuse my remarking that, so far as I am concerned, I don't understand the position at all."

"You will, Andrews, shortly. I always have felt that your mental processes were perhaps a trifle slow."

"I have been in this office, boy and man, practically my whole life long; I'm older than your uncle was, and I was here before he came. He was with Harding and Fletcher before he took this business over, and, so to speak, he took me with it. It was a solid business then, and it's a solid business still—indeed, it's even better than it was. I'm almost—if not quite—as well known in the City as he was; he would have been the first to tell you that with the continued success I have had something to do. He was, in some ways, a difficult man to deal with; but no man had a better head for business—if he gave his confidence, you might be sure it was deserved, and he had entire confidence in me."

"Hear, hear! Go on; I like to hear you."

"When he said a thing he meant it. It's always been a joke among those who knew him that Graham Patterson's word was as good as a bank-note. He has told me more than once that when he was gone—"

"He anticipated going?"

"Not more than other men; only, he was methodical and liked to have everything in order, and, if he could help it, leave nothing to chance. He has told me, as I have said, more than once, that when he was gone—since he only had a daughter—he had arranged that the whole management of the business should be in my hands, and that he had left me a small share in it. He said, frankly, some time ago that he would give me a share in it then and there; if it weren't that he was the kind of man who never would get on with a partner; and that was the case—often he was difficult. I am sure, from what he told me, that it will be found that he has left the management of the business in my hands, as well as a share. What I don't understand, therefore, is on what grounds you are taking up the position you appear to be doing. I am far from wishing to have any unpleasantness with you, Mr. Elmore, but I do not understand."

"I represent Miss Patterson."

"But I represent the business—which was her father's, not hers."

"But it's hers now, you yourself admit that you only expect to be left a small share."

"But I'm left the management."

"That's—I am far from wishing to have any unpleasantness with you, Mr. Andrews, but—you must know that that's all tuppence."

"Pray, Mr. Elmore, what do you mean by that? A will's a will; its terms are not to be lightly set aside."

"You have not told me how old you are, Mr. Andrews, but you have told me that you are my uncle's senior."

"So far as head for business goes, I am as young as ever I was."

"I will not contradict you. I am inclined to think that you are as you were—thirty, forty years ago—that is, in a commercial sense, a thousand years behind the times."

"You have no right to say that. What do you know about business—a young man like you?"

"I am a man of business, Mr. Andrews."

"I was not aware of it until this moment."

"You will be more clearly aware of it before long. I was prepared to marry my cousin had she been penniless, as only the other day—if she married me—she bade fair to be. In that event I would have made her fortune, and my own, as sure as you are sitting there. As events have turned out, so far from being penniless, she is, shall we say, the three-fourths proprietor of a flourishing business, with, probably, all the capital at her command which is needed for its development. Under such circumstances, why should I not devote my energies to the aggrandisement of her business? If I do, do you suppose for one instant—will or no will—that the management of affairs will be in your hands? That you will lead, and I shall follow? Absurd, Andrews; the business has reached a stage at which it can branch out advantageously in a dozen different directions."

"I believe there's something in what you say—if it's in the hands of the right man."

"I am the right man! In the case of equipment of the modern man of business, if he has a head upon his shoulders, youth is his strongest card—it assures his being abreast of the procession. I know what can be done with this business, and it shall be done; I'll do it. In ten years it shall rank among the greatest of its kind in the City of London—in the world; if you live till then you'll own it."

"I'm a bachelor. I've saved enough to keep me in comfort. The business has been to me both wife and child, I could not love it better if it were my own. If I were sure that it would grow and flourish, always on a solid basis, I shouldn't care so much about myself; but it would break my heart, if, for any cause whatever, it were to go to pieces."

"It won't; you'll see. We'll talk about it again when the exact conditions of my uncle's will are known. Whatever they turn out to be, I shouldn't be surprised if you and I get on better together than at this moment you may suppose—you'll find that I like to get on with everyone. By the way, there is one disagreeable matter which, if we are to arrive at a perfect understanding, I ought to speak to you about. Are you aware that during the last few years various small acts of dishonesty have taken place in this office?"

"Mr. Elmore! I never heard of it."

"My uncle knew; he was speaking to me on the subject only a day or two ago. I fancy he even knew who the culprit was. He told me that there were proofs of what he more than hinted at locked up in one of his drawers. It was because of what he said that I was so anxious to go through his papers before anyone else could get at them."

"I hope, Mr. Elmore, you are not imputing dishonesty to me?"

"To you, my good Andrews! Do you think I don't know an honest man when I see one? In that respect I am like my uncle. I am as sure as I am sure of anything that you are as honest a man as I am—rest quite easy on that score. I only wished to point out that while you supposed yourself to be keeping a sharp eye on everything, and that nothing which took place in the office escaped your notice, these irregularities were taking place beneath your very nose. However, on that subject also I may have to speak to you again later. Still another point. The inquest on my uncle is to be held to-day at Victoria Station. As you will readily understand, Miss Patterson is not in a condition to appear at such an inquiry, if her presence can be dispensed with; we are advised it can. She wishes me to ask you if you will appear at the inquiry, and give such formal evidence as may be required. I don't know what questions will be asked you. Frankly, can you throw any light on any cause which may have induced his rash act? I take it he had no financial reason?"

"Absolutely none, of that I'm convinced. He had all the money he wanted, and there was nothing wrong with the business. It's a mystery to me."

"I fancy it will remain a mystery. Why some men and women make away with themselves is a mystery which only they themselves could have solved."

"I don't understand why you and he didn't get on better together."

"Nor I; to me it was a great disappointment. As you have said, he was difficult. He may have felt that my ideas on business matters were different from his, and didn't like it."

"Perhaps if he had lived it would have been different."

"We shall never know what, in that case, might have happened. May I take it that, in the matter of the inquest, you will do as Miss Patterson asks?"

"I will—certainly."

"Thank you. You increase the debt which she is conscious she owes you as her father's right-hand man, and which, whatever the terms of his will may be, she will never forget."

The lad entered to whom he had entrusted the letter.

"Mr. Parmiter has come back with me, sir; he's outside."

"Good; show him in. I think, Mr. Andrews, that, as the inquest is timed for noon, you had better be starting."

The old man went out, and a young one came into the room—a young man, with a student's face and fair hair. Although his cheeks were pale, his appearance was not unprepossessing. Elmore greeted him with outstretched hands.

"Clarence, old man, it's very good of you to come right away like this. I hope it's not seriously inconvenienced you."

"Not a bit. Between ourselves, I was sitting in the office twiddling my thumbs and wondering what I should do now I'd finished reading the paper."

"I'll give you something to do. Sit down. You've heard what's happened to my uncle?"

"I remember your telling me you were with an uncle, but I don't know how many uncles you have nor to which of them you're referring."

"I have, or, rather, had, only one uncle, and last night he committed suicide in the Brighton train."

"Great Scott! Whatever for?"

"That's it. I'll tell you in as few words as possible what the position is. He's left a daughter, an only child, who is now an orphan, to whom I'm engaged to be married. To her he was not—well, all that a father might have been; he drank, and he womanised."

"Did he? Nice man!"

"That's precisely what he was not—a nice man. She knew very little about his private affairs, though quite as much as she wanted. He may have killed himself because he was financially wrong, though, personally, I doubt it, or for any one of a score of reasons. You'll guess the state of mind she's in."

"Naturally; in a case like that it's those who are left who suffer most."

"Of course. She's anxious, before all else, to know where she stands—that is, to know the worst. His affairs were in the hands of a solicitor named Wilkes."

"I know him—Stephen Wilkes; he's an able man."

"Maybe. But she doesn't want him for her solicitor all the same for that, for reasons on which, later, I may enlarge. She's asked me if I knew anyone who would act for her. I suggested you."

"Thank you, Rodney. You always were a fellow who'd do a chap a good turn if you would."

"Nonsense! Do you think that I don't know you—even in the old schooldays? You're as clever a man as you'd be likely to meet in a long day's journey, and as dependable. You mayn't have the largest practice in London to-day, but you will have. What's more, I'd trust you with my bottom dollar, which is more than you can say of the general run of solicitors nowadays. I told her so."

"I'll try my best to prove worthy of your commendation."

"I've no fear of that, not the least. You may consider Miss Patterson your client, and me; and we may both of us turn out to be quite good clients before we've done. I've asked you to come here in order to give you your first instructions."

"I'm all ears."

"Mr. Wilkes is in possession of my uncle's will; he himself says so. Miss Patterson wanted him to hand it over to me to pass on to her, but he declined. Can't you persuade him, acting on Miss Patterson's behalf, to produce the will at the earliest possible moment—say this afternoon at four, in her house in Russell Square—and make known its contents then and there? She'll not sleep till she knows the worst."

"I can try what my persuasive powers will do. Presumably he knows its contents?"

"Presumably, since it is even probable that he drew it up."

"By it he may be appointed to some office of trust."

"Exactly. That's one of the things she wants to know; because, if he is, she'll leave no stone unturned to get him out of it. His relations with her father were such that she'll not be induced to have relations of any kind with him."

"I see; that's how it is. Persons may be interested whose presence he may think desirable at the reading and who are not accessible at such short notice."

"There's nothing in that, Clarence. Candidly, some woman may be interested; it's only surmise on my part, but it's possible, and her presence would neither be essential nor advisable. There's the feeling that whatever her father may have done, Wilkes will not be considering her interests only—that's why she wants you. Get him to attend this afternoon in Russell Square with the will; that'll prove to her that I knew what I was about in suggesting you."

"I'll do my utmost, but you clearly understand that I can't force the man. There's an etiquette in such matters; he'll be perfectly in order if he stands on it."

"Do your best, Clarence—that's all I ask, and, if possible, let me know how it's going to be inside an hour. I want to keep Miss Patterson posted in what is taking place. If you only knew what a state of mind she's in!"

When Mr. Parmiter had gone, Rodney, having given instructions that, if it could be avoided, he was not to be disturbed, subjected the contents of the drawers in his uncle's writing-table to a thorough examination. He came across some interesting items. There was a small leather-bound memorandum-book, which was locked. He opened it with a key which was on his uncle's private bunch. In a flap attached to the cover were some cheques which had been duly presented and paid and some other papers. A glance at the contents of the book showed that they principally related to him, after a fashion which occasioned him surprise, blended with amusement. He had no idea that in his uncle the detective instinct had been so strongly developed. He tore the cheques and other papers into tiny bits, made a bonfire of them on an iron shovel, and ground the ashes into powder. The book itself he slipped into his jacket pocket. In one of the drawers was a canvas bag, containing quite a number of gold coins, while in a letter-case were several bank-notes. He put the bag into another of his pockets, just as it was, and transferred the notes to a letter-case of his own. He chanced just then to be hard pressed for ready cash, as, indeed, was his every-day condition. Should certain eventualities arise, the possession of that money might prove to be of the very first importance. In still another drawer he found an envelope which was endorsed, in his uncle's handwriting, "Draft of my Will." He studied the sheet of ruled foolscap which he took out of it with every appearance of absorbed interest. It was not a very lengthy document. When he had read it he laid it on the table, drew a long breath, and smiled.

"That's all right! It mayn't be all that Gladys would have liked it to be, but it might have been so much worse; it will serve. A good deal may depend on the exact wording; but, anyhow, between us we ought to be able to shape a will like that so that it shall mean, in the not very far-off future, that I shall be a millionaire—unless I'm a greater fool than I suppose. I'd like to wager a trifle that in me there's the stuff that goes to the making of a modern millionaire, and if the will as it stands is on those lines, it ought to give me at least an outside chance of proving it. Here's to you, Uncle P., and, if people can see from the other side, how happy the knowledge that your daughter and your business are in such capable hands should make you."

A lad came in with an envelope.

"A messenger boy has just brought this, sir."

The note within ran:

"DEAR RODNEY,—I have carried out your first instructions to the letter, so I have begun well. Mr. Wilkes will be in Russell Square this afternoon at four with the will. Unless I hear from you to the contrary, I shall be there at half-past three—to be introduced to Miss Patterson, to receive any further instructions, and to be at hand in case I am wanted generally. You might let me have a message by bearer.—Yours sincerely,

"CLARENCE PARMITER."

CHAPTER XIV

BUSINESS FIRST, PLEASURE AFTERWARDS

That afternoon there were five persons in the drawing-room of the house in Russell Square. Miss Patterson, who was already attired in garments of orthodox hue, in which Rodney felt that she did not look her best. It is your fair, slender women who appear to advantage in black—she was too big and dark. There was Rodney, who was also in mourning, which did become him; but, then, anything became him. He was one of your tall, graceful, well-set-up, debonair, handsome young fellows whom any tailor might find it worth his while to dress at reduced prices for the sake of the advertisement. The other three men also were in black: Mr. Wilkes's dark blue cheeks almost matching his attire; Mr. Parmiter's light hair and pale face standing out in marked relief; Mr. Andrews's general air of colourlessness causing his sombre attire to make him seem older than it need have done. The proceedings were short—unexpectedly short—and to the point. Mr. Wilkes had met Miss Patterson before, and while her almost sullen manner suggested no fondness for him, his brusqueness hinted at no particular attachment for her. The keen-eyed Rodney, observing their demeanour, told himself that the lawyer had been too much the father's friend to care overmuch for the child, which was, perhaps, as well, since it might make things easier.

The inquest was already over. Mr. Wilkes had been present, and had taken with him a physician whom he was aware that Graham Patterson had consulted. He testified that Mr. Patterson was suffering from a malady which would certainly have grown more painful as time went on, and was probably incurable. This statement, since it supplied the motive, caused the inquiry to assume briefer limits than it might have done; the obvious inference was that the knowledge of his parlous state had prompted Graham Patterson to take his fate into his own hands. Nothing could have been clearer to such men of the world as the coroner and his jury. All else that was said and done was mere formality. The doctor who had conducted the autopsy, Mr. Andrews, a police officer connected with the railway company, the guard of the train—all these gave formal evidence. The latter said that he had seen the deceased man come running down the platform at Brighton station just as the train was about to start; that he had noticed him getting into a carriage; that he recognised him when, at East Croydon, his attention had been called to him by the ticket collector, who, going to collect his ticket, found him sitting up in the corner of the carriage, dead. In view of the physician's evidence, the whole affair was so transparently simple that no one thought of asking if anyone was in the compartment when he entered it at Brighton station. One of the jury did inquire if the train stopped between Brighton and East Croydon. When he was informed that it did not, it was generally felt that there was nothing more to be said. The hackneyed verdict was recorded as a matter of course—suicide while temporarily insane.

The whole affair struck Rodney, when he learnt all the particulars from Andrews, as distinctly droll. He realised that he owed Mr. Wilkes a debt of gratitude of which that gentleman had no notion. The physician had been an unknown quantity; Rodney, who, through devious channels, had heard of a good many things, had never heard of him. Had not the lawyer brought him on to the scene the situation might easily have become very much more difficult—for him. He would not be so hard on Stephen Wilkes as he had meant to be, but in his treatment of him would recognise that, as Parmiter had put it, he was an able man.

The will was the usual wordy, legal document. Stripped of its verbiage it was plain enough. It began with the legacies. A sufficient sum was to be set apart to buy an annuity of one hundred pounds a year for Agnes Sybil Armstrong, of an address at Hove. She was also to have five hundred pounds in cash and the furniture of the house in which she was residing.

Gladys, who had been warned by Rodney that she might expect something of the kind, pursed her lips together and looked at her cousin. Sitting with expectant eyes fixed on her, he had been waiting for her look, and greeted it with a reassuring smile.

Various legacies were left to servants in Russell Square, to clerks in St. Paul's Churchyard, and to certain trade charities. Five thousand pounds was left to Stephen Wilkes, in recognition of a life-long friendship and of valued services—the lawyer's voice was a trifle hesitant as he read this clause. One thousand pounds in cash and a tenth share in the business were left to Robert Fraser Andrews; and, since the testator's only child was a daughter, he directed that the said Andrews should be appointed manager of his business, under the conditions which followed.

The whole residue of his estate, real and personal, he left to his daughter, Gladys, unreservedly. At this point the cousins again exchanged glances. Andrews was to manage the business for five years; at the end of that period, or in the event of his death, Gladys might appoint his successor, or dispose of the business, whichever she chose. No radical change in the conduct of the business was to be made without consulting her, and she was to have the right of veto. She was to have access to the accounts at all times, with right of comment.

The testator went on to say that Stephen Wilkes had acted as his legal adviser for many years, and to express a strong wish that he would continue in that capacity for his daughter. He hoped that she would consult him freely, both in the conduct of the business and in her affairs generally, and act on his advice. He appointed Robert Fraser Andrews and Stephen Wilkes his executors.

So soon as he had finished the reading of the will Mr. Wilkes observed:

"In order to avoid misunderstanding, I wish to state that, since I have reason to believe that my services would not be welcome—and, indeed, learn that another solicitor has already been retained, whom I see present—I wish to withdraw at the earliest possible moment from all connection with Mr. Patterson's estate and affairs, and also that I renounce administration. I will not act as executor."

When the lawyer stopped, Mr. Andrews had his say:

"I'm very much in the same position as Mr. Wilkes. If Miss Patterson would rather I did not act as manager, I have not the slightest wish to press my claim. I'm given to understand, Miss Patterson, that Mr. Elmore here is likely to become your husband. From a conversation I had with him this morning, I— I'm inclined to think that I am older than I supposed, and that it would be to your advantage and to the advantage of the business that the management of affairs should be in his hands. Also, if you wish it, so as not to be a clog on you in any way, I will not act as executor."

Rodney answered for his cousin:

"You must act as executor, Mr. Andrews; Miss Patterson will very unwillingly release you from that duty. The other point she will discuss with you later; you will find that she is as anxious to consider your wishes as you are to consider hers. I may remark to you, Mr. Wilkes, as well as to Mr. Andrews, that Miss Patterson is grateful for the delicate thought which prompts your proposed action, and she will endeavour in all she does to show that she appreciates at its full value all that you have done for her father, and, by consequence, for her. I think, gentlemen, that, at present, that is all."

The meeting was dissolved. The three gentlemen dismissed. The cousins were left together. Kneeling before the armchair on which Miss Patterson was seated, Rodney drew her towards him and kissed her with a sort of mock solemnity.

"My congratulations, lady! if I may venture to kiss one who is now a person of property and importance. I hope you won't mind, but I almost wish, for my sake, that you hadn't quite so much money."

She put out her hand and softly stroked his hair.

"That's nonsense. How much money have I got?"

"Roughly, I suppose that the business brings in four or five thousand a year, and you've forty or fifty thousand pounds in what represents cash. You're a rich woman."

"Then, if you do marry me, you'll be a rich man."

"There's one thing—put the business at its highwater mark, say that in its best year it brings in five thousand pounds—in ten years it shall bring in fifty thousand."

"Rodney, don't be too speculative. We've enough to get along with; let's be sure of having a good time with what there is."

"My dear lady, I'm no speculator—not such a fool; but I don't want to see a gold-mine producing only copper. You've twice the head your father had, and keener, because younger, eyes. Shortly I shall hope to lay my ideas before you; when you have assimilated them, you will be able to judge for yourself whether or not they're speculative. You'll see, what even old Andrews already sees, that you're the possessor of a gold-mine—a veritable gold-mine—which hitherto has been worked as if it were merely a copper-mine. When you begin to work it as a gold-mine, in less than ten years it will be bringing you in fifty thousand pounds a year; I shouldn't be surprised if it brings you twice as much—honestly."

"A hundred thousand pounds a year, Rodney!"

"Wait—you'll see! This is the age of miracles, which, when you look into them, have the simplest natural causes. Seriously, Gladys, there's no reason why, properly handled, the business of which you are now the sole proprietress—because you can easily get rid of Andrews—should not make you rich beyond the dreams of avarice. Wilkes has been quick in taking the hint, hasn't he?"

"I don't like him—I never did. I think I shall like Mr. Parmiter much better."

"I'm sure you will. He's an awfully good sort and as clever as they make them—and straight! He'll make your interests his own."

There was a momentary pause. The gentleman was still kneeling in front of the armchair, and the lady was still stroking his hair. There was a look on her face which was half comical and half something else as she changed the topic.

"Rodney, who's Agnes Sybil Armstrong?"

"I don't know, and don't you ask. Let her have her hundred a year, and go hang!"

"Does every man have an Agnes Sybil Armstrong?"

"Emphatically no; only—I was going to say only men like your father, but perhaps you wouldn't like it."

"I wonder—will you ever have one?"

"Gladys! Lady, if a man loves one woman, that's all the feminine kind he'll ever want, especially—if she's a woman like you. Doesn't your instinct tell you that when you're my wife, I'll—be satisfied, in every sense?"

"I hope so. If you weren't, I—I shouldn't like it."

"I should say not. May I hope that there is some possibility of your being my wife?"

"I have some ideas in that direction now, though on Saturday I thought I never should. How prophetic you were? You almost foretold what has happened—almost as if you saw it coming. Did you know that he was ill?"

"I had a shrewd suspicion; but you don't suppose I foresaw what actually did happen?"

"I dare say that yours was not the prophetic vision quite to that extent. I wonder why he didn't like you?"

"I'm nearly sure that with him it was a case of Dr. Fell—the reason why he couldn't tell. When you came on the scene he hated me because you didn't."

"Didn't you do anything to ruffle him—to rub him the wrong way?"

"Never—consciously. I've a notion—it's only a notion, but my notions are apt to be pretty near the mark—that he had some idea of marrying you to Mr. Stephen Wilkes."

"Rodney! Good gracious! What a notion!"

"As I remarked, it's only a notion; but I can put two and two together, and something in the gentleman's manner this morning put the crown on my suspicions."

"I'd rather have died."

"Or married me? Well—do! How soon could you make it convenient?"

"How soon would you like it to be?"

"This is Monday. Say Thursday—next?"

"Rodney! How can you?"

"Then make it Friday—if you've no prejudice against the day."

"I'll never be married on a Friday."

"Then postpone it to that far-off date, Saturday, or even Monday. I don't know if you want a smart wedding; if you do, what indefinite postponement may the conventions require?"

"I don't want a smart wedding."

"That sounds hopeful. You're all I want; I don't know if I'm all you want."

"Well; you are one thing."

"Am I? Thanks—you have a nice way. I tell you what, I'll get a special licence—hang the expense—and we'll be married on Monday."

"I won't be married in black, and I will have one bridesmaid; I'll have Cissie Henderson. She's my particular friend; she likes you; she's been on our side all through; and she'll strain a point—when I've put it to her as I shall, she'll have to. As a matter of fact, I believe she'll love to."

"And Clarence Parmiter shall be my best man, and old Andrews shall give you away."

"I don't know about old Andrews."

"Then old Andrews shan't! So long as I get you I don't care who gives you away; if it comes to that, we'll make it worth the verger's while. Then we'll go off for a whole month, and have a rare old spree."

"That sounds inviting."

"And while we're away Andrews and Parmiter between them shall get things ship-shape; and when we come back, under her majesty's directions I shall put my shoulder to the wheel and start making her the richest woman in the world—and the happiest."

"The conceit of him! Mind you do make me happy. Will you?"

"Don't you think I shall?"

"If I hadn't hopes in that direction you—wouldn't be where you are."

"Where shall we go to?"

"Wherever you like."

"Then—"

He leaned forward and whispered in her ear. She put her arms about his neck and drew him to her.

CHAPTER XV

MABEL JOYCE

When Rodney Elmore got back to his rooms it was somewhat late. Some letters were on the table in his sitting-room, and a telegram from Stella Austin. One of those voluminous telegrams which women send when they are in no mood to consider that each unnecessary word means another halfpenny. It was, indeed, a little letter, in which she expressed both sympathy and disappointment. She was so sorry to hear the bad news about his uncle, and assured him—with apparent disregard of the fact that the message might possibly pass through several persons' hands—that he had much better come to her if he was able, since she would console him as nobody else could.

"I shall be terribly disappointed if you do not come," it went on, "so please do come. There are heaps of things I wish to say to you—simply heaps. So mind, Rodney, dear, you are to come some time this evening, and you are to let nothing keep you away from your own Stella."

It was a love-letter which this young lady had flashed across the wires at a halfpenny a word, evidently caring nothing if strangers learned what was in her heart so long as he did. He was still considering it when Miss Joyce came into the room with a decanter and a glass upon a tray.

"Miss Austin's been to see you," she observed. "I suppose that telegram's from her."

"Did she tell you it was from her?"

"She came in and looked about her at pretty nearly everything, and saw it lying on the table, and said she'd sent you a telegram, and supposed that was it. I thought she was going to walk off with it, but she didn't. I expected she'd want to stop till you came in, as Miss Patterson did last night; but I told her I knew you'd an important engagement in the City, and knew you wouldn't be in till very late; so she went."

"Thank you; I'm glad she didn't stay."

"I thought you would be. She asked me if I was the servant. I don't think she liked the look of me."

There was something in his attitude which suggested that he was expecting her to leave the room, and would have liked her to. When she showed no sign of going he commented on her last remark.

"That was rather bad taste on her part."

"Wasn't it?"

Having done with the telegram, he began to examine the letters. She watched him with an expression in her pale blue eyes which, if he had been conscious of it, might have startled him. It was plain from his manner that he intended to offer her no encouragement either to continue the conversation or to remain in the room. After a perceptible interval, she said, with an abruptness which was a little significant:

"I was at the inquest."

He glanced up.

"You were where? At the inquest? Oh! What was the attraction? And how did you get in?"

"I believe the public are admitted to inquests. They're supposed to be public inquiries, aren't they? Also, I had a friend at court; and, anyhow, I wasn't the only person there. I suppose Miss Patterson is a rich woman now."

"She'll have money."

"Are you going to marry her?"

"Why do you ask?"

"Or are you going to marry Miss Austin?"

"Pray why do you ask that?"

"When Miss Patterson was here last night I thought there was an air about her as if she considered you her property; when Miss Austin was here this evening I thought the same thing of her. Odd, wasn't it?"

"The only thing odd about it, my dear Mabel, is that you should have such a vivid imagination. Both these ladies are old friends of mine."

"Old friends, are they? In what sense? In the sense that I'm an old friend?"

"No one could be nicer than you have been."

"I see. Have they been nice to you like that?"

"My dear Mabel, in what quarter sits the wind? Where's Mrs. Joyce?"

"Mother's out; she's going to stay at aunt's till to-morrow. You and I are alone together."

"Good business! Come and give me a kiss."

"No, don't touch me; I won't have it."

"There is something queer about the wind! What's wrong? Is there anything wrong?"

"I'm trying to tell you. It's not easy, but I'm going to tell you if you'll give me a chance."

"You've some bee in your bonnet. Let me get it out."

"You give me a chance, I say! I tried to tell you last night, but I couldn't. But I'm going to tell you now; I've got to!"

"Have you? Couldn't you tell me a little closer, instead of standing all that distance off?"

"I wouldn't come nearer for—for anything."

"Mabel! After all these years!"

"Yes, after all these years! How long have you been here?"

"I never had a memory for dates."

"More than four years you have been here."

"So long as that? And it hasn't seemed a day too long."

"I was a kid in short skirts when you first came."

"And a very pretty kid you were. Almost as pretty even then as you are now."

"Rodney, have you ever cared for me a little bit?"

"Have I ever cared? Haven't I shown it?"

"Shown it? You call that showing it? My word!"

"What is the matter with the girl? I've never seen you like this before."

"Suppose—something was going to happen?"

"Well, isn't something always going to happen? What especially awful thing are you afraid is going to happen?"

"Suppose—something was going to happen—to me—because of you? Suppose—I was going—"

Her voice died away, her eyes fell.

"You don't mean that—"

"I do."

"Good God! It's—it's impossible!"

"Why is it impossible? It's true."

"But, my—my dear girl, it can't be."

"Why can't it be? It is."

"But—you're not sure. How can you be sure? You know, my dear Mabel, how you do fancy things. I'll bet ten to one that you're mistaken."

"Do you suppose that I haven't tried to make myself think that I'm mistaken? I wouldn't believe it. But it's no use pretending any longer; it's sure. What are you going to do?"

"What am I going to do? That's—that's a nice brick to aim at a fellow without the slightest warning."

"I'm sorry; I can't help it; I must know. What are you going to do?"

"My dear girl, you know that you've no more actual knowledge on such a subject than I have. I hope—and I think it's very possible—that you are wrong. Let's, first of all, make sure."

"Very well—we'll make sure. And when we've made sure what are you going to do—if it is sure?"

"We'll discuss that when we've made sure. Give me a chance to think; you've had one. It seems that you've guessed, goodness knows how long. Give me a chance to get my thoughts into order."

"I can't wait; I must know now. What are you going to do—if it is sure?"

"I'll do everything that a man can do—you know that perfectly well. You've knocked the sense all out of me! Do give me a chance to think! Don't look at me with that stand-and-deliver air! Come here, old lady, and let me kiss those pretty eyes of yours; I can't bear to have them look like that."

"Don't touch me—don't dare! You say you'll do everything a man can do. Does that mean you'll marry me?"

"Marry you! Mabel!"

"Don't you mean that you will marry me?"

"My dear girl, it's—it's impossible!"

"Why is it impossible? Are you married already?"

"Good Lord, no!"

"Then why can't you marry me?"

"As if you didn't know!"

"What do I know?"

"As if there weren't a thousand reasons! As if you weren't almost as well posted in my financial position as I am myself! As if you didn't know how hard I've found it to pay my way—that, in fact, I haven't paid it! If I were to marry you, financially there'd be an end of me; and in every other way! Not only should I be worse than penniless, but there'd be absolutely no prospect of my ever being anything else."

"I shouldn't be worse off as your wife than I am now."

"Oh, wouldn't you? You would; don't you make any error! I've never said a word to you about marriage."

"That's true, nor should I have said it to you if it hadn't been for this."

"There you are—that's frank. There's been no deception on either side. After all that there's been between us don't let's have any unpleasantness, for both our sakes. I'm as sorry for the position to which we've managed to bring things as you can be; you must know I am. At present I'm stony, but shortly I hope to have the command of plenty of money."

"Are you going to get it from Miss Patterson or Miss Austin?"

"What does it matter where it comes from?"

"So far as I'm concerned it matters a good deal."

"It'll be my own money."

"If you'll have so much money of your own why can't you marry me?"

"If I do marry you I'll have no money?"

"Are you going to get it with your wife? Which wife?"

"I can understand how you're feeling, so I'll try not to mind your being bitter, though it isn't like you one scrap. I can only implore you to trust me, to leave it all to me; I'll arrange everything. If you're right in what you fear you'll find a place ready for you when the time comes, in which you'll be comfortable, in which you'll have everything you want, and when it's over, if you like you can come home again, and no one will be one whit the wiser, and you won't be an atom the worse. It's done every day."

"Is it? And the child—what about the child?"

"The child? If it is my child—"

"If? if? if? What do you mean by 'if'? You'd better be careful, Rodney, what you are saying. What do you mean by 'if'?"

"My dear girl, it was only a way of speaking."

"Then don't you speak that way. 'If' it is your child! When you knew me I was innocent, and I'm innocent now except for you. Don't you dare to say if! You know it is your child!"

"My dear girl, of course I know it's my child. You won't let a fellow finish what he is going to say. I was only going to say that the child shall want for nothing; it shall have everything a child can have. So shall you; you'll be much better off than if you were my wife."

"If the child is born, and I am not your wife, I'll kill myself—and it. Or, rather, if I'm not going to be your wife, I'll kill myself before it's born, as sure as you are alive."

"Mabel, don't talk like that—don't! I can't bear it. If you only knew how it hurts!"

"Hurts! As if anything hurts you! Nothing could hurt you, nothing; you're not built that way. Do you suppose that I don't know what kind of man you are—that you're an all-round bad lot?"

"To say a thing like that, after pretending to care for me!"

"Pretending! There wasn't much pretence about my caring; I proved it. You wouldn't let me rest until I did. Not only did I care for you, but I do care for you; and I shall continue to care for you as long as I live. No other man can ever be to me what you have been."

"That's more like the Mabel I know."

"But don't imagine that I'm under any delusion about you; you'll know better by the time I've done. You're the kind of man who's not to be trusted with a girl. You make love to every woman you meet— what you call love! You're entangled with no end of women. I know! I don't know how many think you're going to marry them, but I shouldn't be surprised if Miss Patterson and Miss Austin both think you are. If I were to go and tell them, do you think they'd marry you? Not they; they're not that sort."

"But you won't tell them. You're not that sort either. I, perhaps, know you better than you know yourself."

"It's this way. Even you mayn't know who you're going to marry, but I do. You're going to marry me."

"I wish I were. I'll admit so much. But—we can't always do what we wish, my dear."

"You can, and do; that's what makes you dangerous—at first to others, in the end to yourself. Rodney, I don't want to say something which will change the whole face of the world for both of us, but I'll have to if you make me. Don't you make me! Say you'll marry me."

"My dear child—"

"Don't talk like that to me; don't you do it! You're duller than I thought, or long before this you'd have seen what I was driving at. Now, you listen to me; I'll tell you. To-day I was at the inquest."

"That fact, I assure you, in spite of my dullness, I have appreciated already. What I still fail to understand is what the attraction was."

"Attraction! You call it an attraction! You wait. I've always thought that an inquest was to find out the truth, not to hide it up. The idea of that one seemed to be to conceal, not to reveal. The coroner was an old idiot, as blind as a bat. He'd got a notion into his head, and as there wasn't room for more than one at a time—why, there it was! I went there knowing nothing, guessing nothing, suspecting nothing. The inquest hadn't hardly begun before I saw everything, knew everything, understood everything. But the coroner, the jury, and the witnesses—they knew less at the end than the beginning."

"Your words suggest that nature erred in making you a pretty girl, and therefore incompetent to be a coroner."

"According to the guard of the train, your uncle was found sitting up in a corner of the carriage, with a box in his hand, in which were some of the things with which he is supposed to have poisoned himself. The box was handed round for the coroner and jury to look at. Directly I saw it I knew it."

If Elmore changed countenance it was only very slightly, and the change went as quickly as it came; yet one felt that for an instant it had been there.

"Is that so? What sort of box was it? It must have been something rather out of the common run of boxes for you to have recognised it at what, I take it, was some little distance."

"I was close enough, close enough to take it in my hand if I had wanted; and it was all that I could do to keep my hand from off it. And it was very much what you call out of the common run of boxes. It was a silver box, Chinese, with Chinese engraving on it, about an inch and a half long, round, and a little thicker than a fountain pen."

"You seem to have observed it pretty closely."

"It was not the first time I'd seen it. The first time I saw it it was on your dressing-table."

Again, if Elmore's expression altered, it was only as if a flickering something had come and gone in his eyes.

"You may have seen a box like it on my dressing-table. You certainly never saw the one you saw this morning."

"The box was on your dressing-table. I picked it up and asked you what it was. You said you believed it was a Chinese sweetmeat box. I said that if it was it did not hold many sweets. You laughed and said it was very old, and that you believed it came from Pekin, and that some of the carvings on it were Chinese characters, but you didn't know what they meant. I opened it. Inside it were some of the white things which were in it when they handed it round this morning. I asked you if they were sweets. You said that those who wanted a long, long sleep would find them sweet enough; and you took the box from me as you said it. I thought there was something queer about you and the box, and when you put it down for a moment I picked it up again, and, with some scissors which were on the table, scratched some marks on the bottom—I myself hardly know why. But when I saw that box this morning it was all I could do to keep from asking the coroner if they were on the bottom. I could describe them perfectly; I should know them again. I can see them now."

"What a vivid imagination you have, and what powers of observation! Even granting that, by some odd coincidence, that box was my box, what's the inference you draw from it, when the simple explanation is that it was a present to my uncle from his affectionate nephew?"

"I daresay it was a present, but not in the sense you mean. You went to Brighton yesterday by the Pullman, but you didn't come back by it."

"Pray, who is your informant, and what's the relevancy to your previous remarks?"

"George Dale, who has the bed-sitting-room upstairs, and who cares for me in a different way to what you do, because he wants me to be his wife."

"Then why the—something don't you oblige him? Isn't he respectable?"

"Oh, he's respectable."

"Then could there be a sounder proposition? A man who loves you, who would be all that a husband ought to be! I tell you what, on the day you marry him an unknown benefactor will settle on you a thousand pounds—something like a fortune."

"You can talk to me like that, knowing what you know! After what you've done to me you want to pass me on to someone else. That finishes it! Now you listen. George Dale's a booking clerk at Victoria Station. He recognised you, though you didn't him."

"Quite possibly, if he was on the other side of the peep-hole, and seeing that I've only seen him two or three times in my life."

"He gave you your ticket for the Pullman. All the seats are numbered; he made a note of your number. Your ticket wasn't among those which were given up by the passengers who came back by the Pullman, but it was among those which were collected from the train which reached Victoria at 11.30. The guard saw you get into the train at Redhill Station. You got into a first-class compartment with a little man. You two were the only first-class passengers who got in at Redhill, so he took particular notice. You were in the London Bridge part of the train. At East Croydon someone else got into your compartment. You got out and went back to the Victoria part. The guard, shutting your carriage door, took particular notice of you again."

"Your friend the guard appears to be as quick to observe as he is to impart the fruits of his observation."

"He wasn't my friend, only Mr. Dale introduced me to him, and he was kind enough to answer a question or two. Mr. Dale also introduced me to the guard of the train in which your uncle was. I asked him if it stopped anywhere. He thought a bit, and then said that it did once, for about a minute, in Redhill tunnel, because the signal was against it. I haven't made inquiries yet, but I shouldn't be surprised if someone saw you get into your uncle's train at Brighton. As that train stopped in Redhill tunnel, it's not hard to understand how, or why, you got into another train a little later at Redhill Station."

"You surprise me, Mabel. I hadn't a ghost of an idea that you had such a genius for ferreting."

"It's easy enough. If that coroner hadn't had a notion in his head when he started, he might have got at the facts as easily as I have."

"And, from what you call the facts, what is the inference you draw? What dreadful charge against me have you been formulating in your mind?"

"Rodney, a wife can't give evidence against her husband in a charge of murder."

"I believe I have heard as much. And then?"

"I'm the only creature in the world who has any suspicion. If you marry me you're safe."

"You, pretending to love me, can marry the sort of man you believe I am?"

"It is because I do love you that I am willing to marry you, knowing you to be the kind of man you are.

"Your standard of morality is not a high one."

"It's what you've made it."

"Mabel, while you have got parts of your story right, the inferences you draw from it are all wrong; but I'm not going to attempt any denials."

"I shouldn't; lies won't help you—not with me."

"So you also think that I'm a liar?"

"I'm sure of it; you're a born liar. Sometimes I don't believe you know yourself if you are speaking the truth."

"One thing I've learnt this evening—that you're a born actress. I am speaking the absolute truth when I assure you that I never for one second dreamt that you had the opinion of me you seem to have."

"I never really began to understand you myself till last night. Just before you came in Mr. Dale had gone to bed. He told me, as he went upstairs, that your uncle had been found dead in the Brighton train, and that you had gone to Brighton in the Pullman; and he wondered, laughing, if it was you who had killed him. Then Miss Patterson came with her air of owning you, and you came and went out with her again as with one whom you were going to make your wife, and something happened inside my head and I began to understand. All night I scarcely slept for thinking, and in the morning, somehow, I knew; and all day I have been learning much more, until now I know you—for the man you are."

"My dear Mabel, one thing I do see plainly, that you're not very well, that your nerves are out of order, and play you tricks. Let's both turn in. I, for one, am tired, and I'm sure that a good night's rest will do you good; and to-morrow we'll continue our talk where it left off."

"Rodney, you'll give me at once a written promise of marriage, or I'll communicate with Inspector Harlow, and in the morning you'll be charged with murder."

"Do you wish me to suppose that you are speaking seriously?"

"We'll be married at a registrar's—it doesn't matter where, so long as we are married, and at a registrar's it's quickest. You can get a licence for £2 3s. 6d.; I'll get it, I've enough money for that, and then the day after you can be married. If I get the licence to-morrow we can be married on Thursday—and we will."

"We can be married on Thursday, can we, you and I? This sounds like comic opera, and, as the song says, 'When we are married, what shall we do?'"

"You can do as you please. I shall have my marriage lines, and that's all I care about."

"So you propose to haul me to the registrar, and chain me to you, and souse me in the gutter, and ruin my career, and render life not worth living, not because you've any special ambition for yourself, nor even because you crave for the sweets of my society, but in order that you may have somewhere locked up in a drawer what you call your marriage lines. This seems to me like using a steam hammer to crack a nut."

"I've got a sheet of paper; you sit down and write what I tell you."

She laid on the table a sheet of paper which she had taken out of her blouse. As he looked at it he laughed.

"Stamped—a sixpenny stamp, as I'm a sinner! Do you know, my dear, that this is a bill form which you've got here, good for any amount up to fifty pounds. Wherever did you get the thing? And what use do you suppose it is to you? What a practical-minded child it is! And I never guessed it till now! Tis a wonderful world that we live in!"

"You get a pen and write."

He took a fountain pen and a blotting pad from a table at the side, and spread out on the latter the crumpled bill stamp.

"Here we are. Now for the writing. 'Three months after date I promise to pay.' Is that the sort of thing I'm to write?"

"You write what I tell you."

"Tell on; I'm waiting."

"Write: 'I, Rodney Elmore, promise to marry on Thursday next Mabel Joyce, who is about to bear a child of which I am the father.' Have you got that? Why aren't you writing?"

"Before I start I want to see the finish; that is, I want to know all that I am to write."

"Except your signature and the date, that is all."

"Rather a considerable all, eh? What use do you suppose this will be to you when you've got it?"

"That's my business."

"What do you propose to do with it?"

"Nothing. If you marry me I'll give it you before we leave the registrar's."

"And if I don't?"

"You'll be in gaol."

"I see; that's it. If I don't write I'm in the cart, and if I do write and don't marry I'm also in the cart."

"I'm fighting for my life."

"And I lose mine either way."

"How do you make that out? Who's there to be afraid of except me?"

"If I do marry you I might as well be dead, and if I don't you'll do your best to bring my death about."

She was silent. They eyed each other, she standing at one side of the table, he sitting at the other. In the white-faced woman, with the rigid features and close-set lips, who looked at him with such unfaltering gaze, he scarcely recognised the pretty, dainty, blue-eyed girl whom it seemed only yesterday he had wooed and won. He was sufficiently a physiognomist and student of character to be aware that this woman meant every word she said. As this knowledge was borne more clearly in on him a curious something came into his own eyes—the something which had been there last night in the train. He spoke very softly.

"Mabel?"

Her voice fell as his had done.

"Well?"

"We are alone together in the house, you and I."

"We are; as you were alone with your uncle in the railway carriage."

"Why shouldn't I serve you as you persist in hinting that I served him? What reason is there?"

"None."

"Then—why shouldn't I?"

"You can."

"I can—what?"

"Kill me."

"Knowing me, as you pretended to know me, you're not afraid?"

"I shall never be afraid of you."

"You seem to flatter me all at once."

"I don't care what you do to me. I'd rather you killed me than not marry me—much."

"You wouldn't be so easy to explain. You'd want a lot of explaining if they found you dead."

When he stopped she was still looking at him with eyes which never flinched. He went on:

"You wouldn't be difficult to manage."

"I shouldn't resist. If you broke my head to pieces with the poker I wouldn't make a sound."

"The poker? Not such a fool! He would be sanguine who hoped to explain a poker."

He had been sitting back in his chair; now, leaning forward, he rested his arms on the table.

"Suppose I had another of those things which were in the silver box. If I gave it to you would you take it?"

"No."

Her face had become all at once so pale that her very lips seemed white.

"I should have to go through the form of making you."

"You would have to do to me what you did to your uncle."

"And if I did, what then?—what then?"

If he expected an answer it did not come. She stood confronting him, so immobile that she scarcely seemed to breathe. The smile was on his face which had seemed the night before to give it such unpleasant significance, as if unholy thoughts were chasing each other through his mind.

"I'll be frank with you."

If he expected her to speak he was again disappointed.

"If I could explain you—I'd do it, but I don't see how I could. How can I? Suggest an explanation."

"You won't kill me; you dare not. You only killed your uncle because you thought you wouldn't be found out."

"You think that was the only reason? You don't think that I had a choice of evils, and that I merely chose what seemed to be the lesser?"

"I wonder why you killed him?"

"In your case you wouldn't wonder?"

"Was it because of Miss Patterson?"

"As how?"

"Because you've treated her as you've treated me, and her father found out. If I thought—if I thought—Take that paper and write on it what I told you—now! now! now!"

"And if I don't?"

"If you don't kill me—and you won't, you're afraid—I'll have you hanged!"

"So with you also it is a choice of evils."

"Write what I told you—write it—"

She had raised her voice nearly to a scream. All at once she was still, leaving her sentence unfinished. There were sounds without of a key being put in a lock, of a door being opened, of steps in the passage. She spoke in a whisper, hurriedly, eagerly, and the fashion of her countenance was changed:

"That's Mr. Dale come back from the station. If you don't write what I told you now, I'll call him in—I will!"

He also spoke in a whisper, and in some subtle fashion his countenance was also changed:

"Mabel, don't—don't be hard on me."

"Then write, write what I told you; write it now. If I do call him in it'll be too late. Write!"

He drew the bill stamp towards him and picked up the fountain pen. His air was more than a trifle sullen.

"What am I to write?"

"You know perfectly well. Write: 'I, Rodney Elmore, promise to marry on Thursday next Mabel Joyce, who is about to bear a child of which I am the father.' Write that. Now sign it, put your name at the bottom, and the date. I'll blot it."

Drawing the pad to her she blotted what Elmore had written; then, after a glance at what was on it, began to return it to her blouse, while the young gentleman sat and watched.

"I'm going to put this into an envelope with a note I'm going to write, and give it to Mr. Dale, and tell him to keep it for me till I ask for it; and if I don't ask for it he'll know why."

"So, in writing that, I have not only put myself in your power, but also in Mr. Dale's."

"I tell you that if you do marry me on Thursday I'll give it you again before we leave the registrar's; but if for any cause you don't, even if you put me out of the way, Mr. Dale will see that you are made to smart."

A voice was heard calling to her without:

"Miss Joyce."

She replied to it.

"All right, Mr. Dale. You'll find your supper all ready for you in the parlour; I'm coming now."

She went, the bill form inside her blouse. Mr. Elmore was left to his own reflections. He remained just as she had left him, leaning forward, his arms upon the table, looking with unblinking eyes straight in front of him, as if he hoped to find in space an answer to a problem which was difficult to solve.

CHAPTER XVI

THOMAS AUSTIN, SENIOR

Miss Joyce came into Mr. Elmore's bedroom the next morning before he was out of it. As a matter of fact, he was arranging his tie before the looking-glass with that nice care which is becoming to a young gentleman of looks.

"There's a gentleman come to see you—a Mr. Austin. I should say from the look of him that he's the father of the Miss Austin who was here last evening."

"The thing is possible."

"I don't know what he's come about."

"It's conceivable that you soon will know if you keep your ear close enough to my sitting-room door. Mr. Austin has rather a hearty way of speaking."

"Don't you talk to me like that! You know I've never played the spy on you yet, and you know I never will. But don't you make any mistake about last night. Mr. Dale's got that paper you wrote and my letter in a sealed envelope, and if you don't turn up on Thursday you'll be sorry."

"Thank you so much for the information. Now, let me clearly understand. If, as you put it, I do turn up on Thursday, what is going to happen—after the ceremony?"

"All I want is my marriage lines. I'm coming straight back home; you can do as you like."

"If I like can I go through a similar ceremony with Miss Jones or Miss Brown?"

"If I thought you were going to be up to any game of that sort I'd—I'd—"

"Yes—you'd what?"

"I'd go and talk to your Mr. Austin to begin with. Don't you get any ideas of that kind in your head; don't you try it on."

"I've no intention of, as you again put it, 'trying it on,' not I. I only wondered. Then, at least, you won't insist on the position being made instantly public?"

"I don't care if it's made public or not. All I want is my marriage lines—when the time comes."

"And you quite understand that, whatever the relations may be, from the legal point of view, in which we stand to each other, you'll get no money out of me, for the sufficient reason that I shall have none to give you."

"I don't want your money. I don't want anything from you except that one thing; and—and—mind you do turn up!"

"I've been thinking things over in the silent watches of the night, and I've quite decided that I will turn up."

"Mind you do!"

"I will, I will; be assured I will. Now I believe I'm ready. I was thinking of troubling you to tell Mr. Austin that I'll be with him in a second, but I'll save you that trouble."

"Mind—"

Standing by the door she was beginning a sentence. He cut her short.

"All right, my dear; I'll mind. Would you mind getting out of the way?"

She moved aside to let him pass. He went down the stairs to his sitting-room below, quickly, lightly, humming a tune as he went, as if he had not a care in the world; and with a face which was all sunshine he entered his visitor's presence.

"My dear Rodney, this is an unconventional hour at which to pay a call, but I didn't think that in my case you'd mind about conventions, and I thought that, as I didn't get a chance of speaking to you last night, I'd have a few words with you before you started for the City. I suspect that I needn't tell you that I was glad to hear the news from Stella."

The speaker was a short, sturdily-built, fresh-coloured man, probably somewhere in the fifties, whose neatly trimmed beard was a shade whiter than his hair. A pair of bright eyes looked out from behind gold-rimmed spectacles; about his whole appearance there was a suggestion of health, vigour, and clean living. He took both the young man's hands in his, looking up at him as at one whom he both esteemed and liked.

"You're on the tall side. Stella always did like six-footers. I shouldn't wonder if that's the main reason why she's contracted a fondness for you."

Rodney laughed.

"It's very good of you, sir, to look me up in this unceremonious way. You must join me at breakfast."

"On this occasion I've been an earlier bird than you—I've breakfasted—but I will join you in a cup of coffee."

Rodney rang the bell. Miss Joyce entered with the breakfast on a tray. As she was placing the various articles on the table the two men scarcely spoke. The young man was examining the outsides of three or four letters which the morning post had brought; the elder, who had taken up his position before the fireplace, was for the most part observing Miss Joyce. When she had gone he said:

"That's not a bad-looking young woman. Who is she?"

"She's the landlady's daughter."

"Don't they keep a servant?"

"I fancy they do at intervals, someone who does the rougher work; but I'm out all day, and I never see her. So far as I'm concerned, either the mother or the daughter does the waiting."

"Are you the only lodger?"

"Oh, no; there's another man upstairs, who's by way of being a booking clerk or something. I rather fancy he has an eye in her direction."

"Is that so? Then perhaps that's what worries her. I never saw a young girl with a whiter face, or one with such an odd look in her eyes. It quite troubled me."

"How are you, sir? Though I don't think I need ask."

"No, you needn't. As always, I'm in the enjoyment of vulgar health; nothing ever seems to ail me, though in saying so perhaps I ought to touch wood. When I heard from Stella yesterday morning I made up my mind that I would come up to town at once and say what I had to say by word of mouth, instead of putting it on paper. I arrived in the afternoon, hoping to see you in the evening; but I didn't. I can tell you that Stella was very badly disappointed. I think she was unreasonable; but girls are! You'll have to make your peace to-day. I daresay you won't find it very difficult. This is very bad news about your uncle. I see the inquest is in the morning's paper."

"Is it, sir? As yet I haven't seen a paper."

"From what I can gather he was suffering from some form of malignant disease, and, it seems, in a fit of despair, took his own life. Poor fellow! It's easy to judge such cases, but I often feel that God, who is love, understands and pardons. I hope I'm saying nothing that I ought not to say. Mrs. Austin will have it that I oughtn't to talk like that, but that's how I do feel. Will his death make any difference to you?"

"Do you mean has he left me anything? No, sir; not a penny."

"What becomes of the business?"

"According to the will it's to be carried on by the managing man for the benefit of those mentioned in the will."

"Of whom you're not one?"

"No, sir, I am not."

"Then that makes what I have to say all the easier. I am glad to hear that you're going to be Stella's husband; Mrs. Austin is glad to hear it; I'm sure Tom will be glad to hear it—in fact, we're all of us glad to hear it."

"It's very kind of you to say so, sir, considering what an ineligible son-in-law I am. Here is a letter from Tom this morning. Shall I open it and see what he says?"

"You needn't. I've no doubt it conveys his congratulations in his own vernacular. I know Tom and his letters. There are some things about the governance of this world which I don't understand, which shows I am not omniscient. Experience teaches me that when a man has a son and a good business the son will have none of it, and can with difficulty be brought to believe that the business offers a good opening for him; whereas if a man has a son and no business, the son is apt to look upon it almost as a grievance that his father has no business in which to give him an opening. Instances of the kind are so common that I've nearly come to look upon them as illustrations of a general rule. Now, here am I, and there is Tom, and there's the business, producing, even in these competitive days, quite a comfortable number of thousands a year. Tom's a born optimist. The only time Eve seen him at all pessimistic is when I've suggested that those thousands might as well find their way into his pockets; then he's pessimism gone mad. He'd sooner raise sheep in Australia, or ranch in Manitoba, or do some other ridiculous thing. In fact, he once told me—in such matters he's frankness itself—that he'd rather sweep a crossing than be what he called imprisoned for life in the warehouse at Leicester. I'll do him this justice—that I believe his instincts are right, because I've never seen anything about him to lead me to suppose that in him are the makings of a business man. That's a pretty quandary for a man to be in who has a good business and an only son. Now, Rodney, I've always liked you. It's true that I've sometimes felt that a decent-looking young fellow occasionally finds it difficult to steer clear of quicksands which are represented by nice-looking persons of the opposite sex; but I've never had any tangible or serious charge to bring against you, and I've no doubt that when you're married there'll be only one woman in the world to you, and she will be your wife."

As the speaker paused, apparently with the intention of giving the other an opening, Rodney said with a smile:

"I'm at least glad, sir, that you've no tangible or serious charge to bring against me."

"Well, no, I haven't. At the same time—however, we'll let bygones be bygones. I daresay I'd an eye for more than one pretty girl before I'd a Mrs. Austin. I do know you're clever, with great charm of manner. I sometimes wonder if your manners are not almost too charming; but then, I come of a stocky school—no one's ever accused an Austin of having a charming manner, and I quite realise that, as things are, in business personal charm's a valuable asset; and I've been frequently struck by the fact that you're the possessor of a singularly quick perception. I think you have what is in reality an instinct, but what is called on the Stock Exchange a 'nose.' Again, a thing which in a business man is well worth having."

"You seem to have been observing me with unexpectedly flattering attention, sir."

"Oh, I've had an eye on you for quite a while. I want you, when you are Stella's husband, to come into my business. If you turn out as I hope and expect, I'll make you a partner. I've been imprisoned in the warehouse all my life, so, as I would like to see more of the world, soon as you're ready to take my place I should like you to take it. How would that meet your views?"

"Nothing could please me better, sir. I don't know where I shall find words with which to thank you even for the suggestion."

"I want no thanks; I want deeds. I'm hopeful that the arrangement will turn out to our mutual advantage. Now, Rodney, tell me candidly do you love my girl?"

"Let me put question for question. Do you think I'm the kind of man who would ask her to be my wife if I didn't?"

"Then why didn't you ask her before?"

"Mr. Austin, you're not quite fair to me."

"How am I unfair?"

"I've loved Stella ever—ever since we were boy and girl together. I've tried to break myself of loving her, but I haven't succeeded. I've never been able to dream of anyone but her as wife. You were a rich man; I was not only penniless, but without prospects. Over and over again I've been on the point of telling her what I felt, but I've checked myself. It hasn't been easy, but I've done it. I meant to wait till I'd some shadow of a right to ask her to be my wife, but last Saturday, when I saw her dear face, I—I couldn't hold myself in any longer, and that's the truth."

"I'm glad you couldn't. While I'm quite aware that your sentiments do you honour, all the same I rather wish that you'd shown a little more of the perception with which I've credited you. Rodney, is there any reason why the marriage should be postponed?"

"Mr. Austin, I haven't at the moment five pounds in the world to call my own. That's the only reason, so far as I'm concerned; but some fathers would think it a quite sufficient one."

Mr. Austin's eyes twinkled behind his glasses as he settled his spectacles on his nose.

"I suppose they would, if you look at it in that way. You don't paint your position too attractively."

"It couldn't be worse than it is."

"You're not in debt?"

"Oh, I'm not in debt; I don't know who'd give me credit if I wanted it. I've just enough to live on, as it were, from hand to mouth; but, with all the goodwill in the world and all the management, I don't see how it's going to be enough for two."

"I see. You put the position with some clearness. As you say, some fathers would think it a sufficient reason for postponement, but I'm not one of them. As you perhaps know, Stella has some means of her own."

"Isn't that one of the reasons why I—I kept quiet for so long?"

"And on her marriage I shall settle a further sum on her, besides making other arrangements. For instance, I shall, as I have said, be glad to receive you in my business, giving you at the commencement a salary which will enable you to contribute towards some of the expenses of a wife, with the prospect of a partnership in the early future. Now, do you see any reason why there should be any postponement so far as you're concerned?"

"I shall be only too delighted to marry Stella next week."

"Next week is a little early perhaps; but what do you say to next month?"

"If I'm Stella's husband next month I shall be the happiest man in the world."

He looked and sounded as if he meant it.

"You understand that in matters of this sort it is the lady who has the final word, but you have my authority to tell Stella that if she can see her way to stand with you at the altar in a month or earlier, she will make her mother and father happy, to say nothing of you. Now suppose you come and spend the day with us?"

"My dear sir! I must go to the City."

"Meaning to your late uncle's office? Why? Can't you scribble a note as soon as you've finished breakfast, and make an end of that?"

"It's impossible; I must go to-day."

"Very well. Go to-day, and say you're not coming to-morrow, or ever again. Say good-bye."

"I'm afraid that that wouldn't be playing the game. I ought to go, at any rate, till the end of the week."

"Very well. Perhaps you're right in not wishing to leave them in the lurch, if the departure of such a junior clerk as I understand you are would be leaving them in the lurch. Then on Saturday you'll come down with me to Leicester, and on Monday I'll introduce you to the warehouse. It will be just as well that you should have a look round before you're actually installed."

Here was Mr. Austin mapping out everything for him, as he had foreseen long ago would be the case if he ever committed himself to Stella; treating him as a puppet who would be content to dance when he pulled the strings. He had no doubt that Mrs. Austin would be ready to play the same motherly part in the management of his domestic affairs. He smiled as he thought of it. His would-be father-in-law went on:

"I'm going to write to Mrs. Austin and wire to Tom; I want to arrange a little dinner for to-morrow in honour of a certain auspicious event. Stella tells me she wants you all to herself to-night, and I'm not to interfere. I don't know what she wants you for, I'm sure, but I've promised not to interfere. She'll pull a face when she sees you've not returned with me, so you come early; after disappointing her twice—on Sunday and last night—she'll think that you can't come too early."

"I'll leave the office as early as I can—trust me for that!—rush back here, dress, and come right on."

"Dress! You needn't dress! They're homely folk at Kensington, and Stella will excuse you; she won't want you to waste, in dressing, valuable time which might be spent with her. You come straight on from the office in your toil-stained garments. She'll want to know what time. Shall I say five? I dare say, at a pinch, you can manage to be in Kensington by five."

Rodney considered. If he did go straight on from the office he would at least escape the risk of another heated discussion with Miss Joyce—that would be something.

"Very well, sir; if Stella will forgive me coming as I am, as you say, all toil-stained, I'll try my best to be with her as near as possible to five."

CHAPTER XVII

THE ACTING HEAD OF THE FIRM

Mr. Austin and Rodney left the house together, and so disappointed Miss Joyce, who was waiting to have one or two last words with Mr. Elmore. Having parted from Mr. Austin, Rodney paid a few calls on his way to St. Paul's Churchyard.

To begin with, he went into a jeweller's shop, and bought a ring set with pearls and diamonds—a simple, inexpensive trifle, which cost six pounds. It was designed for Stella's finger, and was to be her engagement ring.

"It won't do," he said to himself, "for it to cost too much, for one of her inquiring family will want to know where I got the money from. She'll value it none the less because 'I can no more, though poor the offering be.'"

Then he looked in at the offices of the White Star Steamship Company, and paid a deposit on a berth which he booked on a steamer which was to sail from Liverpool to New York on the following Thursday, booking it in the name of John Griffiths; then into the offices of the Royal Mail Steam Packet Company, where he booked a berth for the following Friday, from Southampton to Buenos Ayres, in the name of Charles Dickinson; then to the Cunard offices, where he booked for Saturday to New York, in the name of Adolphus Ridgway. Afterwards he visited the Bishop's Registry, in Doctors' Commons, and there, having made certain affidavits, received, in exchange for two sovereigns, a strip of paper which authorised him to marry Gladys Patterson, spinster, at any church in the London diocese. Thus prepared, as one might suppose, for more than one emergency, he paid still another call before proceeding to St. Paul's Churchyard—on Clarence Parmiter, solicitor. From him he wanted to know what forms it would be necessary to go through to enable Miss Patterson to draw on her late father's banking account. Mr.

Parmiter explained that to do this it would be necessary, first of all, to prove Mr. Patterson's will—and it was not usual to do that, at any rate, till after the testator was buried. When, Mr. Parmiter asked, was the funeral to take place. In spite of himself, his visitor smiled; so fast had events come crowding on him that the fact that the dead man would have to be put into his grave had entirely escaped his notice—so far as he was aware, no arrangements for the funeral had been made of any sort or kind. Mr. Parmiter looked as if he felt that the smile with which this announcement was made was a little out of place. He said that probably Rodney would find that the matter had been arranged by one of the executors, or by Miss Patterson herself. If cash was wanted in the interim; if Miss Patterson and Mr. Andrews, as executor, would attend with him at a bank with which Mr. Patterson had an account, he did not doubt that arrangements might be made which would provide the lady with such advances as she required; and, of course, if she chose, she might instruct the bank to honour any cheques which he—Rodney Elmore—might draw, acting on her behalf.

Mr. Elmore left his friend's chambers with a feeling strong upon him that the business of getting his uncle's money out of the bank was not going to be as simple as he had hoped it would be. Clarence Parmiter even told him that the bank would not now honour any cheque which Graham Patterson might have drawn while still alive. This he did feel was unreasonable; it rendered even forgery futile. If he could wait he did not doubt that matters would be perfectly all right; but—could he wait? If only certain difficulties could be smoothed away, and he was given time, he did not doubt that he would be able to load himself with money; but could they be smoothed away, even for a week? Danger threatened from so many quarters; he really had been such an utter fool. If he had only realised what a fool, he would have taken precious good care to walk more warily; he would have been a wiser and a better man. But wisdom after the event was easy; what he needed was to be ready at a moment's notice for whatever came. He had planned escape in three different directions on three following days—if he could only get away with enough money to count! There was that nest-egg which he had found in his uncle's drawer, but what was that to a man in his plight? What he wanted was ten, or even, say, five thousand pounds. With five thousand pounds he might do very well on the other side of the world.

As, strolling leisurely along, he considered the matter in all its bearings calmly, it appeared to him that nothing worth calling money could be got at least until the morrow. In the morning he would meet his cousin at the bank, with Parmiter and Andrews; the arrangements would be made of which Parmiter had spoken; then, immediately after, he would be free to lay hands on as much ready cash as the arrangements permitted. He had no doubt that everything would be all right until to-morrow—he would so manage that it should be; all the same, he would have liked to have had a good supply of coin at his command, in case. However, it was no use grizzling at what might not be. He smiled as he arrived at this conclusion; he was still smiling when he reached the office. He marched, as a matter of course, to the room which had been his uncle's own particular sanctum, and this time no one even as much as hinted nay. Indeed, he was presently followed by Andrews, who informed him, with a countenance of decent solemnity, that he had made arrangements, which he hoped would meet with his and Miss Patterson's approval, for the interment of Mr. Patterson's remains in the family vault at Kensal Green, the interment to take place upon the morrow—Wednesday. Tickled by certain thoughts of his own, Rodney smiled as he listened; but this time, as his face was bent over the table, it is possible that the smile went unnoticed. He expressed himself as greatly obliged by what Andrews had done, and was certain that his feelings would be shared by Miss Patterson. Indeed, he was convinced that Miss Patterson would be willing to leave everything in his charge, since she would feel assured that everything he did would be right and proper and for the best. Mr. Andrews put his hand up to his mouth and coughed—the cough of one who was sensible that he deserved the compliment which was paid him.

He wanted to know if Mr. Elmore did not think it would be well to close the office for the whole of to-morrow, so as to give the staff an opportunity of at least attending at the graveside. They had all been remembered in the will, and would like to show the last tokens of respect for their dead master. Rodney, to whom the notion of marking such an occasion as a sort of holiday was novel, informed Andrews that the idea was excellent, and that he was at liberty to act in the matter as he thought was right. Andrews then wanted to know if Miss Patterson would be present, or if he—Rodney Elmore— would represent her as chief mourner. The suggestion moved Rodney in a way he would not have cared to admit. He had had no intention of attending his uncle's funeral at all—and as chief mourner! He to represent his cousin in such a capacity! That would be indeed to mock the dead. He was conscious of a feeling which surprised himself; he had not supposed he was so sensitive.

"I think," he told Andrews, "we must leave these points till later. I will consult with Miss Patterson and— observe her wishes. There is another matter," he went on. "Access to Mr. Patterson's banking account is not so easy as I imagined. My acquaintance with the procedure in these cases is nil; I don't know what yours amounts to."

"I know no more than you; this is the first time I find myself in such a position. Two payments of some importance are to be made this week; I was wondering how they would be met. Of course, if representations are made, time will be given."

"But, all the same, you would rather the payments were made? Exactly my feelings, Andrews; I want everything to be done in due order. I am going to arrange for Miss Patterson to meet you and Mr. Parmiter at the bank to-morrow morning, when I am advised that it will be possible to make arrangements which will enable us to meet all liabilities as they fall due. By the way, I believe that the trading account pass-book is in your charge; you might let me look at it."

Rodney examined the book when it was brought to him with great attention. He was already posted in certain figures which had to deal with his uncle's private account. Customers were brought in to him; some who had called in the ordinary course of business, others who had come to offer condolences, and so on. Their being brought straight to him showed a frank acceptance on Andrews' part of the fact that he was to be acting head of the firm; none the less, therefore, he was careful that Andrews was present at each of the interviews, referring certain matters to him with a little air of deference which won, as it was intended to win, the managing man's heart. The customers were favourably impressed, agreeing, as they went out, that Graham Patterson's mantle had descended on to capable shoulders.

"I shouldn't wonder," declared Mr. Brailson North as he shook hands with Mr. Andrews at the outer door, "if he turns out to be every bit as good a man as his uncle."

This, coming from a member of one of the largest firms in the City, was praise indeed. The managing man's eyes glistened. Anything which suggested a compliment to the business, so wrapped up in it was his whole existence, was a compliment to him. Since yesterday his ideas on the subject of Mr. Elmore had changed.

"Mr. North," he addressed the visitor in a confidential whisper, "Mr. Patterson was a good man, an excellent man of business in his way, sound and discreet; but between you, me, and this doorpost, I shouldn't wonder if the young one was better, with all his uncle's soundness and discretion, together with something that his uncle hadn't got. He's surprised me! You mark my words, I shouldn't be surprised if the house of Graham Patterson—there's going to be no alteration in the title—takes its place among the greatest City houses—mind you, in the front rank."

Mr. North laughed.

"There's no reason why your prophecy shouldn't come true. This is the day of the young man. Your young man has evidently got a head on his shoulders; he's a good foundation to build on. If he has grit, steadiness, caution, and knows just what sort of structure he would raise on it, there's no reason that I know of why he shouldn't build anything he likes. I agree with you in thinking that it is possible that the house of Graham Patterson is destined to be, in all respects, one of the finest in the City of London."

While these things were being said in his praise Rodney Elmore was writing to Miss Patterson. He enclosed for her inspection the marriage licence he had bought, asked in what church she would like the ceremony to take place on Monday, and added that he hoped to be able to make all final detailed arrangements with her to-morrow after the funeral. He told her of the difficulty which had arisen about getting money, asked her to meet him at the bank in the morning at 11.30; hoped that afterwards they might lunch together, pointing out that he never had lunched with her yet. Since after to-morrow he looked forward to being able to spend most of his time with her till Monday, and then for ever and a day—and that wouldn't seem a day too long!—he said that he felt that it would be better to devote the evening to doing certain little things of his own, which, sooner or later, would have to be done. By doing them he would clear the decks for action, so that, when the time for action came, he would be able to devote the whole of his time and, indeed, the whole of his life to her. All of which meant that he would not be able to tell her, except on paper, that he loved her till they met at the bank to-morrow morning.

Before actually slipping it into the envelope, together with this edifying epistle, he read the marriage licence carefully through. The perusal started him on what, for him, was an unwonted train of thought. Already, while still in the first flush of youth, he had spoilt his life, brought it to final wreck and ruin. What an extremely silly thing to have done! It was characteristic of this young gentleman that he never could bring himself to look at anything through serious eyes—even death. Whatever his first impulse might be, his second was to smile. Life, with all that appertained thereto, was such a funny thing. Here was he, with a career on either hand, each of which would lead at least to fortune; yet he might have neither. That did seem droll. Each was represented by a woman; personally he would have preferred that which was represented by Gladys, if only because he had no doubt that ere long he would be master not only of the business but of her. He was not so sure of Stella. In her he suspected an obstinate streak which he feared might be congenital. He had always felt that the Austins were, as the head of the house had put it, "stocky." He would find them more inclined to manage than to be managed. One thing he did know of himself: that he never could be managed. He might not put up an open fight—open fighting was not precisely in his line—but, if a sustained attempt were made to manage him, he would slip away—somehow, that was sure. Therefore, if only for the sake of peace and quietude, it would be better to avoid the risk. All the same, there was something about Stella which did appeal to him. With a sudden smile, slipping the licence and the letter into the envelope, he closed the flap.

Then, with pen in hand, as he was about to write the address, he started again to think. It was women—girls—who had brought him to his present pass, that was how he put it to himself. What Mabel Joyce said was perfectly true: he could not be alone with a girl without making love to her. It was a physical impossibility; he did not know why, but it was. The mischief was that his instinct had not warned him they were dangerous, hence his horrid situation. Indeed, it was hard that they should be dangerous; they were so pleasant to make love to. There were men who cared nothing for women, who went through life without making love—real love!—to a single one. How they managed he could not think. To him life under such conditions would not be worth living. He was a Sybarite. Life meant to him its good things; were there better things than women? He doubted it. He thought little of men; he had a very high opinion of women; he doubted if he had ever met one in whom there was not something to be desired.

Take Mabel Joyce. She was showing him a side of her character whose existence he had not suspected. Yet he understood her, quite believed her when she said that she was fighting for her life. No one could have been sweeter to him than she had been; then she was such a pretty little thing, from the tips of her little pink toes to the top of her fluffy little head. It could hardly be set down to her as a fault if she was sweet no longer. Let him be just! Then there was Gladys, a girl of quite a different type; but that was the charm about women, there were so many types. He was persuaded that they would have the best possible time together, if the fates could only manage to be kind. He would make her a model husband, he really would; he rather wondered what it would feel like to be a husband, but he did not doubt that it would be all right. A little cramped, perhaps; but he would study her, and her interests, in every possible way. She should never regret the father she had lost, who was precious little loss after all. He would be better to her than a father; he should rather think so! Then there was Mary Carmichael; but at the thought of Mary Carmichael his pulses began to dance—that any man should be ass enough to care nothing for women when there was Mary Carmichael! Also, let him not forget little Stella—why, what an idiot he was; she was waiting for him now! He glanced at his watch. Great Scott! how the time had flown! And that poor child was longingly waiting for him to put his arms about her and stifle her with kisses. That he should be brute enough to let her wait!

He addressed the envelope, rang the bell, bade the lad who answered take it at once to Russell Square, took his hat off its peg, and, after a few hurried words to Andrews as he went out, started off for Kensington.

CHAPTER XVIII

THE PERFECT LOVER

Stella, opening the door for him herself, was at him like a small wild thing.

"I thought you were never coming!"

"Why, it's not yet half-past five."

"Half-past five! when I expected papa to bring you with him, and he said you'd be here by five! Come in here; I'll talk to you!"

She took from him his hat and stick and gloves, and placed them on a table in the hall; then she led him by the sleeve of his coat into a room on the left, and shut the door, and drew a long breath.

"Oh—h—h! So you've come at last, my lord! Let me look at you, to make sure that it is you. Oh, Rodney, why have you been so long in coming?"

She put her arms about his neck and drew him down to her and kissed him. He said, softly:

"I do believe you have grown shorter."

"You wretch! To let a thing like that be your first word to me!"

"It's such a long way down, though it's well worth stooping for."

He kissed her again, tenderly, on her pretty lips—he was an expert in the art of kissing. Because he did it so well, she, not knowing that such skill came of practice, had him kiss her again and again and again, till the breath had half gone out of her body and she was all rapturous palpitation.

"If you only knew what ages it seems since I saw you!"

"Stella, what do you think it has seemed to me? If you only knew what I have gone through!"

"Poor boy! I suppose you have had to bear a good deal."

"You have no notion what I've had to bear."

That was true enough, or she would not have been as close to him as she was.

"It was bad enough when you didn't come on Sunday. I suppose you didn't get back from that Mrs. What's-her-name, your mother's friend, in time?"

"My dear, I had a chapter of accidents, and nearly missed the last train; I'll tell you all about it some day, and you'll laugh. I didn't feel like laughing then, I can tell you that."

"And I didn't feel like laughing, and I can tell you that. In fact, I—I cried."

"Stella!"

"I did; it seemed so awful. That was the longest Sunday I ever knew; and then when the evening came I kept expecting you every moment; I kept rushing out of the front door to look for you. Every footstep in the street I thought was yours, and every vehicle the hansom which was bringing you; when it kept getting later and later, and still you didn't come, I—I fancied all sorts of things, and I simply had to cry."

"My darling, I would infinitely rather have been with you than where I was."

That again was true enough; part of the time he had been in the tunnel—a gruesome time.

"What time was it when you did get back?"

"Frightfully late; but—Stella, you won't tell anyone if I tell you something? Promise!"

"Of course I promise. What—what is it?"

"You can laugh if you like; I don't mind your laughing a little bit; but I don't want them to laugh."

"Why should they laugh?"

"I did come to see you—after I came back."

"Rodney!"

"At least, I came as far as the outside of the house. I dismissed the cab at the corner; then I walked—or rather sneaked—along the pavement; if a bobby had seen me he'd have been all suspicion—till I reached the house. It was all in darkness; there wasn't a glimmer of light anywhere."

"What time was it?"

"About one, perhaps later."

"Rodney, I'd been in my room hours and hours; but I wasn't asleep; I was crying in bed."

"Stella! You were crying! Great Scott! if—if I'd only known it, I'd—I'd have done something."

"What would you have done?"

"I'd—I'd have done something if—if I'd had to break a window!"

"But what good would your breaking a window have done me?"

"Anyhow, it would have been a beginning; but, you see, I didn't even know which your room was—whether you were at the front or the back."

"I'm on the second floor in the front; my window's over the hall door."

"I kept staring at it all the time; I had a sort of feeling—I swear I had a sort of feeling! If I'd only been sure I'd have whistled."

"Whistled! At one in the morning! What would have been the good of that?"

"Suppose, say, I'd whistled 'The Devout Lover'—or what I should have meant for 'The Devout Lover'—you'd have heard."

"I probably should have heard; Miss Claughton would probably have heard also."

"Oh, hang Miss Claughton!"

"Rodney! Miss Claughton's a dear—and your hostess!"

"Miss Claughton may be an absolute angel for all I know—you know what I mean—so long as you heard I shouldn't have cared who heard. Then you'd have wondered who was kicking up that awful row."

"Do you think I should?"

"Certain! I can't whistle for nuts. Then you'd have got out of bed, crossed the room with your dear little bare feet—"

"Rodney!"

"And lifted the corner of the blind."

"I might."

"When you'd seen me hanging on to the railings for all I was worth, trying to get my breath and whistle at the same time; you'd have stopped crying, whatever else you did."

"Rodney, how absurd you are! Fancy your hanging on to the railings for all you were worth! What did you really do?"

"Oh, I hung about and hung about, and then I slunk off home. Wasn't it silly to come and see you at that time of night? I knew you'd laugh!"

"If I'd known you were there I shouldn't have cried. The idea, you darling! But, Rodney, why didn't you manage to get a peep at me the whole of yesterday?"

"Do you think I didn't try?—but I couldn't; it was a day of horrors! Just as I was wondering if I couldn't manage to get at least a kiss by making out that Kensington was on the way to the City, the news came of what my uncle had done. That was a facer, for a man to get news like that just as he was finishing his breakfast."

"But I thought you didn't get the news till you reached the City? You sent your first telegram from there."

"I got the news before, but I didn't understand; I didn't want to understand, I didn't dare to understand. Then I had to go to the inquest."

"Did you? It doesn't say anything in the paper about you being there."

"Of course not; my evidence wasn't wanted after all, but we all of us had to be there. It was awful!"

"You poor, poor boy! Afterwards why didn't you come straight to me?"

"I couldn't; I had to rush off to the City."

"But why?"

"Everything was in the most frightful confusion; no one knew why he had done it."

"But there was the verdict!"

"The verdict? My uncle was not a man to kill himself for a shadow; there might be a better reason. Say nothing to your father; I wish to impute nothing against my uncle's credit; but at one time it seemed just possible that he had done it, because he knew he was ruined, to save himself from shame, dishonour. We had to find out, to be certain, to make sure; we went all through the books; we went through everything; we were at it till the small hours of the morning."

"My dear! Did they tell you I had called?"

"Did they not! When I heard it I wished that I could have flown to you on a flying machine; but it was impossible."

"But papa tells me that you talk about going to the office every day this week."

"Stella, let me put a case. Suppose Mr. Austin were my uncle, and he had done what my uncle did, and everything were at sixes and sevens, and all the help was wanted that could be got, what would you think of me if I were to cut and run—it would amount to that!—even for the sake of the best and sweetest and prettiest and dearest girl in the world—meaning you?"

"That's all very well, Rodney; but I asked papa if he thought you really had to go—if you ought to go; and he said that so far as he could make out there wasn't the least necessity why you should ever set foot in the office again."

"Your father said that?"

"And I believe he's been making inquiries."

"Has he? When I see your father I shall have to tell him that this is a matter in which I am afraid I shall have to use my own judgment."

"At least you can get one day off to take me out—say to-morrow."

"To-morrow! It's my uncle's funeral."

"Well? There's no reason why you should go to it, if it is. Who expects you to go?"

For a moment it seemed as if the question had left the ready-tongued young gentleman nonplussed; but it was only for a moment.

"My dear Stella, isn't it sufficient answer to say that my uncle was the only relative I have in the world?"

"My dear Rodney, I don't wish to comment on your sudden sensitiveness where your uncle is concerned. I never dreamt that you felt for him what you seem to feel; but I suppose your connection with him will cease when he is buried?"

"In a sense, certainly."

"In all senses?"

"My dear Stella, I have already told you."

"To whom has he left his business?"

"Until the contents of the will are known who can say—positively?"

"Has he left it to you?"

"That I am quite sure he hasn't."

"Has he left you anything?"

"There again, till the will is read, who can be sure?"

"When is the will to be read?"

"To-morrow, after the funeral."

"Where?"

"At his house in Russell Square."

"Are you invited to be present?"

"'Invited' is scarcely the correct word; instructions have been issued that the whole staff is to attend. That rather looks as if he may have left something, possibly some trifle, to everyone who was actually in his employ at the time of his death."

"I see. That explains why you want to be present at the funeral. And afterwards, when the will has been read, will you—dine with us? Papa wants me to dine, I think, at the Savoy, to what he calls 'celebrate' our engagement."

"You may be sure I'll come if I can."

"'If'! It's again 'if.' Is it to be all 'ifs'?"

"My dearest Stella, what do you mean?"

"It doesn't matter. Shall we go to the drawing-room? I think we shall find that the Miss Claughtons and papa are waiting for us there."

The young lady turned as if to leave the room. He caught her by the arm.

"Stella, is it possible, is it conceivable, that you can imagine that what has happened is in the least degree, in any sense my fault? Can you suppose that I would not ten thousand times rather spend every hour of every day with you than do what I have done, what I may still have to do?—that my heart, my thoughts, are not with you every instant I have to spend in that confounded City?"

"Rodney, I am very anxious to believe that there are sufficient reasons which compel you to spend all the time you seem to spend in the City; but you don't manage to make it very clear what they are."

"Stella! Stella! How can you talk like that? What shall I say? What can I do?"

"You can promise to dine with us to-morrow night."

"I gladly promise it—gladly."

"There's no 'if' about the promise?"

"No 'if'! If you only knew how I shall look forward to coming, what pleasure I shall give myself in coming! My dear, if you only knew how I am looking forward to dining with you all the days of all the year!"

"And, Rodney, papa understand that you are coming into his business; is that what you understand?"

"Rather! You bet it is, if he'll have me. Do you think I'd throw away a chance like that?"

"Nothing that may be in your uncle's will will make any difference?"

"You goose! What do you suppose will be there? The probability is that there will be nothing of the slightest interest to me—at the most some trivial legacy—a hundred, fifty, five-and-twenty pounds! But let me tell you this, that in the present state of my exchequer even the latter sum will be a godsend. You don't know what it is to be in a chronic state of impecuniosity—a little millionaire like you!"

"I, a millionaire!"

"You don't appreciate the situation; you really don't. Entirely between us, I wonder that I ever had the courage—the cheek!—to tell you how much I love you; how dear to me is the ground under your small feet; how I long to have you in my arms—you, with the Bank of England at your back; and I! But— Cæsar's ghost!—what am I dreaming about? The sight of you, the touch of you, the sound of you, has so—so got into the very bones of me that I'd clean forgotten. Why—Stella!—what's this?"

He took a small, round, leather-covered box out of his waistcoat pocket.

"My dear Rodney—how should I know what it is?"

As she looked at the outside of the box her eyes began to sparkle—as if she did not know!

"There! Why, it's a ring!"

"What a pet."

"Give me your hand!"

"That's not the proper hand."

"Isn't it? Which is the proper hand?"

"Rodney! How ignorant you are!"

"My dear, have I had your experience?"

"My experience!—silly! I thought everybody knew on which hand the engagement finger was—there!—that is the finger!"

She held out to him a finger which, if it was small, was slim and daintily fashioned. He bent and kissed it.

"Dear digit!—salutation! Now, you unclothed midget, I'll clothe you with this ring."

"Oh, Rodney, what—what a darling!"

She pressed it to her lips.

"Does it fit?"

"As if it were made for me."

"Isn't that wonderful, when I only guessed?"

"Thank you—thank you, Rodney."

"It's only a poor little ring—a love token, to mark you as my own—that's all. But one day I'll give you the finest ring that money can buy, and you can put it in the place of this."

"As if I ever would—or could! Rodney, this is the most beautiful ring I have ever seen—ever, ever, ever! And it always will be the most beautiful ring in the world—to me. No other will ever take its place."

Her voice fell as she moved a little closer to him.

"I shall hope to be still wearing it when I am lying in my grave."

"Dear love!"

He took her in his arms and kissed her again, as it were, solemnly. He was practised in all varieties of the art. And they were silent.

CHAPTER XIX

THE FEW WORDS AT THE END OF THE EVENING

There were five of them at dinner—the lovers, the lady's father, her two hostesses—the Misses Claughton. These were cousins of her mother. Miss Claughton was tall and straight and prim; Miss Nancy Claughton, the younger sister, was stout and tender. Both ladies were disposed to make a fuss of

Rodney, to invest him with a sort of halo, as if, in asking Stella to be his wife, he had done something which marked him out as an unusual young man. Mr. Austin's inclination was towards jocosity. Rodney had long since decided that a sense of humour was not that gentleman's strongest point. Dry he could be, he had rather an effective trick of it; but funny—no. His persistent efforts to be funny did not improve the flavour of what, from the young gentleman's point of view, was a sufficiently homely repast. The soup was doubtful, one could not be sure if it was meant to be clear or thick; the cod was boiled to rags—and, anyhow, he hated cod; the mutton was overdone; the sweets were suited to the nursery. Under the circumstances it was perhaps as well that, between Mr. Austin's jokes, the question chiefly discussed was where they should dine on the morrow. It was some consolation, Rodney felt, that there was a prospect of a decent meal after the passage of another four-and-twenty hours. The gentlemen did not remain at table when the feast was done; Mr. Austin was a teetotaller, and Rodney, when he had tasted Miss Claughton's claret, wished he was; so there was no temptation to linger over the wine. In the drawing-room they had "music." Stella played and sang. Rodney, whose taste in music was as fastidious as in other things, would have been content had she done neither. She had not got a bad little voice; from the point of view of those who liked little voices of the kind; but he had always been of opinion that it was worth more to the professors of singing than to anybody else. Still, she sang straight at him, and for him only; so it was not so bad. Presently Mr. Austin vanished, and the Misses Claughton followed. So he put his arm about Stella's waist, and that was better. She was even more disposed to be made love to after dinner than before, and somehow she seemed prettier and sweeter and more desirable to him. Under such conditions he was the kind of young man who was bound to shine.

After a while—quite an agreeable while—he led the conversation on to the subject which Mr. Austin had broached in the morning. The lady lent a complacent ear.

"Stella, I have a very serious question which I wish to put to you."

"What is it? If you can be serious."

"You will find I can when you have heard my question; I pray you incline your little pink ears unto my question. Will you marry me?"

"Perhaps, some day—silly!"

"When is 'some day'?"

"When would you like it to be?"

"This day; to-night."

"Rodney, you—you really mustn't talk like that."

"Why mustn't I?"

"You only proposed last Saturday."

"Well. Allow a week for that fact to get fixed firmly in your mind, another for preparation, why shouldn't 'some day' be Saturday week?"

"Don't be ridiculous."

"It's you who are ridiculous. If you keep me waiting long I shall kiss you all away."

"Am I the only girl you've ever kissed?"

"Yes."

"That's a fib; I saw you kiss Mary."

"Gracious! When?"

"Have you been so much in the habit of kissing Mary that you need ask when?"

"If by Mary you mean Miss Carmichael, I don't remember to have ever kissed her once."

"Well, I remember. And let me tell you something, sir: there have been times when—I've been jealous of Mary."

"Good gracious me! what an extraordinary child! Miss Carmichael's sole recommendation to me has been that she's your friend; besides, hasn't Tom an eye on her?"

"Oh, Tom! Tom never would see anything—like that; but I see. Honestly, don't you think Mary's very pretty?"

"She's not bad, in a way; but she's not to be compared with you."

"That she certainly isn't; you don't imagine that you can make me believe that I'm—a tenth part as pretty as Mary? Do you take me for a perfect goose?"

"Stella, do you remember what you said before dinner about the ring. You said—I don't know if you meant it."

"I meant every word I said, Rodney."

"Well, sweetheart, you said it was the most beautiful ring you had ever seen. Just as you said that, and meant it, I say and mean that you are the most beautiful girl I have ever seen; and, to me, you will be the most beautiful girl, as long as I live."

"Do you really mean that? Really?"

"By the time we're—Darby and Joan, you'll know I mean it. Now, young woman, I'm as one who speaks with authority. I'm authorised to inform you that if you will stand with me at the altar inside a month you will make your mother happy and your father happy, to say nothing of me. So which day next month is it to be? Shall I put it at the first?"

"Who told you to say that?"

"Your own father, this morning as ever was."

"Was—was the idea yours or his?"

"My very dearest—small one—"

"I'm not so small as all that! You're not to call me small!!"

"Well, all-that-my-heart-desireth, which you are, I will tell you with such precision as is in me. I said to him: 'I want her! I do want her! Oh, I want her badly! But, if I have to earn her, I'll have to wait for her, I dare not think how long.' Then he said to me—exactly what I've told you; and my heart sang. Do you doubt? Ask him! To me the point is: shall we say the first?"

"Rodney, do try to be sensible! You're a man, and you can't understand."

"Is that so? So long as you do."

"To a girl her wedding day is the day of her life."

"Some girls manage to have several wedding days, so I suppose they have two or three days in their lives."

"There will be only one wedding day in my life. Whatever happens I want that to be, in every sense, a wonderful day; I want mine to be a pretty wedding."

"With you as bride that's assured."

"A really pretty wedding can't be arranged at a moment's notice; it takes time."

"Half an hour—or three-quarters?"

"Don't be so silly! Mamma's coming up to town to-morrow. I'll consult her; then I shall have some idea how long a time it will take."

"You mean how short a time! Do mean how short a time!"

"Well, how short a time. Rodney, how many bridesmaids would you like me to have?"

"Bridesmaids? My dear! What are bridesmaids to me, so long as I've the bride? All—all—all I'm going to be married to is the bride!"

"You are—a perfect—"

"Yes? A perfect—what?"

"Oh, I don't know! Rodney?"

She hid her face upon his shoulder.

"I always wondered what there was in a kiss to make a fuss about. Now—I know."

When he left it had been practically settled that the wedding should take place on the earliest possible day of the ensuing month.

He walked home, by way of Kensington High Street and the Park. And as he walked he mused, and more than once his musings moved him to something very much like laughter, out there in the solitude and the dark. Was ever man before in such a complication—promised at three weddings as bridegroom? As he tried to puzzle out how it all had come about it struck him as quite inconceivably comical. If he told the story to the ladies themselves they could scarcely fail to see how funny it was—at least, he hoped they would. The position would be simple enough if, as is still the custom in some of the more civilised countries of the world, a man could have wives galore. But if it came to choosing, why, there would be the rub. Mabel had her points; who knew it better than he? While as for Stella, he had never dreamed she was so charming. With her kisses still on his lips, her soft voice still in his ears, her pretty eyes still looking into his, how could he help but love her! Dear little Stella! A week all alone with her, even a fortnight—he would like to have the chance of it. Perhaps, after a fortnight, a little relaxation might be desirable, a sort of change of air. But why look so far ahead? Then there was Mary—but he dare not think of Mary Carmichael, even then. If he had ten thousand a year, and freedom, he would choose Mary Carmichael before all the girls he had ever met. But that was out of the question; he had better put her out of his mind. Things were already sufficiently complicated without adding her. On the whole, the circumstances being what they were, considering the position with the judicial calmness which was becoming, he plumped for Gladys; and—the business in St. Paul's Churchyard. Gladys Patterson should be his wife; yes, she should be his wife, on all accounts; on all!—if—if it was not necessary to take a voyage to foreign parts.

In that room on the second floor of the house in Kensington, Stella Austin, in her nightdress, her pretty hair hanging in two long plaits down her back, was on her knees beside her bed, seeming such a child. She was thanking God for all His goodness to her—she always began her prayers by thanking God. She thanked Him for many things, but chiefly, and beyond all else, for having given her so thoughtful, so tender, so true a lover. God knew how happy He had made her, and how full her heart was of gratitude to Him. And she prayed that God would make her worthy of the lover He had given. She knew how, in so many ways, he was above her, above anything she might ever hope to be; she prayed God that He would give her strength and grace, so that she might be at least a little more deserving. She had been unkind to-night, and—and wickedly jealous; she knew she had. Please God make her kinder and less selfish! And, when the time came, please God, make her a good wife, a good wife!

At this point articulate utterance ceased, her face fell forward on the coverlet because her eyes were streaming with tears. It was to her such a solemn and beautiful thought that she would before very long be Rodney Elmore's wife that she trembled with the very rapture of it, so that she could no longer even go on with her prayers.

* * * * *

When Mr. Elmore reached his lodgings, with the exception of the light in his sitting-room, the house was in darkness. But if that signified that the household had retired to rest, it did not follow that everyone was asleep, as he was presently to learn. He had only been in his room a couple of minutes when the door opened noiselessly—to admit Miss Joyce. Coming right in, she stood with her back to the door, which she closed behind her. She was in a state of undress which did not become her ill. As he eyed her Rodney compared her, mentally, with Stella; not to her disadvantage. She really was a good-looking girl; only—he did not like the look which was on her white face and in her eyes. He felt sure someone would notice it, and questions would be asked.

She spoke in so faint a whisper that what she said was only just audible; his voice was lowered in sympathy with hers.

"Mother's come back."

"Has she? That's good hearing. I hope she had a good time at your aunt's."

"I've got the licence."

"The—? Oh, have you? That also is good hearing."

"It cost me two pounds four and six."

"Did it? I hope you consider it to be worth the money."

"I've fixed it for Thursday at noon."

"Noon? Isn't that—rather an unfashionable hour?"

"Mind you're there! You've promised! I've got your promise."

"Am I likely to forget—the circumstances under which you got my promise?"

"If you're not there you'll be sorry."

"Honestly, Mabel, I think we shall both of us be sorry."

"You will! There's—there's another thing; I—I want to warn you."

"Warn me? Haven't you done that once or twice already?"

"I—I want to warn you against Mr. Dale."

"Against Mr. Dale? Why?"

"I believe he suspects."

"Suspects? What? About you and me?"

"About—your uncle."

"What does he suspect about my uncle?"

"He's been finding out things. Ssh! there's someone moving. Perhaps it's mother; she mustn't find me here, like this."

She flitted from the room as noiselessly as she had entered, shutting the door without its making a sound. He stood and listened. Perhaps it was her conscience which had made her fancy noises—all seemed still. If she had ascended to her room on the landing, a ghost could not have moved more silently.

CHAPTER XX

THE FIRST LINE OF AN OLD SONG

Rodney Elmore had the unusual attribute of seeming at his best in the morning, as if calm, unruffled sleep, having removed the cobwebs from his brain, returned him rested and buoyant to a world in which there were no shadows. When, on the Wednesday morning, he came downstairs with light steps and dancing eyes, he found among the letters on the breakfast table one which was addressed in a familiar hand. He gave it pride of place.

"MY DEAR R.,—I don't know what possesses me, but I feel that I simply must write and tell you that I wish you were within kissing distance. Isn't that a ridiculous feeling to have, especially where you're concerned? Do you think that I don't know? I have been conscious of the most extraordinary sensations since Sunday. I made a mistake in asking you to come and console me. You did it so effectually that—well, I would like you to continue the treatment. There's a dreadful thing to say! Aren't I a wretch? Poor dear Tom! I know he has all the good qualities I haven't, and that he'll make me the best husband in the world, but as for his consoling me—oh, dear! oh, dear! oh, dear! I don't like the idea at all! I'm nearly sure that, after all, the best husband in the world is not the one I'm looking for. What makes me feel so all over pins and needles when I'm with Tom, and so comfy when I'm with you? Isn't it odd? Have you any feeling of the kind where I'm concerned? I know you'll say so, but have you? You'd say anything to anyone, but, all the same, I've a feeling somewhere that, if I chose, I could have you on a little bit of string. I daren't ask you to come here again, I simply daren't; but, if you do come, mind you give me proper warning. What would you say if I ran up to town? Should I see Stella at the corner of every street? Sweet Stella! Aren't I a cat? I suppose you couldn't rob a bank or something? If you and I were starting off to-morrow together, ever so far, for ever so long—I dare not think of it, and that's the honest truth. Aren't I insane? No one but you would ever guess it.—M.

"Mind you tear this up the very moment you have read it, and you're to forget that you ever did read it!

"By the way, by which train did you go up on Sunday? You weren't sure that you could catch the Pullman, and, if you did miss it, did you go by the 9.10? In that case you must have been in the same train as your uncle. When I saw about it in the paper it gave me quite a shock. Fancy if he was in the next carriage to yours? I suppose the dear man hasn't left you a millionaire? If he only had! You would—wouldn't you?

"Tear it up!"

He had just finished reading this somewhat interjectional epistle when Miss Joyce came in, the bearer of his morning meal. He greeted her as if he were really pleased to see her.

"The top of the morning to you, Baby! How moves the world your way? Do you feel like dancing on your pink toes?"

When he called her Baby, the pet name he had for her, she glanced up at him, almost as if she were startled.

"Did you understand what I said to you last night?"

"Perfectly; I've been thinking it all over, and I've come to a decision. I think you're quite right in what you wish me to do. As this isn't Leap Year, let me regularise the position. Mabel, I would like you to be my wife. Will you take me for your husband?"

"You say that because you know you can't help yourself."

"You are mistaken. If I didn't want to be your husband, nothing you or anyone could say or do could make me, rest assured of that. I won't pretend that, if things had turned out differently, I—should have suggested it; but, as they are, please, Mabel, let me do the proposing—say you will be my wife."

"I'm going to be your wife; to-morrow, Thursday, at noon, and don't you make any mistake. There's the address of the registrar's office at which you're going to be married, and mind you're there to time."

"Baby—you are only a baby, after all—don't talk like that; don't let's enter the matrimonial state as if we wished to cut each other's throats; let's start afresh on the old terms. I hope that when we're being married you won't have those white cheeks and unhappy eyes, or the registrar will think that I'm frightening you into being my bride, and you know that will be wrong."

"Rodney, do you care for me a little bit?"

"My dear Mabel, I care for you in an altogether different fashion from that which you suppose, as I hope to be able to prove to you before very long. Come, let's be friends."

"Don't touch me—don't! Mother's waiting for me. She wants me for something; she told me not to be long. I—I want to speak to you before I go. I—I want to warn you against Mr. Dale."

"You said something to that effect last night. Is Mr. Dale so dangerous?"

"He's jealous of you."

"Well, does that constitute him dangerous?"

"He always has been throwing out nasty hints about you."

"To whom? Surely not to you? You wouldn't listen to what you yourself call nasty hints about me coming from a man like Dale?"

"It wasn't so much that I listened as that he was always at it whenever he came near me. I couldn't stop him. I suppose that my asking him about your going to Brighton on Sunday, and my going to the inquest, and such-like, made him—made him—"

"Yes? Made him what?"

"Started him thinking. Anyhow, he's—he's been finding out things, and—I don't know that he hasn't found out. You take care of him!"

"My dear Mabel, in what sense am I to take care of him? I'm inclined to think that I should rather like to have a talk with your friend Mr. Dale."

"You'll do no good by that."

"Shan't I? We'll see. Where is he to be found—in the booking office at Victoria Station?"

"One week he goes early and comes back about six; the next he has his dinner first and doesn't come back till after one—this is his late week. He hasn't had his breakfast yet; he's still up in his room."

"Is that so? I'm afraid I can't stop to talk to him just now, but I certainly will take the first chance which offers."

"Don't you say anything to him to make him nasty!"

A feminine voice was heard calling the young lady's name.

"There's mother calling. She'll give me a talking to! Mind, to-morrow at noon; and there's the address upon that piece of paper."

"My dear Mabel, I'm making arrangements which will permit of my placing the whole of to-morrow at your service. I promise that you shall have something like a wedding day."

When the lady had gone the gentleman poured himself out a cup of coffee with the air of one who was in the enjoyment of an excellent joke. He propped Miss Carmichael's letter up against the coffee-pot and read it through again. The second reading seemed to add to his sense of enjoyment.

"Rob a bank? Quite as heinous crimes have been committed for the sake of a woman. I've always had a kind of fancy that you're the type of girl for whom it would be worth one's while to do such things. If I were to ask you to start upon that little trip at which you hint, I wonder what you'd say—if you knew. Hullo! what's this?"

He was staring at a sheet of paper which he had taken out of one of the three or four envelopes which were lying on the table. On it were a couple of typewritten lines:

"If you take a friend's advice you will get clean away while you have still a chance."

He regarded the words as if in doubt as to whether they were intended to convey to him an esoteric meaning.

"No signature, no address, no date; the first anonymous communication I ever have been favoured with. Postmark on the envelope, Kew, dispatched from there last night at eight o'clock, which doesn't convey much intelligence to me. So far as I'm aware I have no acquaintance who resides at Kew; and I suppose an anonymous correspondent, if he had his head screwed on, is scarcely likely to reside in the district from which he sends his letter. It's very good of a friend to make a friendly suggestion, but quite what he means I do not know; nor have I the very dimmest notion who the friend may be. Come in!"

Someone had tapped at the door. In response to his invitation a young man entered of about his own age; not tall, but sturdily built, with close-cut black hair, small dark eyes, and a somewhat voluminous moustache. There was that in his manner which hinted that he was in a state of some excitement; that, indeed, he was an excitable young man. He came right up to the table, with a billycock hat in one hand and a bamboo cane in the other. He looked at Elmore with what were scarcely friendly eyes. When he spoke it was in what evidently were lowered tones and with a curious, staccato utterance, as if he wished to throw his words into the other's face.

"You'll have to excuse my coming in like this, but I'm going out, and I want to speak to you before I do go."

"That's very good of you. I believe you are Mr. Dale."

"My name is Dale—George Dale, as you very well know."

"Pray sit down, Mr. Dale. I don't remember to have had the pleasure of being introduced to you before."

"Thanking you all the same, I won't sit down, and as to being introduced to you, I never have been. It's only for your sake I'm speaking to you now. I want to ask you a question to begin with."

"Ask it, Mr. Dale."

"What are your intentions as regards Miss Joyce?"

"Really, Mr. Dale, I don't know if you are joking in putting such a question. If you aren't I certainly don't know what you mean."

Rodney smiled at his visitor pleasantly; but the smile, instead of affording Mr. Dale gratification, not only caused his scowl to deepen, but induced him to use language of unexpected vigour.

"You're a liar! That's what you are—a liar! You're a liar, because you know quite well what I mean. I'm not afraid of you. You're a bigger man than I am, but I can use the gloves. You wouldn't knock me out so easy as you think. I'd mark you first! But I haven't come here to fight you."

"That, at least, is gratifying intelligence, Mr. Dale."

"Oh, you can sneer—you're one of the sneering sort; but sneers won't do you any good. You take my tip and get as far away from this as you can—out of England, if you can!—between now and this time to-morrow!"

Rodney regarded his visitor with an air of placid amusement, which certainly did not seem to have a soothing effect.

"Mr. Dale, am I indebted to you for this?"

He held out the sheet of paper on which were the two typewritten lines. Mr. Dale eyed it askance.

"What's that? Where did you get it from?"

"It came by this morning's post—from you?"

"That I'll swear it never did; what's more, I don't know who it does come from. That looks as if there were more than one in it. I'll commit myself to nothing. I've got myself to think of as well as you; but, although this didn't come from me, and I don't know anything at all about it, you do what it says here—get clean away while you have still a chance."

Without another word, or giving Rodney a chance to utter one, Mr. Dale bolted from, rather than left, the room; within ten seconds of his going the slamming of the front door announced that he had left the house. For some seconds Elmore sat still; then, getting up from his chair, began to fill a pipe with tobacco. Miss Joyce put her head into the room, noiselessly, unexpectedly, as she seemed to have a trick of doing.

"Was that Mr. Dale? I thought it might be you. Has he been in here?"

"He has. You come in and take away the breakfast things; I've had all I want to eat."

Coming in, she began to do as he had said, talking, as she put the things together, in a half whisper which recalled Mr. Dale's staccato undertones. It seemed to be a house of whispers.

"What did he say to you?"

"He came to offer me a tip."

"A tip?"

"He said that if I took his tip I shouldn't stand upon the order of my going, but go at once, and go as far as possible between now and to-morrow."

She put both hands to her left side, as if unconscious that she had a plate in one and a teaspoon in the other.

"Rodney! Then—then—what are you going to do?"

"Nothing."

"But if he tells?"

"Tells what?"

"He said to me last night that if anyone knows that—that someone has killed a person, and doesn't at once inform the police, that's being an accessory after the fact."

"Well? He was merely acquainting you with what I take is a legal truism."

"Then he said that, whatever I might choose to do, he did not mean to be an accessory, either before the fact or after. Then he looked at me in such a way—I knew what he meant—and he went right off to bed without saying another word."

"What had you been talking about?"

"About—your uncle."

"Had he introduced the subject or had you?"

"He had; he would keep talking about it. Rodney, he knows, and—he's going to tell."

"Then, in that case, it looks as if you will gain little by becoming my wife, and that I shall gain nothing."

"Rodney, I want you to get out of your head what I said the other night. I don't want to force you to marry me, and I never did."

"Then you've rather an unfortunate way of expressing yourself, don't you think so, my dear Mabel?"

"I—I didn't know how else to do what I wanted to do. It's quite true that if I'm not going to be your wife I'll kill myself; but that doesn't matter—I'd just as soon die as live. But I do want to save you, and the only way I can do it is for you to marry me."

"That may keep you from playing the tell-tale, but how is it going to affect Mr. Dale?"

"He won't tell if I'm your wife."

"Won't he? Why? I should have thought, if your story's correct, that he'd have told all the more, that disappointment would have inflamed him to madness."

Rodney, as he said this, struck a match to light his pipe, and laughed. Nothing could have seemed less like laughter than the girl's white face and haunted eyes.

"He'd tell to keep me from being your wife, but if I were your wife he'd never tell. I know him; he'd suffer anything rather than do anything which would give me pain or bring me to shame; if I were your wife he'd never tell. You're a gentleman, Rodney, and I'm not a lady, and I don't suppose I ever shall be; I'm just a girl who has let you do what you like with her, and you're cleverer than I am—much, much cleverer; but, in this, do be advised by me—do, dear, do! There is something here, something which makes me sure that the only way out of it, for you, is for you to make me your wife. I know you don't want to do it, that you never meant to do it, and I can quite understand why; but you'd better have me for your wife than—than that; don't you see, dear, that you had? I shan't be able to tell, and George Dale won't, and no one else knows, and instead of trying to find out more he'll keep others from finding out anything; he'll be on your side instead of against you, for my sake. Rodney, I implore you—for your own sake, dear, your own sake!—to do as you promised, and marry me."

She pleaded to be allowed to save his life as if she were pleading for her own life. He turned to shake the ash from his pipe into the fender, and so remained, for some moments, with his back to her; while her eyes looked as if they were crying out to him. When he turned to her again he was pressing the tobacco down into his pipe before restoring it to his lips, smiling as he looked at her.

"My dear Mabel, I'm not certain that I follow your reasoning, but do make your mind easy; I've promised to marry you to-morrow, and I will—on the stroke of noon—to the tick, for my sake as well as for yours. And, though the fates don't seem over propitious at the moment, I dare say we shall be quite as happy as the average married folk—at least, I'll marry you."

"You mean it?"

"I do—unreservedly; please understand that once more, and once for all. You shall have something like a wedding day."

"I wish—I wish it were to-day; I'm afraid—of what may happen—before to-morrow."

"Of whatever you may be afraid, I'm afraid that it couldn't be to-day. It's my uncle's funeral to-day."

"Rodney! You—you're not going!"

"I am; as chief mourner."

"Rodney, you—you can't do a thing like that! You—you mustn't!"

As she spoke an elderly woman came into the room, of a somewhat portly presence—the lady's mother. Seemingly she was in a mood to be garrulous.

"What mustn't he do? Excuse me, Mr. Elmore, for coming in like this, but really, Mabel, I don't know what you are thinking about. I'm sure Mr. Elmore wants to go to his business, and here's all the work at a standstill—"

"All right, mother; Mr. Elmore doesn't want to hear you grumbling at me, I know."

Without waiting for her mother to continue her observations, Miss Joyce bustled out of the room with the breakfast tray in her hands. Left alone with him, the landlady addressed her lodger.

"What's the matter with the girl I can't think; I never saw anything like the change that's come over her the last few days; she looks more fit for a hospital than anything else—and her temper! She never says anything to me; I suppose you don't know what's wrong?"

"Mrs. Joyce, I'm not your daughter's confidant; she certainly says nothing to me in the sense you mean. Why do you take it for granted that anything's wrong?"

"Because I've got two eyes in my head, that's why. She's not the same girl she was; that something's wrong I'm certain sure; but she snaps my nose off directly I open my mouth. I know she thinks a lot of you. I wondered if she'd said anything to you."

"Absolutely nothing."

"Then I can't understand the girl, and that's flat!"

With that somewhat cryptic utterance Mrs. Joyce went out of the room as impetuously as she had entered. Rodney stood looking at the door for a moment or two, as if in doubt whether she would return. He tore the sheet of paper on which were the two typewritten lines into tiny scraps and dropped them into the fireplace. Re-reading Miss Carmichael's epistle, he obeyed her injunctions, a little tardily, perhaps, and sent the fragments after the others, repeating to himself as he did so a line from an old song:

"Of all the girls that are so sweet!"

Then he took an oblong piece of paper out of a letter-case and studied it.

"'Steamship Cedric.—John Griffiths, passenger to New York, cabin forty-five, berth A.' I wonder if it will be occupied, or if the money's wasted. That's for to-morrow, or is it to be Buenos Ayres on Friday, or New York on Saturday?"

He shrugged his shoulders.

"Who knows if it is to be either?"

He had left the house and was descending the steps when a telegraph boy approached, with a yellow envelope in his hand.

"Who's it for?" he asked.

"Rodney Elmore, sir."

"I am Rodney Elmore. Wait and see if there's an answer."

The telegram which the envelope contained was a lengthy one; it covered the whole of the pink slip of paper. He read it through once, then again. As he read it the second time he whistled, very softly, as if unconsciously, the opening bars of "Sally in Our Alley."

"There is an answer. Give me a form."

He spread the form the boy gave him out upon his letter-case, then he seemed to consider what to say; then read the telegram he had received a third time, as if in search of light and leading. Arriving at a sudden decision, he wrote on the form the name and address of the person to whom the message was to be sent, and then one word, "Right." He added nothing which would show who the sender was; evidently he took it for granted that it would be recognised that the message came from him. As he watched the lad mount his bicycle and pedal away, he said to himself, always with that characteristic air of his, as of one who appreciates a capital jest:

"That settles it! Now the plot does begin to thicken."

CHAPTER XXI

THE DEAD MAN'S LETTER

The final understanding had been that those who were to go to the bank, in order that arrangements might be made which would give them immediate access to the funds of the late Graham Patterson, were to meet at the office in St. Paul's Churchyard. On the way to the City Rodney paid two or three calls. When he entered the office the outer rooms were empty; there was a notice on the outer door to the effect that business was suspended on account of Mr. Patterson's funeral. Mr. Andrews came out of what had been the late proprietor's own sanctum to greet him.

"Mr. Wilkes is here, Mr. Elmore, and particularly wishes to see you."

Rodney said nothing, but his look suggested that he resented something which he noticed in the other's manner, as well as the fact that he had come out of that particular room. Passing on in silence to the private office, he found Mr. Wilkes seated, not in his uncle's own chair, as he had been on Monday, but in one close to it. He did not rise as the young man entered, but contented himself with nodding slightly. Rodney, scenting something antagonistic in the other's presence there as well as in his attitude, did not even nod. He marched straight to the chair behind the writing-table, which he chose now to regard as his own, and which was within a yard of that on which the other was seated, and, remaining standing himself, looked down on the lawyer.

"To what am I indebted, Mr. Wilkes, for your presence to-day? Did you not notice the intimation on the door, informing all and sundry that these offices are closed? If it is a business matter on which you have called, I must ask you to postpone it, at any rate until to-morrow."

Instead of showing any disposition to take himself off, as the other so plainly suggested, the dark-visaged lawyer, leaning back in his chair, looked up at the young man with something in his glance which was not exactly complimentary.

"I have come, Mr. Elmore, a good deal against my own wish, in consequence of a communication which I have received from Mr. Patterson."

"From—what do you mean, from Mr. Patterson?"

"A letter came to my office yesterday evening, after I had left, which was placed in my hands this morning. Before proceeding to take other steps, I thought it might perhaps save unpleasantness, and be fairer to you, if, in the first instance, I acquainted you with its substance."

"From whom is the letter?"

"From your late uncle, Graham Patterson."

"You say it reached you last night? I don't understand."

"Nor I, as yet, quite; I can only form a hypothesis. It seems that the letter was written at Brighton some time on Sunday. Clearly, from the postmark, it was posted at Brighton on Sunday. It ought to have reached me, of course, on Monday, but the presumption is that, owing to some vagary of the Post Office, it went astray, so that it has been more than two days on the road, instead of only a few hours. Under the circumstances that seems rather a curious accident. Here is the letter. I warn you that you will not find it a pleasant one."

"Is it absolutely necessary, then, that I should know its contents? My relations with Mr. Patterson were not of a kind to lead me to expect any pleasantness from him, either on paper or off it."

"The position is this. It is my duty to place this letter before—someone else, when very serious consequences may ensue; but, by taking a certain course, you may relieve me of the duty."

"In that case, let me know what is in the letter."

"I had better read it to you, so that you may understand that the language is the writer's, not mine."

Mr. Wilkes withdrew a letter from an envelope which he took from his pocket; the envelope he held out to Rodney.

"You see? The address is in your uncle's hand; it was post-marked at Brighton on Sunday evening, so there can be no doubt about the date on which it was dispatched."

The lawyer proceeded to read the letter out loud, with a dryness which seemed to give it peculiar point.

"'DEAR STEPHEN' [my Christian name, I may remind you, is Stephen],—'I want you to draw up a codicil to my will, and to have it ready for my signature to-morrow—Monday afternoon.

"'It is to be to the effect that if my daughter marries my nephew, Rodney Elmore, then all that portion of my will which refers to her is to be null and void—she is not to have a penny. All that would have been hers is to be divided equally among the following charities.' [Then follows a list of them; there are eight. Then the letter goes on]: 'I hope that's clear enough. Between ourselves, Master Elmore is an all-round scoundrel; I swear to you that I'm convinced that no rascality would be too steep for him. He is a liar of the very first water, a thief, and a forger; so much I can prove. I would sooner have my girl dead than his wife; the damned young blackguard is after her for all he knows. But I am going to clear him out in charge of a constable when I get back to the office; I doubt if he has got tight enough hold of my girl to induce her to marry a convict—it will be a clear case of penal servitude for him.

"'I know you will think I am writing strongly, but that is because I feel strongly. When I tell you the whole story you will admit that I am justified.

"'Mind you have that codicil ready, on the lines I have given; I will call in on my way back from the office and sign. I know you do not touch criminal business as a rule, but you will have to make an exception in my case. I want you to instruct counsel in the matter of Master Elmore, for reasons which I will make clear to you when we meet. Sincerely yours,

"'GRAHAM PATTERSON.'"

When the lawyer had done reading he lowered the letter and glanced up at the young man, who still stood towering above him. If he expected to find on his face any signs of confusion, still less of guilt or shame, his expectation was not realised. There was a look rather on Rodney's countenance of scorn, of confidence in himself, of contempt for whoever might speak ill of him, which became him very well. His remarks, when they came, possibly scarcely breathed the spirit the solicitor had looked for.

"Have you read that letter to Mr. Andrews?"

"I have not."

"Have you made him acquainted with its contents?"

"I have dropped no hint to him of its existence."

"I have no pretensions to knowledge of the law of libel, but it is pretty clear that no action can be brought against the man who wrote that letter. With you the case is different. It was written, I presume, in confidence to you. If you bring it to the notice of anybody else you make yourself responsible for the statements it contains—you publish them. If you call my honour in question by publishing such a farrago of lies about me I will first of all thrash you, as they have it, to within an inch of your life, and then, if needs be, I will spend my last penny in calling you to account in a court of law. You shall not shelter yourself behind a dead man."

"You use strong language, Mr. Elmore."

"Could I use stronger language than that letter?"

"I understand that you deny the statements it contains?"

"Do I understand that you associate yourself with your correspondent so far as to require a denial?"

"You misapprehend the situation; whether wilfully or not I don't know. I have no personal concern in this matter at all; eliminate that idea from your mind. Graham Patterson was my client living; in a sense he is still my client dead. I have no option but to continue to do my duty to him without fear or favour."

"I presume in return for a certain fee, Mr. Wilkes?"

"You forget yourself, sir."

"In this room, Mr. Wilkes, eliminate from your mind all legal fictions. Don't, for your own sake, drive the fact that you are acting as my uncle's bravo too far home. In the face of that letter I begin to understand why he committed suicide. He was either drunk or mad when he wrote it. When sobriety or sanity returned, realising the situation in which he had placed himself, rather than face the consequences of what he had done, he took his own life. Don't you show yourself to be in possession of the dastard's courage which he lacked."

"You take up an extraordinary position, Mr. Elmore."

"What is the position you take up?"

"Here is a letter from a man to his lawyer, in which he gives him instructions to make certain alterations in his will, stating reasons why he wishes those alterations to be made. It is signed, dated; its authenticity can be readily established. I am not sure that it has not a certain testamentary value."

"Are you suggesting that that letter in any way affects my uncle's will?"

"I am not prepared to give a definite opinion; but this I will say, that if its existence were to come to the knowledge of the societies herein mentioned, they would be justified in taking counsel's opinion, and quite possibly he would advise their taking further action."

"You are, of course, at liberty to take any steps with regard to that tissue of libels you please, especially as I have made it, I think, perfectly clear to you that you will do so at your own proper peril."

"Evidently your uncle was averse to your marrying his daughter. Am I to take it that you admit so much?"

"Oh, I admit so much; he always was averse to that."

"Then, in that case, you will at once resolve the difficulty by withdrawing all pretensions to Miss Patterson's hand."

"Damn your impudence, sir."

"Is that your answer?"

"It is; with this addition—that I hope, and intend, to marry Miss Patterson at the earliest possible moment."

"Then, in that case, you leave me no option but to place this letter before Miss Patterson."

"Is that meant for a threat?"

Andrews appeared in the doorway to announce that Mr. Parmiter was in the outer office.

"Show Mr. Parmiter in at once for a few minutes, Andrews, if you please."

As the young solicitor came in Rodney advanced to greet him.

"Hallo, Parmiter! you come in the very nick of time—you see Mr. Wilkes has favoured me with his company again. Mr. Wilkes, read to Mr. Parmiter the letter you just now read to me."

"I shall certainly do nothing of the kind. With all possible respect to Mr. Parmiter, this is a matter in which he has no locus standi, and in which I cannot recognise him at all."

"Why not? He is my solicitor; he advises me. When you have made known to him the contents of that letter, don't you think it possible that he may give me the advice which, apparently, you would like him to give?"

While he was still speaking the door opened to admit Miss Patterson. He moved to her with both hands held out.

"Now, here is someone whom, I presume, you will recognise—the very person. Gladys, here is Mr. Wilkes. He has something which he very much wishes to say to you."

Returning the letter to its envelope, Mr. Wilkes rose from his chair.

"My hands are not going to be forced by you, Mr. Elmore, don't you suppose it. In making any communication to Miss Patterson which I may have to make, I shall prefer to choose my own time and place."

"That's it, is it? I quite appreciate the reasons which actuate you, Mr. Wilkes, in wishing to make what you call your communication to Miss Patterson behind my back; and I think that Miss Patterson will appreciate them equally well. Mr. Wilkes has in his hand what he claims to be a letter from your father. If you take my advice you will insist on his showing it to you at once."

Miss Patterson was quick to act on the hint which her lover gave her. She moved close up to the lawyer.

"Mr. Wilkes, be so good as to let me see the letter to which my cousin refers."

"With pleasure, Miss Patterson, at—if you will allow me to say so—some more convenient season; the sooner the better. For instance, may I have a few minutes' private conversation with you this afternoon? The matter on which I wish to speak to you is for your ear only."

"You have spoken of it to my cousin?"

"Oh, yes; he has spoken of it to me."

"Then, why can you not speak of it to me in his presence?"

"I will write to you on the subject, Miss Patterson, and will endeavour to make my reasons clear."

He made as if to move towards the door. She placed herself in front of him.

"One moment, Mr. Wilkes. Any letter from you will be handed to Mr. Elmore, unopened. I will have no private communication with you, nor, if I can help it, will I have any communication with you of any sort or kind."

"I regret to hear you say so, Miss Patterson, and can only deplore the attitude of mind which prompts you to arrive at what I cannot but feel is a most unfortunate decision."

"You are impertinent, Mr. Wilkes."

The lawyer, with his dark eyes fixed on the lady's face, raised the hand in which was the envelope which contained the letter with the intention of slipping it into an inner pocket of his coat. Her quick glance recognised the handwriting of the address.

"It's from dad!" she cried. "It's a letter from dad!"

She had snatched the letter from between the lawyer's fingers before he had the faintest inkling of what she was about to do.

"Miss Patterson," he exclaimed, "give me back that letter."

She retreated, as he showed a disposition to advance. Mr. Elmore interposed himself between the lawyer and the lady.

"Steady, Mr. Wilkes, steady. You told me that it would be your duty to place that letter in Miss Patterson's hands. It is in her hands. What objection have you to offer?"

Whatever protest the lawyer might have been inclined to make he apparently came to the conclusion that, at the moment, it would be futile to make any. He withdrew himself from Elmore's immediate neighbourhood, and observed the lady, as she read the letter. She read it without comment to the end. Then she asked:

"When did you get this letter?"

"It reached my office last night, and me this morning; but, as you see, it was written on Sunday, and would appear to have been delayed in the post."

She turned to Rodney.

"Have you read this letter?"

"It has been read aloud to me, which comes to the same thing."

"You know—what he says at the end?"

"I do; Mr. Wilkes took special care of that."

"Is it true?"

"It is absolutely false. There is not one word of truth in it. It comes to me as a complete surprise. Never by so much as a word did your father lead me to suppose that he had such thoughts of me. I cannot conceive what can have been the condition of his mind when he wrote in such a strain. But that letter enables me to begin to understand that something must have happened to him mentally, and that when he committed suicide he actually was insane."

Miss Patterson tore the letter in half from top to bottom. The lawyer broke into exclamation.

"Miss Patterson! What are you doing? You must not do that! Not only is it not your letter, but it is a document of the gravest legal importance."

Paying him no heed whatever, the girl continued in silence the destruction of the letter, going about the business in the most thorough-going manner, reducing it to the tiniest atoms. When she had finished with the letter itself, she proceeded to dispose of the envelope, Mr. Wilkes expostulating hotly all the time, but kept from active interference by the insistent fashion with which Mr. Elmore prevented him from getting near the lady. Compelled at last to own that it was useless to attempt to stay her, he called upon his colleague to take notice of the outrage to which the letter was subjected, to say nothing of himself.

"Mr. Parmiter, you are witness of what is being done. This young lady, with the connivance and, indeed, assistance of this young man, is destroying a document of the first importance, which is not only in no sense her own property, but which was obtained from me by what is tantamount to an act of robbery, accompanied, in a legal sense, by violence. Of these facts you will be called upon, in due course, to give evidence."

Mr. Parmiter was still, but the lady spoke.

"Are you not forgetting that Mr. Parmiter is my solicitor, and that a solicitor cannot give evidence against his own client? I am sorry to have to seem to teach you law, Mr. Wilkes. Rodney, have you a match? If so, will you please burn these?"

She held out the fragments of the letter. Mr. Wilkes made a final attempt at salvage.

"Miss Patterson, I implore you to give me those scraps of paper. It may still not be too late to piece them together, and so save you from consequences of whose gravity you have no notion."

Once more the young gentleman interposed.

"Steady, Mr. Wilkes, steady!"

"Remove your hand from my shoulder, sir! You are only making your position every moment more and more serious!"

Again the lady spoke.

"To use a phrase of which you seem to be rather fond, Mr. Wilkes, in a legal sense, I believe this is my room. I must ask you to leave it at once."

"Not before you have given me those scraps of paper, Miss Patterson!"

"If you won't go, I shall reluctantly have to ask Mr. Elmore to put you out, and, in doing so, to use no more violence than is necessary."

"I entreat you, Miss Patterson, to accept sound advice, and to do something which may permit of my repairing the mischief you have caused. Give me those scraps of paper."

"Rodney, will you please put Mr. Wilkes out? But please don't hurt him!"

The young man put the lawyer out, doing him no actual bodily hurt. He conducted him through the outer office to the landing, then addressed the astonished Andrews.

"Andrews, this is Mr. Stephen Wilkes; I believe you know him. Give instructions that, under no pretext, is he to be admitted to these offices again. I shall look to you to see that those instructions are carried out. Good-day, sir."

Shutting the door in the lawyer's face, he audibly turned the key on the inner side.

"Now, Andrews, would you mind coming into the other room?"

Miss Patterson greeted her cousin with the request she had already made. She still had the fragments of the letter between her fingers.

"How about that match, Rodney? Please burn these."

He made a little bonfire of them on the hearth, while she went on:

"I don't suppose you will be very eager now to attend my father's funeral in the capacity of mourner."

"I am not. I would much rather not go at all, if you will pardon the abstention."

"I would much rather you did not go either—so, Andrews, that is settled. Also, be so good as to understand that I should prefer that the funeral should not start from Russell Square."

Mr. Patterson's body had been removed from the station to the undertaker's, where it at present reposed in a handsome example of the undertaker's art. The idea had been to bring it in a hearse to Russell Square, whence the funeral cortège was to start. It was this arrangement which Miss Patterson wished to have altered. The managing man silently acquiesced; there was still time to give instructions that all that was left of his late employer was to be taken straight from the undertaker's to the cemetery.

CHAPTER XXII

PHILIP WALTER AUGUSTUS PARKER

The four of them went together to the bank, which was within a minute's walk. There, the necessary forms being quickly gone through, a sum of two thousand pounds was credited to Miss Patterson, power being given to Rodney Elmore to draw on her account for such sums as were needed for the proper conduct of the business, it being tacitly understood that he would draw only such sums as were needed for the business. That matter being settled, they separated; Mr. Andrews and Mr. Parmiter going their own ways, Miss Patterson and Mr. Elmore departing together in a cab to lunch. The cab had not gone very far before the young gentleman made a discovery.

"I've left my letter-case on the table in the bank?"

"Your letter-case? Did you? What a nuisance; I never noticed it. Are you sure it was on the table?"

"Quite; I remember distinctly; it was under a blotting-pad. What an idiot I am! I'm frightfully sorry, but I'm afraid I shall have to go back and get it."

"Of course, we will go back."

The cab returned to the bank. The lady remained inside; the gentleman passed through the great swing doors—through first one pair, then a second—it was impossible to see from the street what was taking place beyond. Once in the bank, the young gentleman said nothing about his letter-case—it had apparently passed from his memory altogether; but he presented at the counter a cheque for a thousand pounds, with his own signature attached. He took it in tens and fives, and a hundred pounds in gold. If the paying clerk thought it was rather an odd way of taking so large a sum, he made no comment. He came back through the swing doors with a letter-case held in his hand.

"I've got it," he explained.

He emphatically had, though she understood one thing and he meant another. When they had gone some little distance in the direction of lunch she observed:

"I wish I were not in mourning. I've half a mind to go back and change."

He observed her critically—he was holding one of her hands under cover of the apron.

"My dear Gladys, I can't admit that you do look your best in mourning."

"Do you think that I don't know that?"

"But you look charming, all the same."

"No, I don't; I look a perfect fright."

"I doubt if you could look a fright even if you tried; I'm certain you don't look one now. In fact, the more I look at you the harder I find it to keep from kissing you."

"I dare say! You'd better not."

"That's a truth of which I'm unpleasantly aware. Still, if you did look like anything distantly resembling a fright, I shouldn't have that feeling so strong upon me, should I?"

"You're not to talk like that in a hansom!"

"I'm merely explaining. I suggest that if you do feel like changing, you should lunch first, and change afterwards."

"You're coming back with me to Russell Square?"

"Rather!"

"I won't wear mourning—people may say and think what they choose—I declare I won't. Did you ever see anything like that letter?"

"It was by way of being a curiosity."

"But, Rodney, he said you were—he said you were all sorts of things! What did he mean?"

"Your father was one of those not uncommon men who always use much stronger language than the occasion requires—it was a habit of his. For instance, when, in spite of his very positive commands, I showed an inclination to continue your acquaintance, he as good as told me I was a murderer—he said that it was his positive conviction that for the sake of a five-pound note I'd murder you."

"Did he really?"

"He did. And I dare say that when you showed no desire to cut me dead, he said one or two nice things to you."

"Oh, he did—several. He made out that I was everything that was bad."

"There you are—that's the kind of man he was."

"But didn't he say something about a policeman—and giving you in charge?"

"I am sure that he would have given me in charge to twenty policemen if he could, and that nothing would have pleased him better than to have had me sent to penal servitude for life."

"What I can't make out is—why did he dislike you so?"

"My dear, I'm afraid the explanation is simple—too simple. I don't want to hurt your feelings, but I've a notion—a very strong one—that he didn't like you. He regarded you as a nuisance; you know how he kept you in the background as long as he could; you interfered with the sort of life he liked to live; you were in his way."

"He certainly never at any period of his life or mine, showed himself over-anxious for my company."

"When you did become installed in town, he had formed his own plans for your future. What precisely was the arrangement between them I don't pretend to know; but I dare say I shall find out before long—it won't need much to induce Wilkes to give himself away; but I am persuaded that it was his intention that you should become Mrs. Stephen Wilkes."

"But what makes you think so? It seems to me so monstrous. Fancy me as Mrs. Stephen Wilkes!"

"Thank you, I'd rather not. It's only a case of intuition, I admit, but I'm convinced I'm right, and one day I may be able to give you chapter and verse. He was not over-fond of me to begin with, but when you appeared on the scene, and he saw that his best laid plans bade fair to gang agley, he suddenly began to develop a feeling towards me which ended as it has done. It's not a pretty one, but there's my explanation. But, sweetheart, that page is ended; let's turn it over and never look back at it; and all the rest of the volume—let's try our best to make it happy reading."

They ate a fair lunch, considering, and enjoyed it, and afterwards returned together in a taximeter cab to Russell Square, feeling more tenderly disposed to each other, and at peace with all the world. When Miss Patterson had ate and drunk well she was apt to discover a turn for languorous sentiment which appealed to Mr. Elmore very forcibly indeed. Since, therefore, it was probably their intention to spend an amorous afternoon, the shock was all the greater when, on their arrival at No. 90, they were greeted in the hall by a tall upstanding, broad-shouldered, soldierly-looking man in whom Gladys recognised the officer of police who had brought her the news of her father's tragic fate.

"Inspector Harlow," she exclaimed. "What—what are you doing here?"

It was perhaps only natural that, drawing away from the policeman towards her lover, she should slip her hands through his arm as if she looked to him for protection from some suddenly threatening danger. Rodney pressed his arm closer to his side, as if to assure her she would find shelter there; though, as she uttered the visitor's name, he glanced towards him with a look which, as it were, with difficulty became an odd little smile. The visitor's manner, when he spoke, suggested mystery.

"Can I say half a dozen words with you, Miss Patterson, in private?"

She led the way to the first room to which they came, which chanced to be the dining-room, she entering first, then Rodney, the inspector last. When he was in he shut the door and stood up against it.

"I said, Miss Patterson, in private."

The inspector had an eye on Rodney.

"We are in private; you can say anything you wish to say before this gentleman. This is Mr. Elmore, to whom I am shortly to be married."

"Mr. Elmore?"

As the officer echoed the name the two men's glances met. In the inspector's eyes there was an expression of eager curiosity, as if he were taken by surprise; Rodney's quick perceptions told him that while his name, and probably more than his name, was known to the other, for some cause he was the last person he had expected to see; the man was studying him with an interest which he did not attempt to conceal. The young man, on his side, was regarding the inspector as if he found him amusing.

"Well, inspector, when you have quite finished staring at Mr. Elmore, perhaps you will tell me what it is you have to say."

The girl's candid allusion to the peculiarity which it seemed she had noticed in his manner had the effect of bringing the officer back to a consciousness of what he was doing.

"Was I staring? I beg Mr. Elmore's pardon—and yours, Miss Patterson. I was only thinking that, under the circumstances, it is a fortunate accident that Mr. Elmore should be present."

"You have omitted to state what are the circumstances to which you allude."

"I will proceed to supply that omission at once, Miss Patterson. You will probably think that they are strange ones; and, indeed, they are; but you will, of course, understand that I am only here in pursuance of my duty. I have come in consequence of a letter which I received this morning. I will read it to you."

He took an envelope from a fat pocket-book.

"It bears no address, and is not dated; but the envelope shows that it was posted last night at Beckenham.

"'To Inspector Harlow.

"'Sir,—Mr. Graham Patterson did not commit suicide; he was murdered.

"'If you can make it convenient to be at Mr. Graham Patterson's late residence, No. 90, Russell Square, to-morrow, Wednesday, afternoon at 3.30, I will be there also, and will point out to you the murderer.

"'Your obedient servant,

"'Philip Walter Augustus Parker.'"

Silence followed when the inspector ceased to read. The officer was engaged in folding the letter and returning it to its envelope; Gladys looked as if she were too startled to give ready utterance to her feelings in words. Rodney was possibly trying to associate someone of whom he had heard with the name of Parker—and failing. His memory did not often play him tricks; he was pretty sure that no one of that name was known to him. The inspector was the first to speak.

"You will, of course, perceive, Miss Patterson, that the probabilities are that this letter is a hoax; the signature, Philip Walter Augustus Parker, in itself suggests a hoax. Then there is the absence of an address. And, of course, we have the verdict of the coroner's jury, and the evidence on which it was found. I am quite prepared to learn that I have come to Russell Square, and troubled you with my presence, for nothing. But at the same time, in my position, I did not feel justified in not coming, on the very off-chance of making the acquaintance of Philip Walter Augustus Parker. It is now on the stroke of half-past three; we will give him a few minutes' grace, after which—if, as I expect will be the case, there are still no signs of him—I'll take myself off, with apologies, Miss Patterson. But should he by any strange chance put in an appearance, I would ask you to have him at once shown in here."

Hardly had the inspector done speaking than there was the sound of an electric bell and a rat-tat-tat at the front door. The trio in the dining-room could scarcely have seemed more startled had they been suddenly confronted by a ghost. The inspector's voice sank to a whisper.

"If the name's Parker, would you mind asking the servant—in here?"

A gesture supplied the words he had omitted in his sentence. He held the door open so that Gladys could speak to the maid who was coming along the hall. She did so, also in lowered tones.

"If that's a person of the name of Parker show him at once in here."

She withdrew; the inspector shut the door; there was a pause; no one spoke; each of the three stood and listened. They could hear the front door opened and steps coming along the hall. Then the dining-room door was opened by a maid, who announced:

"Mr. Parker."

There entered the little man who had followed the example set by Rodney of getting out of the train in Redhill Tunnel.

CHAPTER XXIII

NECESSARY CREDENTIALS

The moment he appeared Rodney knew that he had been expecting him; that somewhere at the back of his mind there had been a feeling that it was he who was coming. His impulse was to take him by the throat and crush the life out of him before he had a chance of saying a word; which was the impulse of a badly frightened man. But he seldom lost his presence of mind for long; and, on that occasion, he had it again almost as soon as it had gone; indeed, within the same second he was smiling at himself for having allowed himself to be disposed towards such crass folly.

So far as Rodney was able to judge the little man was clad just as he had been on Sunday evening—in the same shabby tweed suit, the old unbrushed boots, with the same suggestion about him that he might easily have been improved by a more intimate acquaintance with soap and water. He had his hat in one hand, and with the other he rubbed his scrubby chin. No one could have seemed more at his ease. Without offering any sort of greeting he immediately proceeded to address the inspector, while the maid was still closing the door, in that thin, unmusical, penetrating voice which Rodney had so much disliked.

"So you are there, Harlow, are you? I wondered if you'd have sense enough to come."

He rounded off his sentence with the snigger which had so jarred on the young man's sensitive nerves, and which affected Gladys so unpleasantly that, with what seemed to be a start of repulsion, she moved closer to her lover's side. The stranger noted the movement, and commented on it—again with the uncomfortable snigger.

"That's right; get as close as you can; he'll keep you safe; anyone will be safe who gets close enough to him. You're Miss Patterson; I could tell you anywhere by your likeness to your father. You're not the kind of girl I care about, any more than he was the kind of man. Who's the youngster? Now, there is someone worth looking at; why, he's as handsome as paint, and of quite unusual force of character for so young a man. Miss Patterson, the girl who gets him for a lover will have a lover of a kind of which she has no notion. He's a most remarkable young man."

With a view, perhaps, of checking the stranger's volubility, the inspector administered what was possibly meant for a rebuke.

"If you would confine yourself to the business which has brought you here, sir, it would be as well. Are you Mr. Parker?"

"I am; Philip Walter Augustus Parker—a lot of name for a man of my size."

"You sent me a letter last night from Beckenham?"

"I did."

"Stating that Mr. Graham Patterson did not commit suicide."

"Exactly."

"But was murdered?"

"He was."

"You went on to say that if I were here this afternoon you would point out to me the murderer."

"I will."

"Point him out."

"I am."

"I thought so."

"I knew you did. I saw on your intelligent visage that you knew what was coming. You have some experience of cranks who accuse themselves of crimes of which they are innocent; you take it for granted that I am one of them, which shows what a dunce you are. I am a lunatic. That's right, Harlow, smile again. I knew that would tickle you. A policeman's sense of humour is his own."

"It is necessary, Mr. Parker, that I should warn you that anything you say will be taken down and used against you."

"Quite right, Harlow; take it down; but as for using it against me, that's absurd. The law does not punish lunatics; whatever they may do it holds them guiltless. I'm an example of the inadequacy of the law to protect the public from what I may describe as the lunatic at large. It is not sufficiently recognised that there is an order of dementia which may at any time develop into homicidal mania, and that, therefore, a lunatic, unless he is kept in safe keeping, may kill, with impunity, whom he pleases—as I have done. I have killed Graham Patterson; yet no one may venture to kill me. My life is more sacred than that of a sane man in the eyes of the law."

The inspector looked at the girl significantly.

"I think, Miss Patterson, that I had better deal with Mr. Parker alone."

"And, Miss Patterson, I think not. What I am about to say will be found of interest not only by you, but also by—that extraordinary young man. Harlow, your duty is to take down what I am about to say in writing; don't exceed it. Shut the door. Miss Patterson will stay where she is."

The inspector looked at the lady, as if for instructions. As she gave no sign, beyond drawing a little closer to her lover, he shut the door, which he had opened a few inches. Mr. Parker beamed at him with a grotesque little air of triumph.

"There, Harlow—you see! Now attend to me. Suppose, before I go any further, we all sit down; my tale may take some minutes; I don't want anyone to get tired of standing. You won't? Very good—then stand. There are plenty of chairs, and very comfortable some of them seem; but, of course, I don't propose to force you to occupy them if you would rather not. Now—attention! To begin at the beginning."

Again he indulged in the uncomfortable sort of laughter which, more than anything else, revealed the disorder of the creature's mind.

"On Sunday evening I bolted from my keeper, one Metcalf, in whose charge I have been for six or seven months, and of whom I was tired to extinction—an unclubable fellow who never talks unless he has something to say. I left Brighton station on the 9.10 train. Until the train started I was the sole occupant of a first-class carriage, at which I was not displeased. I had some idea of committing suicide myself. Life, I assure you, has little to offer me. I am just sane enough to know that I never shall be saner. There's a wall—a wall which I shall never climb, and which shuts me out—from I don't know what. If I were left alone—I so seldom am; they won't leave me alone!—here would be an excellent opportunity to consider the best way out of it. You may fancy, then, what my feelings were when, just as the train was starting, another passenger entered—bundled in by an extremely officious porter. He would never have caught the train if it hadn't been for the porter—in which case he would have been still alive—so that one may say, logically, the porter killed him. The fellow certainly ought to be punished."

He waved his hat with a gesture which was possibly intended to represent the execution of the porter in question.

"The man who had entered my compartment, Miss Patterson, was your father—in every respect a most objectionable person, combining in himself nearly everything that I most object to—bloated, overfed, nearly drunk, horrible to contemplate. He sat there perspiring, puffing, panting, gasping for breath; I half expected he would have a fit. But, instead of having a fit, before the train had gone very far he was asleep, fast asleep. Could any conduct have been more disgusting?—drunken sleep! With a man of my stamp at the other end of the carriage, could anything have been more insulting? And he snored—such snores! I declare to you he made more noise than the train did; if that extraordinary young man had been in the next compartment he'd have heard him. And his jaw dropped open—it was that gave me the idea. Who is it says that trifles light as air lead to I don't know what? It was that trifle which led to my killing your father, Miss Patterson."

Again the cackling giggle, which made the girl try to draw still nearer to her lover, as if the thing were possible.

"Some time before I had come into possession of quite a quantity of potassium cyanide; I won't say how—I had. The artfulness of lunatics is proverbial, and I'm as artful as any of them; on that point I refer you to Metcalf, as well as to others who have had me in their charge, both in asylums and out of them—they'll tell you! It was in the form of tabloids, looking just like sweeties, in a nice little silver box; enough to kill a street. I had meant to use it to kill myself, but at the sight of that dreadful man, with his bulging mouth, I thought—why not use it to kill him? Pop one into his mouth, and the trick was done! I moved inch by inch and foot by foot along the seat towards his end of the carriage; he still snored on, paying no attention of any sort to me; he was a horrid, vulgar man. At last I was right in front of him; I might have been ten miles away for all he knew. How he snored, and how his jaws did gape! I had the silver box in one hand and a tabloid between the finger and thumb of the other, and I leaned forward and popped it into his open mouth."

Mr. Parker illustrated his words by his gestures, with the air of one who was telling an amusing tale.

"Oh, what a change came over him! You should have seen it! He snored the tabloid right down his throat, and he gave a great gasp and was dead. He had not even waked; I am sure that he never knew I was on the seat in front of him, or that I was in the carriage at all. There was his huge carcase bolt upright in front of me, and I knew that he would never snore any more. It made me feel quite odd; it was all so sudden and so funny. I daresay it would have made that extraordinary young man feel odd, eh?"

He looked up at Rodney with a leer which made his mean, wrinkled face all at once seem bestial. But he never faltered in his story, which he told with a sniggering relish which lent it a quality of horror which no display of dramatic, conscience-stricken intensity could possibly have done.

"My idea had been to tell the porters all about it the first time the train stopped; it would have been funny to see the fuss they'd have made; I shouldn't have cared. But it so happened that the signal was against us, and the train stopped in the middle of Redhill tunnel."

The inspector allowed no hint to escape him of what he knew or did not know. He kept his eyes fastened on the little man, as if his wish were not so much to follow his actual words, but to see something which might be behind them.

"When it stopped I had another idea, quite as brilliant as the first. Why should I go through the nuisance of a trial for murder? With a little management, if this objectionable person were found in a carriage by himself, it might be taken for granted that he had committed suicide, which would be too funny. So I put the silver box open in his fingers, slipped out of the carriage into the tunnel—in the darkness no one saw me—waited for the train to go, then walked after it, out of the tunnel, up the banks, across the fields to Redhill Station; had a drink or two, which I was in want of; went on by the 10.40, until at Croydon I was joined by Metcalf, who had got there first. For the rest of the tale refer to him."

Continuing, Mr. Parker seemed to address his remarks particularly to Rodney:

"You never would have thought that it could be so easy to kill a man, and have it brought in as suicide, would you? When I read the report of the inquest in the papers, I was amazed to find how easy it really was. Then it occurred to me that as, of course, he had been murdered—I knew that—why shouldn't I communicate with the police, after all? No harm would come to me; lunatics are protected by the law. It would be different if he had been murdered by—you; you would quite certainly be hung. I shall go to Broadmoor. I have rather a fancy for Broadmoor. I am told that they are all of them lunatics there; I should like to see. At any rate, they have all of them done something; no lunatic I've met ever did anything worth doing. They must be interesting people. But certain credentials are necessary for Broadmoor, and now I think I've earned them. If the part I've played in this little affair of Graham Patterson doesn't qualify me for Broadmoor, then I should very much like to know what would. Eh, young man, eh?"

CHAPTER XXIV

LOVERS PARTING

Inspector Harlow having gone, with Mr. Parker as close companion, the lovers being again alone together, it was pretty plain that they were conscious that, since entering the house, the situation had materially changed. Rodney, try how he might, could not erase from his mind, so quickly as he wished, the impression that he had been assisting at some hideous nightmare. He had supposed, at the sight of the little man, that his accuser had come into the room. His nerves were strained in the expectation that every moment the charge would be made. Even as the instants passed, and he began to see the drift of the tale which the man was telling, inventing it as he went on, he had a feeling that he was only playing with him as a cat does with a mouse, and that, just when it seemed least likely, he would right-about-face and, perhaps with that diabolical snigger of his, place the onus of the guilt on him. Now that the fellow had actually gone, a self-accused prisoner in the inspector's charge, the feeling that he was still taking part in some fantastic drama seemed stronger than ever.

Gladys, on her side, when at last she broke the curious silence, which prevailed longer than either of them supposed after they had been left together, quickly showed that she was obsessed by a mood in which he did not know her, in which, as it were, she had slipped out of his reach.

"Rodney, do you think that what that man said is true?"

"He seemed to give chapter and verse for most of it."

"But if it's true—dad didn't take his own life!"

"If it's true."

"But don't you see what a difference that makes?"

"Of course it makes a difference; but in what sense do you mean?"

"In every sense—every sense! Do you think—that while he's being buried—I should be here—if I had known that he was murdered? He was my father."

"In any case he was that."

"Not in any case, not in any case! I may have got him all wrong! I may have misjudged! I may—I don't know what I mayn't have done. There's the letter!"

"What letter?"

"To Mr. Wilkes. You said, when he wrote it, he was mad, and that taking his own life proved it. I thought so. But, if he didn't take his own life, what then?" Rodney made an effort to regain his self-possession, and partially succeeded.

"My dear Gladys, the whole business is a bad one, whichever way you look at it. We are to be married on Monday."

"Monday? Married—to you?"

The knowledge of women on which he was apt to pride himself ought to have warned him that this was not the same girl as the one with whom he had come back from lunch in the cab. But at the moment he was not yet quite himself; his perception was at fault. He made a mistake.

"My dear Gladys, you are perfectly well aware that the arrangement, as it stands at present, is that we are to be married on Monday. I was merely about to suggest that, as it would seem that this whole unfortunate affair is likely to prove too much, we should be married to-morrow instead, and then we shall be able to get out of this unpleasant atmosphere at the earliest possible moment."

"Stop! stop!"

She shouted at rather than spoke to him.

"Perhaps I shall not be married to you at all."

He stared at her in genuine amazement.

"Gladys! What are you talking about? What do you mean?"

"I don't know what I mean; I almost hope I never may know."

"My dear child; that wretched man."

"Have you ever seen him before?"

"Seen whom?"

"You know quite well. That—wretched man."

"So far as I'm aware, never in my life. What makes you ask such a question?"

"Are you sure? Do you swear it?"

"How can a man swear to a thing like that? But I do swear that, to the best of my knowledge and belief, I have never seen him before."

"Then how came it that he knew you so well?"

"Knew me so well? Gladys! What are you dreaming about? Why, he never even addressed me by name."

"No, I noticed that; but he addressed you all the same. Most of what he said was especially addressed to you, as if he knew that you would understand."

"What are you driving at?"

"What's more, he saw that I was afraid of you."

"Afraid? You? Why, you could hardly have snuggled closer."

"That was because I was afraid to let you know how afraid of you I was."

"Gladys! Has that creature turned your brain?"

"I—I don't know. Oh, if I could only say a few words to dad—if I only could!"

"What would they be?"

"I would—ask him—how—he died."

"You have two stories offered for your choice. Are you content with neither?"

"Rodney, if my father were standing here now, and his spirit may be, would you tell me, in his presence, that you don't know why he disliked you?"

"Are you going into that all over again? To what end?"

"What does that man know of you? What does he know?"

"How can I tell what a half-witted man knows of me, or thinks he knows? Certainly he knows nothing to my discredit."

"Rodney—don't."

"Don't what?"

"You know! You do know! I can see in your eyes you know! Please go!"

"Sweetheart!"

"Don't—speak to me—like that—now. Go!"

"You surely are not in earnest. You cannot wish me to leave you before this extraordinary misunderstanding which has so inexplicably sprung up is cleared away. Tell me what is in your mind—frankly, all! I quite understand how this wretched man, Parker, may have turned your thoughts into unexpected currents and filled you with miserable doubts. I assure you he has upset me more than I care to tell you."

"I know that he upset you! I felt you were upset when I was so close to you. I can see it now."

If for the moment he was disconcerted—and the lady's manner was disconcerting—he slurred it over with creditable skill.

"Come, Gladys; let's try to get back to where we were—to perfect understanding. Tell me your doubts, no matter how insoluble they may seem to you. I promise you I'll solve them."

"I'm sure you will; I feel you could solve anything, but I am afraid of your solution."

Before he had an inkling of her intention she had passed rapidly across the floor and from the room.

"Gladys!" he exclaimed.

But it was too late; she had gone. He stood staring at the door through which she had vanished, irresolute. Should he follow her, possibly to her bedroom, and entreat her for a hearing? For once in his life he had been taken wholly unawares; he had not suspected that this Gladys was in the Gladys he had known. Often a man lives to a ripe old age, ignorant how many women are contained in the one woman he knows best. Then, as if unwittingly, his fingers strayed to the pocket in which were the proceeds of the cheque he had cashed while Gladys, without in the cab, had supposed him to have gone into the bank for his letter-case. Apparently the touch decided him; often a little thing brought him to an instant decision. Without making any further effort to gain the lady's ear, he buttoned his coat across his chest, took his hat and stick from off the table, and quietly left the house.

CHAPTER XXV

STELLA'S BETROTHAL FEAST

That evening Rodney Elmore was at a dinner given at a famous restaurant in honour of his engagement to Stella Austin, quite a different sort of meal from that at which he had assisted at the Misses Claughton's house in Kensington. If in his manner there was an unusual touch of nervousness, it was not unbecoming; the bride that was to be was not entirely herself. He met her as, with her father and mother, she entered the hall. She said to him, as he fell in by her side:

"I did hope, Rodney, that you would have come to fetch me."

"My dear, it's only by the skin of my teeth that I've got here myself! Do you think that I wouldn't have come if I could?"

She said nothing in reply, but as she passed towards the ladies' cloak-room there was a look on her face which almost suggested tears. Her mother's manner, as she greeted him, was not too genial:

"So you are here? Well, I suppose that's something!"

Mr. Austin, as he deposited his hat and coat with the attendant, seemed very much in the same key.

"We should have been here some minutes ago, only Stella would have it you were coming to fetch her; we should have been waiting for you still if she had had her way. How was it you didn't come? She's quite disappointed; rather a pity that the evening should have begun with a misunderstanding of that sort."

Rodney drew the gentleman aside.

"I take it, Mr. Austin, that you haven't heard the news?"

"To what news do you refer?"

"It is now stated that my uncle did not commit suicide, but was murdered."

"But I thought the coroner's jury had returned a verdict of suicide."

"That is so; but this afternoon a man named Parker gave himself up to the police, on his own confession, as having murdered my uncle. You will understand that I—I have had rather a trying day."

"On his confession? Is the man a lunatic?"

"That's just it; he is, yet it seems only too likely that—he did what he says he did."

"But how came he to make his confession in your presence? Do you know the man?"

"Not I; he's an entire stranger to me; but I'll tell you all about it later. I don't want you to say anything to the ladies or anyone; I only mention it to you because I want you to understand how it is that I am not in such—such good fettle as I might be for an occasion of this kind; and also because I want you, if needs be, to help me with Stella."

"My dear boy, of course I will. It is only natural that, at a time like this, a girl should think that there's nothing of much consequence except her own affairs; but I'll stand by you, never fear. I rather wish that the whole thing had been postponed, but Stella wouldn't hear of it. There's Tom not at all himself; he wanted Mary Carmichael to come, and Stella wanted her to come, in fact, we all wanted her to come, but she hasn't. I've been told nothing, but I can see there's some trouble there. Altogether the evening doesn't look as if it were going to be quite such a merry one as I had hoped it would have been; however, we must make the best of it. Cheer up, lad; put your troubles behind you for this night only."

That was a prescription which at any rate the prescriber's son did not seem at all disposed to follow, as Rodney quickly learnt when Tom appeared a little tardily. Tom's naturally good-humoured face wore an expression of unwonted gloom, and there was that in his air and general bearing which accorded ill with a time of feasting and making merry.

"You know, old chap, I oughtn't to be here, I really didn't. I shall queer the whole show. Unless I drink too much, and put my spirits up that way, I shall give everyone the hump; and when I start on that lay I'm apt to get my spirits up a bit too much, so I don't know that that will have a good effect either."

Rodney laughed as he put his hand on the speaker's shoulder.

"Why, Tom, what's wrong?"

"I don't know what's wrong, but something's wrong. I do know that. When the governor told me about this kick-up to-night, I wrote to Mary and told her all about it, and asked her to come up, and so on, and said I'd run down to Brighton this morning to bring her up, and told her the train I'd come by, and asked her to meet me at the station. She didn't meet me at the station—that was shock number one; and then when I got to the house, if you please, the servant didn't want to let me in—she wanted to make me believe that Mary was out. I wasn't taking that; I would go in, and I saw her old aunt—she's an old dear, she is. After a while, and she'd told no end of them, she owned up that Mary was in all the time she'd been telling them. She was up in her bedroom, and had given word that if I called she wouldn't see me. You might have bowled me over with an old cork."

"The lady wasn't well."

"Her health was all right; the old girl owned as much. She said Mary was perfectly well, but beyond that she wouldn't say anything; and she made out that she couldn't; and she wouldn't send a message up, or a note, or anything. She said that she knew her niece well enough to be sure that that would be no use. But when she saw that I was set, she said that if I chose I might go up and try my luck. So, if you please, up I went, and rapped at her bedroom door."

"Summoned her to surrender, quite in the good old style; and she did?"

"Not much she didn't. I spoke to her through the bedroom door, I called out to her, I as nearly as possible howled; I daresay I rapped as many as twenty times—I know I made my knuckles sore But she took not the slightest notice, not a sound came from the other side; she might have been stone deaf or dead. In fact, I wanted to tell her that I felt sure that something dreadful had happened, and that if she wouldn't speak I should have to break down the door to see what was wrong. But the old girl wouldn't have it. She said that she had had enough of that folly, and when I talked about camping out on the door-mat she marched me off downstairs, feeling all mops and brooms, and all over the place. Then it came out that when I was at the front door she had told the old girl that she wouldn't see me, and nothing would make her see me, and had rushed up to her bedroom and locked herself in. So I came back from Brighton all alone, and the wonder is I didn't start to drink and keep on at it; only I had a sort of feeling that if I began by being squiffy when I got here things wouldn't be so very much brighter; besides, there's always time to start that sort of thing if you are set on it."

"My dear old chap, you've done something to upset the lady's apple-cart; you'll have a letter telling you all about it in the morning."

"I hope so, but I doubt it; I might have known I was feeling too much bucked up. You know she never said exactly yes; she sort of let me take it for granted, and perhaps I took it a little too much for granted; I feel that perhaps that's how it is. But if she's off with me, I'm done—clean. She could make a man of me, even the kind of article the governor thinks a man; but no one else could. If she won't have me, I shall emigrate, that's what I shall do; I shall go to one of those cheery spots where you get knocked out by blackwater fever, or sleeping sickness, or something nice of that sort, three months after you've landed."

Notice being given that dinner was ready, Rodney led Stella into the private room in which it was to be served cheerfully enough, bestowing on her admiring glances and whispering what he meant to be sweet things into her pretty ear as they went.

"My hat! that's a duck of a frock you're arrayed in; you do look scrumptious."

"I'm glad you think so."

The maid's manner was a trifle prim; she plainly wished him to understand that she was still a little out with him. He smiled at her.

"I don't know what you're laughing at."

"Would you rather I cried?"

"I'm afraid poor Tom feels like crying. Isn't it strange Mary not coming, and sending no message, or anything—nothing to explain? Have you heard how she treated Tom?"

They had reached the dinner-table, and were settling themselves in their places.

"Stella, be so good as to understand, once for all, that there's only one subject to-night, and that's you. All other subjects are tabooed. Are you quite comfortable? Don't put your chair too far off; so that, if you feel like it, you can put your baby foot out towards mine and with your wee slipper crush my favourite corn."

"Rodney, I'm glad you are going to talk to me at last, though I don't suppose you have thought of me once all day."

"Shall I tell you what I've been looking for ever since I came?"

"I expect for somewhere to smoke."

"I've been looking for—say, a curtained nook, where I can have you alone for about five minutes, and have a few of those kisses of which I have been dreaming this livelong day."

"If you had come and fetched me you might have had one kiss—in the cab."

"I'll have one kiss when I take you back—one!"

"Oh, you are going to take me back?"

"I am; and I'm going to eat you on the way; then you'll understand what you escaped by my not fetching you."

"You're not to talk like that; people will hear you."

"Let 'em. Fancy if you'd arrived here with that lovely frock all crumpled—two in a cab! People would have wondered what you had been doing."

"Rodney, if you will talk like that I shall crush your favourite corn."

"Crush it!"

"Please pass me the salt."

Whether, while he passed her the salt, she did crush it, there was nothing to show.

The feast passed off better than, at one time, it had promised to do. There were about twenty people present. Mr. Austin had whipped up, at a moment's notice, various relations, and also certain persons who were intimately connected with the firm of which he was head; he desired to introduce to them not only his future son-in-law, but also the probable partner in his business. Most of these people were very willing to be entertained, simple souls, easily pleased, and the dinner was a good one. Even Tom, who found himself next to a girl with mischievous eyes and a saucy tongue, was inclined to shed some of his melancholy before the menu was half-way through.

"I never did meet a girl who says such things as you do," he told her, with a frankness which was perhaps meant for laudation. "You are quite too altogether."

"You see," she said, with her eyes fixed demurely on her plate, "it doesn't matter what one does say to some people, does it?"

"What do you mean by that?"

"Of course some people don't count, do they?"

"By that I suppose you mean that I'm a—"

She did not wait for him to finish.

"Oh, not at all."

She looked at him with innocence in her glance, which was too perfect to be real.

"How many times have you been ploughed?"

"Who's been telling you tales about me?"

"I was only thinking that it doesn't matter if one hasn't brains so long as one has looks, and you have got those, haven't you?"

Tom's face, as the minx said this, in a voice which was just loud enough to reach his ears, would have made a good photographic study. Beyond a doubt he was in a fair way to lose some of his sadness, at least for the time.

When the cloth had been removed the giver of the feast, getting on to his feet, made the usual half jovial, half sentimental references to the occasion which had brought them together; and, in wishing the young couple well, made special allusion to the fact that he was not only welcoming a son, but also a colleague. The toast he ended by proposing could not have been better received. Then, while the young maiden sat blushing, the young man stood up, and, in a brief yet deft little speech, told how happy they all had made him, how the hopes which he had cherished for years had at last been realised, how dear those hopes had been to him, how unworthy he was of all the good gifts which had descended on him. But of this they might be sure, that if he had health and strength—and at present he was very well and pretty strong, thanking them very much—he would do his very best in the years to come to prove that he could at least appreciate those things which Providence had bestowed on him. The young man sat down on quite a pathetic note, and the girl by his side pressed his hand and looked as if this were indeed one of those moments of which she had dreamed.

Then there were other speeches and all sorts of kind things were said, which, at such times, one takes it for granted should be said. The young man was made much of, and the maiden, if possible, even more. And when the feast was really ended, and all the good wishes had been wished again and again, and there came the time of parting, even Mr. Austin was obliged to confess to himself that everything could scarcely have gone off better. His wife was radiant, some of the shadows had gone from Tom's face; apparently the young lady with the mischievous eyes had in some subtle way, the secret of which she only possessed, acted the part of the sun in dispelling the clouds; Stella could not by any possibility have looked happier or Rodney prouder. Tom, it is believed, saw the young lady with the mischievous eyes home in one cab, and it is certain that Rodney was with Stella in another. What took place during that journey in the cab between the restaurant and Kensington it is not perhaps easy to determine precisely, but beyond a doubt Rodney had that one kiss which had been spoken of, and probably others; for when the house in Kensington was reached, and the young lady ran up the steps to the front door, she was in a state of the most delightful agitation. And in the house there was the final parting, which occupied a considerable time, for they had to say to each other the things which they had already said more than once, and which Rodney at least could say so well and to which the girl so loved to listen.

"I think that, after all, to-night has made up for to-day. Do you know, Rodney," and she looked up into his face with something shining in her pretty eyes, "that to-day I have had the most curious fancies? I was actually frightened; I don't know at what, but I do know that somehow it was because of you. Wasn't it silly?"

"I am not sure that it's ever silly for you to be frightened because of me; I'm in the most delicious terror all day, and sometimes all night, because of you; but you are a goose."

Then he held her perhaps a little closer, and whispered:

"It has been something of a night, hasn't it? For the first time in my life I feel as if I were a person of some importance. You couldn't have your betrothal feast again to-morrow, could you?"

She smiled.

"I doubt it; but we might have a silver betrothal feast as well as a silver wedding. Hasn't that sort of thing ever been done?"

He laughed at the conceit, and when the parting really did come she was looking forward as through a dim mist, towards that silver time at which he had hinted; and when she went upstairs she prayed that after five-and-twenty years of married life she might be as happy as she was then. And all night she slept sweetly, dreaming the happiest dreams of all that took place during the passage of the years, through which she walked with the husband whom she loved so dearly, ever heart in heart and hand in hand. That night was to her a halcyon time.

CHAPTER XXVI

GOOD NIGHT

When Rodney Elmore went home, as his cab drew up in front of his lodgings a man came quickly across the road and stood so that he was between him and the entrance to the house.

"Mr. Rodney Elmore?"

Rodney looked him up and down. It was not a very good light just there, but it was clear enough for him to recognise the man who had greeted him. For the first time in his life a feeling that was something very like dizziness went all over him, so that he all but reeled; but that self-control which so seldom quitted him except for the briefest instant was back before it had actually gone. He did not reel, but stood quite still, and, with a smile upon his face, looked the man fairly and squarely in the eyes.

"That is my name—I am Rodney Elmore; but you, sir—pray, who are you?"

"My name is Edward Giles. But I don't think that that can mean much to you, Mr. Elmore."

"I am very pleased to meet you, Mr. Giles, but, as you say, your name does convey absolutely nothing to me. What is it that I can have the pleasure of doing for you at this latish hour?"

The man was silent for a moment. Then a curious smile flitted across his face as he came a half-step nearer.

"Think, Mr. Elmore. I shouldn't be surprised if you had rather a good memory. Don't you remember me?"

"Not the least in the world, Mr. Giles."

"It isn't so very long ago since you saw me."

"Indeed! I presume it was on rather a special occasion, Mr. Giles, since you appear to be rather anxious to recall it to my recollection."

"It was rather a special occasion for you, Mr. Elmore; and a still more special occasion—for Mr. Patterson."

"My uncle?"

"Yes, Mr. Elmore, your uncle. Don't you remember last Sunday evening at Brighton station?"

Rodney hesitated.

"Why do you ask?"

"You do remember, Mr. Elmore, and so do I. I can see you still, coming sauntering down the platform smoking a cigarette and looking into the first-class carriages to see which of them would suit you best. You chose one, and then stood for a moment or two at the door, looking up and down the platform, to see, as it were, if there was anything which caught your eye. Then you got into the carriage, and took the seat at the farther end, facing the engine. You thought you were going to journey up all alone, but just as the train was starting a stout, elderly gentleman came bustling along. Yours was the only carriage door that was open, and I helped him in. I shut the door, and you went out of the station together. Don't you remember that? Look at me carefully. Don't you remember that I was the party who helped your uncle into your carriage? Just look at me and think."

Again Rodney hesitated, and seemed to think. Then he said, in a tone the indifference of which was perhaps a trifle studied:

"Really, Mr. Giles, I don't quite know what it is you expect me to say."

The man gave a little laugh.

"Anyhow, Mr. Elmore, you've said it."

Without an attempt at a farewell greeting, he walked quickly back across the street, to where, as Rodney had been aware, another person had been waiting.

The pair walked briskly off together side by side, and Rodney went up the steps into the house. He knew that, as he had expected, the presence of that platform inspector was going to prove awkward for him; more awkward than he cared to think. But he did think, as he turned into his sitting-room; and still stood thinking as the door was gently opened and Mabel Joyce came in. Her agitation was almost unpleasantly evident. One could see that her hands were trembling, that her lips were twitching, and that, indeed, it was all she could do to keep her whole body from shaking. She came quickly towards the table, and leaned upon the edge; plainly it was a very real assistance in aiding her to stand. And her voice was as tremulous as her person.

"Did—did you see him?"

"My dear Mabel, did I see whom?"

She seemed to clutch the table still more tightly.

"Rodney, don't! It's no good. Do you think I don't know? What's the good of pretending with me, when you know—I know? What cock-and-bull story is this about some man, some fool, some lunatic, who says—he did it? Do you think that I don't know, that Mr. Dale doesn't know, that they all don't know? Rodney," and her voice trembled so that it was with pain she spoke at all, "there'll—there'll—be a warrant—out—in the morning. Oh, my God! my God!"

And the girl threw herself forward on the table, crying and trembling as if on the verge of a convulsion.

"What on earth, Mabel, is the use of spoiling your pretty face like this? I am a little worried to-night, and that's the truth. If there's anything you want to say to me, old girl, say it, and have done with it."

He sighed. She raised herself from the table, and looked across at him.

"Rodney, it won't be any use our marrying." There was a big sob. "That won't save you—now. God knows what will."

"It's really very good of you to worry about the sort of man that I have been to you; take my tip, my dear, don't worry. I'll win through."

"But how? How? You don't understand! This—this fool, whoever he is, who pretends he did it, has only made them all the keener. They—they mean to have you now."

"They? And who are they?"

"There's Dale, and Giles, and Harlow, and—and don't ask me who besides. They're all wild because—because you tricked them; because they made such idiots of themselves at the inquest."

Rodney raised his arms above his head, and stretched himself, and yawned, as if he were a little weary.

"They were a trifle premature; coroner, and jury, an eminent specialist, and Harlow, and all—the whole jolly lot of them. I don't wonder they feel a trifle wild. But why with me?"

"You know, Rodney—you know! You know! Oh, don't—don't pretend!"

"On my word of honour—if it's any use employing that pretty figure of speech with you—I am not pretending. I've still another trick in the bag; that's all. And that's what you don't give me credit for, my dear."

"What—what trick's that? You've too many tricks—you're all tricks! It's—Rodney, it's—it's too late for tricks!"

"But not for this pretty trick of mine. Mabel, it's such a pretty one! But now you listen to me for a moment. Pull yourself together. Stand up; let me see your face."

She did as he bade her, and stood, leaning on the table with both her hands, looking at him with eyes from which the tears were streaming.

"Mabel, you asked me to marry you. I said I would, and I will."

"But—what's the use of it now? You don't understand."

"Oh, yes, I do; I don't know if I can get you to believe me, but I do understand much better than you suppose; and, indeed, I rather fancy even better than you do. Anyhow, the supposition is that we're to be bride and bridegroom, dear, to-morrow; let's for goodness' sake be friends to-night. Let's try to say, at any rate, one or two pleasant things, as, not so very long ago, we used to do. What's going to come of it all you seem doubtful, and I can hardly pretend that I'm quite sure. I don't suppose, Mabel, that you ever read Dante, or, perhaps, even heard of him. But, in a tolerably well-known poem by Dante, there is this story. He goes down, with a party named Virgil, into one of the lowest depths of hell, and there he meets a poor devil who seems to be having an uncommonly bad time. They ask him what he has done that he should suffer so, and he answers something to this effect. He has it that his creed was a very simple one. He believed, and he acted on his belief, that one moment of perfect bliss was worth an eternity of hell, He had that perfect moment, the lucky bargee! And now for ever he's in hell. Yet, do you know, he isn't sorry; he thinks that moment was worth the price he paid. That's a moral story, and I don't pretend that I've got it quite right; but that's what it comes to; and, upon my word, I'm sometimes half disposed to think that that man's creed is mine. I guess it would be rather too much to ask you to make it yours; but—this you'll grant—we have had our moments of bliss, which was nearly perfect. Now, haven't we?"

"I—I don't know why you're talking to me like this. I—I know we have. Oh, Rodney, how—how I wish we hadn't!"

"Well, I don't—and I rather fancy I'm in a worse fix than you. But, as I live, when I think of the fun we've had, I don't care—that." And he snapped his fingers. "They can do as they please, but they can't take from me my memories; and if I'm face to face with hell—I'll carry them there."

He held out his hands to her with a little gesture of appeal. "Lady, talking will do no good, so let's say pretty things. Sweetheart, I'll be shot if I won't call you sweetheart, look you never so sourly at me!"

"Oh, Rodney, I—I don't want to look sourly at you! Sourly! Oh, my dear, if you only knew!"

"I do know, and that's just it. I want you to know. Sweetheart, good night!"

He still held out his hands to her. As she looked at him, with straining eyes, she seemed to waver.

"Rodney!"

"Good night. Come here and say it—or shall we meet half-way?"

He moved towards her round the table, and she, as if she could not help it, moved towards him. And they said good night.

CHAPTER XXVII

THE GENTLEMAN'S DEPARTURE AND THE LADY'S EXPLANATIONS

In the morning early Mabel Joyce knocked at the door of Mr. Elmore's bedroom with a jug of shaving water in her hand; knocked softly, as if she did not wish to rouse the sleeper too abruptly from his rest. When no answer came she clung to the handle of the door, as a tremor seemed to pass all over her; then, presently, knocked again. Still no reply. She bent her head towards the panel, listening intently. Then, suddenly, decisively, rapped three times and waited. Still no reply. With a quick movement she turned the handle and passed into the room; and, when in, closed the door rapidly behind her, standing with her back against it, in an attitude of one who was afraid. She looked towards the bed. It was empty; the sleeper had awaked himself from slumber, had risen, and had gone. Putting the jug beside her on the floor, she passed quickly towards the bed; leaning over it, she stared at something which caught her eye upon the pillow. On the white slip was a dark red stain. She put out her hand, clutched it with her finger, withdrew her finger, and looked at it. Part of the redness had passed from the pillow to the tip of her finger. All at once she dropped on to her knees beside the empty bed, and, bowing her head upon the coverlet, stayed motionless. Then rose again to her feet, looking round her. Her glance caught something on the dressing-table—an envelope. Moving towards it, she snatched it up. It was addressed, simply, "Mrs. Joyce." Although it seemed scarcely likely that such an address was intended for her, she ripped open the flap, and took out the sheet of paper it contained.

"DEAR MRS. JOYCE,—I'm off, to another world—the world beyond the grave. I'm more of a coward than I thought; and yet I don't know that it's quite that. I have tried to cut my throat in bed—your bed; but my hand bungled. I have made rather a mess—and then I stopped. It seemed rather a pity to spoil your bedclothes, and I did not like to feel the razor. I am going to do it another way—outside your house, in a place I know of, where I hope no one will ever find me. I want no coroner to sit upon my body, and I want no jury to make me the subject of their silly verdicts.

"I have heaps of reasons—I dare say you'll hear enough about them before long. I'd rather you heard of them than other people heard of them, when I am not here. It is because I am so anxious that the hearing should take place behind my back that I am going. I don't quite know what I owe you, but I believe I'm a little in arrears. You'll find ten pounds on the table; it should more than pay you, and even make up for the week's notice which I have not given. All my possessions that I leave behind—and there are quite a number of decent suits of clothes—are yours. Do as you like with them. If you sell them, and get the price you ought to get, you should not do badly.

"Tell everybody what I have told you, and, if you like, show them this letter. You have not been a bad landlady; I don't suppose I shall be better suited where I am going; nor have I been a bad lodger; if you get a better you'll be in luck.

"Say good-bye to Mabel. There is a portrait of a kind in the locket which you will find near this envelope. I think I should like her to have it, as one to whom I am indebted for many favours.—Your one-time lodger,

"RODNEY ELMORE.

"Do you think I shall find it lonely where I am going? I wonder!"

The girl, having read this letter to the end, caught up an old-fashioned locket; doubtless the one referred to. Opening it, there looked out at her the young man's face—a miniature, not ill-done. She pressed it to her lips, not once, nor twice, but again and again and again. Then, shutting it, slipped it inside her blouse. She gave another rapid glance about the room, moved hither and thither as if to make sure that there was nothing left which might tell more than need be told; then, passing hastily from the room, went not downstairs to her mother but upstairs to the lodger overhead. At his door she also knocked. Response was instant.

"Who's there? Come in!"

She went in. Mr. Dale was sitting up in bed She stayed close to the door.

"He's gone!" she said.

Mr. Dale, although he seemed but recently roused from sleep, seemed to grasp her meaning in a moment.

"Gone where?"

"He's left this."

She tossed the letter she had been reading so dexterously that it fell just before him on the bed. He caught it up and read.

"What's it mean?" he asked. She seemed to consider for a moment.

"You know as well as I do."

"I suppose I do—when you come to think of it. He's a beauty—a shining star!" He stared at the letter. "What does he mean?"

"At any rate, he means one thing—he's gone." Mr. Dale leaned back, looking at the girl as if he were endeavouring to find something on her face which should give him a hint what to say next. When he spoke again it was slowly, as if he measured his words; yet bitterly, as if behind them was a meaning which scarcely jumped to the eye.

"Look here, Mabel, this isn't going to be an easy thing to do. I'm going to have all my work cut out if it's to be managed. You know what I mean by managed. And, as I'm alive, I don't want to do it for nothing—and I don't mean to."

"What do you mean?"

"If the tale's not to be told—you know what tale—it must be on terms. I won't ask what this chap's been to you, because I believe I know. He's been—a blackguard; that's what he's been to you; and, on my word I believe you women like a man who's a blackguard. But I don't want to talk about that now."

"I shouldn't, especially as I expect mother will be calling me before you've done."

The shade of sarcasm in the girl's tone made the man regard her with knitted brows.

"Never you mind about your mother; I know all about her. For once in your life you'll just listen to me. Mr. Rodney Elmore has gone, vanished from the scene—he's dead; here's this letter to prove it to anyone who doubts it." The speaker grinned. "I'm not dead; I'm alive—very much alive; and I want you to take a particular note of that."

"Do you think I don't know that you're alive?"

Mr. Dale's tone grew suddenly fierce.

"I haven't got Mr. Rodney Elmore's pretty tone, nor his pretty manners, nor his pretty words; but I do care for you." He laughed. "Care for you! Why, I'd eat the dirt you walk on; and you've made me do it more than once. Mabel, if I keep my mouth shut, and get others to keep theirs shut, will you stop treating me as if I were dirt, and treat me as if I were a man?"

"I'll treat you as you like; I'll do whatever you like; I'll be your slave, if—if you do that."

She stood close up against the door, with both hands pressed against her breast, and her words seemed to come from her in gasps. As he saw that in very truth she suffered, his whole bearing underwent a sudden change. He all at once grew tender.

"Mabel, I'll make no bargain; I'll do it—for your sake; and—I'll trust to you for my reward."

With odd suddenness she turned right round, so that her back was towards him, and her face pressed against the panel of the door. Her pain seemed to hurt him.

"For God's sake don't—don't do that! I'd rather—do what he's only pretended to do than give you pain. Cheer up—just try hard to cheer up, if it's only just enough to help you to know what ought to be done next."

The suggestion affected her in a fashion which perhaps took him a little aback. She turned again as suddenly as she had done before, this time towards him. Her eyes blazed; the words came swiftly from her lips.

"Do you think that I don't know what I'm going to do next? Do you think it hasn't been in my mind all night? Why, I've got it all cut, and planned, and dried. Leave that to me; all I want is for you to see"—her voice fell—"the tale's not told."

"It sha'n't be if I can help it; and I think I can."

The words still came swiftly from her.

"Say nothing to mother, say nothing to anyone; leave me to do all the telling—you know nothing; that's all you've got to know. You understand?"

His voice as he replied was grim.

"Oh, yes, I understand."

"Then, for the present, it's good-bye."

She opened the door. He checked her.

"I shall see you to-night when I come in."

"You shall; if—if nothing's been told."

She went from the room to her own on the landing below, put on her hat, her coat, and her gloves, and went quickly down the stairs. Seldom was a pretty girl ready more quickly for the street. She already had the front door open when her mother called to her.

"Mabel, what to goodness is the matter with you? Where are you going?"

The girl seemed for a moment to be in doubt whether or not to let her mother's question go unheeded; then decided to vouchsafe her at least some scraps of information.

"Mother, I believe Mr. Elmore's gone."

"Gone? Mr. Elmore? What's the girl talking about?"

"His bedroom's empty, and there's ten pounds on the dressing-table, and I'm going straight off to the City to see."

"To the City!"

The astonishment of the lady's voice was justified; she came quickly along the passage as if to learn what might be the significance of the mystery which she felt was in the air. But her daughter did not wait for her approach; she was through the door, had shut it with a bang, before her mother had realised what it was she meant to do.

Miss Joyce did not go to the City; she went instead to No. 90, Russell Square. There she inquired for Miss Patterson. She was told the lady was at breakfast.

"Tell her—tell her that I'm Miss Joyce, and that I must see her—at once."

She was in the hall, and looked so strange as she leaned against the wall, with her white face and frightened eyes, that the maid looked at her as if she could not make her out at all.

"Miss Joyce, did you say the name was?"

"Yes—Joyce—Mabel Joyce; tell Miss Patterson that Miss Joyce must see her at once."

The maid went into a room upon the right—the dining-room—presently reappeared, with Miss Patterson behind her. Gladys came out into the hall.

"Miss Joyce! You wish to see me? On what business?"

"Somewhere—somewhere where we'll be private."

Gladys observed her with curious eyes; then she held open the dining-room door.

"I'm at breakfast; but, if you don't mind, you'd better come in here."

Mabel went in, Gladys followed. The stranger, now that they were alone, presented such a woebegone picture that, in spite of herself, Gladys was moved.

"You don't seem well—are you ill? Hadn't you better sit down?—here's a chair."

She pushed the chair towards her visitor, but Mabel would none of it.

"No, it doesn't matter, I'd—I'd rather stand. My mother was Mr. Elmore's—landlady."

"Joyce? Oh, yes, of course, I thought I knew the name; I remember." Perhaps unconsciously to herself, Gladys's tone hardened; she drew herself a little straighter, she even moved a little away. In spite of her obvious trouble, Mabel noticed.

"You needn't be afraid of me—I shan't bite."

"I was not afraid that you would bite. What is it you wish with me, Miss Joyce?"

"That."

She stretched out towards the other a letter. Gladys eyed it askance, almost, one might have thought from her demeanour, that she feared that it might bite.

"What's that?"

"If you take it—you'll see. You're right this time in being afraid; you've cause to be more afraid of that than of me. But it's written by somebody you know well, and—you'd better read it."

Still doubtfully, as if she really were in awe of what the sheet of paper might portend, she took it gingerly from the other's fingers. Then she read it. And as she read, a curious change came over, not only her countenance, but her whole bearing. When she had reached the end her hands dropped to her side, she stared at the girl in front of her as she might have done at a visitant from another sphere.

"What—does this letter mean?"

For answer, Mabel took another piece of paper from that woman's universal pocket—her blouse. She held it out to Gladys, and, even more cautiously than before, Gladys took it with unwilling fingers. This time, as she read it, it was with an obvious lack of comprehension.

"What on earth is this?"

"Can't you see? Isn't it plain enough? It's a marriage licence—now can you see?"

Gladys seemed to make an effort to achieve steadiness, not with entire success. As if to hide her partial failure, she went down the room to the seat which she had been occupying at the other end of the table. Resting her hand on the top of the chair, raising the paper again, she re-read it. Her back was towards Mabel, her face could not have been more eloquent, one saw a spasm pass right across it. She was still; there was a perceptible interval; she turned towards her visitor. Her face seemed to have aged; one saw that as she grew older she would not grow better-looking.

"I see that this purports to be a licence of marriage—I don't know much about these things, but I take it that the marriage was to be before a registrar—between Rodney Elmore, who, I presume, is my cousin—"

"He's your cousin right enough."

"And—Mabel Joyce. Are you the Mabel Joyce referred to?"

"I am; we were to have been married to-day—at noon sharp; the registrar—he'll be waiting for us, but he'll have to wait. Mr. Rodney Elmore, that's your cousin and my husband that was to be, he's bolted."

"Bolted? I see. Is that what this letter means?"

"That's just exactly what it means."

"It doesn't mean that—he's—he's killed himself?"

"Not much it doesn't; I know the gentleman. It simply means that, for reasons of his own—I'm one of them and I daresay you're another—he's cut and run."

Gladys's tone could scarcely have been more frigid or her bearing more outwardly calm; unfortunately both the frigidity and the calmness were a little overdone.

"I see. I'm much obliged to you for bringing me—this very interesting piece of news. I believe this is yours. I scarcely think I need detain you longer."

She returned to Mabel both the licence and the letter. Enclosing them one in the other, the girl passed from the room out of the house. Gladys stood staring at the door through which she had left, exactly, if she could only have known it, as Rodney had stared when she had vanished the afternoon before. Then she clenched her fists and shook them in the air.

"To think that I should ever have been such a fool! That I should ever have let him—soil me with his touch! Dad was right; what a fool he must have thought me! If I'd only listened, what might not—have been saved!"

Shortly afterwards she entered the office at St. Paul's Churchyard. Andrews advanced to greet her.

"Mr. Elmore has not yet arrived."

"I know he hasn't; I wish to speak to you."

She led the way towards her father's private room; as he followed Andrews seemed to recognise something in her carriage which recalled his master. There could be no doubt that this was his daughter. When they were in the room and the door was closed, Miss Patterson seated herself in her father's chair. She looked the managing man in the face, with something in her glance which again recalled her sire.

"Andrews, I suppose you can observe a confidence?"

Andrews smiled; he rubbed his hands together; one felt that he could not make out the lady's mood, still less achieve a satisfactory guess at what was in the air.

"I hope so, Miss Patterson, I'm sure. Your father reposed many and many a confidence in me, and I never betrayed one of them—I'm not likely now to betray yours."

"Right, Andrews, I believe you. I believe my father knew the kind of man who may be trusted; he trusted you, and I will. Shake hands." She offered him her hand. As if doubtful whether or not he was taking a liberty, he took it in his. They gravely shook hands.

"It's very good of you, Miss Patterson, I'm sure, to say so; but what you do say is true—your father trusted me, and so can you."

She eyed him for some seconds as if debating in her mind what to say to him and just how to say it. Then it came from her, as it were, all of a sudden.

"Andrews, I told you that my cousin, Rodney Elmore, and I were engaged to be married. I was mistaken—we are not. Stop! I don't want you to ask any questions; that's the confidence I'm reposing in you, I want you to ask none, I simply tell you we're not. Another thing. You told me when I came in just now that Mr. Elmore had not come yet. Andrews, he never will come again—to this office."

"Indeed, miss! Is that so, miss?"

The girl smiled—gravely.

"There, again, Andrews—my confidence! You are to ask no questions. Neither you nor I will see Mr. Elmore again—ever. Still one other thing. You remember what my father said in his will about leaving the conduct of his business in your hands? I echo my father's words; I want you to manage it for me on my father's lines."

The old man was evidently confused. He stood staring at the girl and rubbing his hands, as if he found himself in a quandary from which he sought a way out.

"I'm sure, Miss Patterson, that I'm very gratified by the confidence you place in me, and I want to do my best to ask no questions, but—but there's one remark I ought to make." He bent over the table as if he wished the remark in question to reach her ear alone. "I don't know, Miss Patterson, if you are aware that yesterday morning Mr. Elmore drew a thousand pounds from the bank."

"Yesterday morning? When did he do that? Not when we were there?"

"It appears that he returned directly after we had left, and cashed a cheque for a thousand pounds across the counter, took it in tens and fives and gold—rather a funny way of taking a cheque like that."

The girl said nothing; just possible she thought the more—it is still more possible that hers was disagreeable thinking. It came back to her; she understood; the letter-case which had been left behind; her sitting in the cab while he had gone into the bank to fetch it. Letter-case? So the letter-case was a cheque for a thousand pounds; and while she'd been sitting in the cab he had been putting her money into his pocket. What a pretty fellow this cousin was, this lover of—how many ages ago? Could she ever have cared, to say nothing of loved, a thing like this? This girl had a sense of humour which was her own; at the thought of it she smiled—indeed, suddenly she leaned back in her chair and laughed outright.

"Cashed a cheque for a thousand pounds, did he? Well, Andrews, dad left him nothing in his will—I wonder why. How funny! Then there's still another thing to tell you, Andrews. Let them understand at the bank, as quickly as you can, that they're not to cash any more of Mr. Elmore's cheques which are drawn on my account. Now, Andrews, will you be so very good as to send someone to Mr. Wilkes, and give him my most respectful compliments, and say, if he can possibly spare a moment, I should like very much indeed to see him here at once."

When Miss Joyce got home she found, waiting in the sitting-room which had so recently been Rodney's, Mr. Austin. The gentleman regarded her as she came in with an air of grave disapprobation.

"You are, I believe, the landlady's daughter."

Mabel nodded.

"I have just had a few words with your mother, who appears to be an extraordinary woman, and who has told me an extraordinary tale."

"My mother's not in the habit of telling extraordinary tales to anyone."

"Then, what does she mean by—by talking stuff and nonsense about Mr. Elmore's having gone, and—and I don't know what besides?"

Miss Joyce drew a long breath, and seemed to nerve herself for an effort. She had had a good deal to bear that morning, and to retain even a vestige of self-command needed all her efforts.

"Mr. Austin, Mr. Elmore has gone, and he's left a letter behind him in which he pretends that he has committed suicide; but he hasn't, I know better. But here's the letter; you might like to look at it."

He read the letter with which we are already familiar; and it had a very similar effect on him to that which it had had on others, only in his case he read it over and over again, as if to make sure that its meaning had not escaped him, yet that its meaning had escaped him his words made plain.

"You—you may understand this letter, young woman, but I certainly do not. What—what does this most extraordinary, and, as it seems to me, inconsequent, letter mean?"

"I'll tell you just as shortly as I can exactly what it means. And, perhaps, when I have told you you won't ask any more questions than you can conveniently help, because—I've had just about as much to bear as I can manage. Rodney Elmore—I'm not going to call him Mr. Elmore, I've as much right to call him Rodney as anybody in this world; he's got himself into a mess, and I'm one of them. Why, he promised to marry me to-day at twelve o'clock."

"He—promised! Young woman!"

"Here's the licence to prove it; but—I suppose he daren't face it; so he's gone, and he's done me, and I'm not the only one he's done. Has he done your daughter?"

"Your question, put in such a form, I entirely decline to answer."

"You needn't; I know. And, mind you, I don't believe he's gone alone either, wherever it is he has gone to. What's the name of that girl down at Brighton that he was so thick with, and your son's sweetheart?"

Mr. Austin started as if something had stung him. He stared at the girl with growing apprehension.

"You can't mean—?"

"Yes, I can. Wasn't her first name Mary? I have heard the other—it's a queer one—and I forget it. But you ask your son, if he cares for the girl, to make inquiries, and if she's missing, and he wants her new address, to find out Rodney Elmore's, and—he'll find hers."

CHAPTER XXVIII

A CONSPIRACY OF SILENCE

There are few worse half-hours in life than that in which a man finds that the one person whom he has liked, and respected, and trusted, and believed in before all others, is a scamp, a liar, and a cur. As Mr. Austin sat cowering in the corner of his cab it was to him almost as if he had been these things, instead of Rodney Elmore. He ascended the steps of the Kensington house a little stiffly, a little bowed, a little shorn of his full height; he bore himself, indeed, as if he were ashamed; it was with a sense of shame that he spoke to his son, who was apparently just about to go out as he went in.

"Tom, I want to speak to you."

The lad looked at his father with a look of surprise.

"Why, pater; what's wrong?"

The father closed the door of the room into which he had preceded his son. There was something shifty in his bearing; he seemed unwilling to meet the youngster's glances.

"Tom, what was that you were saying about—about Mary Carmichael?"

The lad smiled, ruefully enough; there was an awkwardness about his manner. He turned away, as if on his side he had no wish to meet his father's eyes.

"All I can make out is that she has gone. It seems that while that old aunt of hers was out yesterday afternoon—she vanished. She just left a note behind her to say that she was going, and that they weren't to bother, because she wasn't coming back; but they'd hear from her some day—she couldn't say just when."

"Tom, she's gone with Rodney Elmore."

The lad swung round as on a pivot.

"Pater! What do you mean?"

The father told the story as he knew it, the lad listening—first as one in a dream, and then as one in a rage. Then, with a gasp as of astonishment, he blurted out:

"But what about Stella?"

"Yes; what about Stella? Stella's here, and—why, where's Rodney? I thought, father, he'd come with you."

Miss Austin had come running into the room eagerly, happily, laughingly, taking it for granted that her lover was within. As she looked from her father to her brother, and noted the oddity of their manner, her eyes grew wider open.

"Father, where—where is Rodney?"

Then the father told the tale to her; it was the hardest task he had ever had to perform. The girl first scorned him, then laughed, then doubted, and then, in a fit of what was very like fury, announced her intention of going in search of Rodney, whom she declared she believed to be cruelly aspersed, and learning the truth from his own lips. It was with difficulty she was stayed. When she, at last, was brought to understand, she was already another Stella to the one her father had known. She was not to be comforted. And when her mother came, and heard the story, too, she put her arm about her daughter's waist and led her to her room, and there remained alone with her an hour or more. When she came out she also was another woman; and her daughter was in her room, alone.

And that, to all intents and purposes, so far as it is known, is the end of the story, though the real end is not yet. Such stories take a long time ending. Sometimes they are continued in the generation which comes after, and never end. Mr. Philip Walter Augustus Parker was tried for the murder of Graham Patterson, and, apparently to his complete satisfaction, was found guilty. The law plays such pranks oftener than is commonly supposed. The story he told was so well put together, all the joints fitted so well. As the judge instructed the jury they really had no option; on the evidence there was only one possible verdict; and that was returned. Mr. Parker earned his credentials; he was sent, as he desired, on a lengthy visit to Broadmoor. The whole story might have fallen to pieces and his visit to Broadmoor indefinitely postponed had the platform inspector at Brighton station—Edward Giles—given his evidence in another way. A few questions would have changed the whole face of affairs, but they were not asked. He told that it was he who had helped Graham Patterson into the carriage, and also that there already was someone in it when the dead man entered. At that point the questions which were put to him went awry. He was asked if the prisoner was that other person; he replied that he did not recognise him, but as, when the witness had entered the box, Mr. Parker had greeted him with that unpleasant little chuckle of his, and had proclaimed that he recognised him, even before he opened his mouth, as the porter, as he put it, who had been of assistance to Mr. Patterson, for the judge, as for the jury, that was sufficient. Giles himself was evidently taken aback, and while he declared that he did not recognise the prisoner, he admitted that if Parker had not been the man in the carriage, he could not understand how he recognised him. So Mr. Parker had his wish.

Mr. Andrews is still the managing man, as well as a partner, of the firm of Graham Patterson, which continues to thrive on the same sound old lines. And Gladys Patterson is the wife of Stephen Wilkes—that strikes even her, when she thinks of it, as queer. How it came about, she has told her husband more than once, she does not understand; she wonders sometimes, so she tells him, if her father could ever have had it in his mind that that was the match he would have chosen. She is thinking of Rodney's words. Her husband laughs, and assures her that to the best of his knowledge and belief her father never dreamt of anything of the kind. Whereat she thinks all the more of Rodney's words, having a dim suspicion hidden in her somewhere that it was because of what he said that this strange thing had happened, and, in what she feels is in quite an uncanny way, that it was he who brought it all about.

Mabel Joyce is Mrs. George Dale, fairly happy, as the average wife's standard of happiness goes, and Dale is happy too; but there is about him a suggestion of solicitous anxiety, as if he would be glad to be as certain of her satisfaction with the way that things have turned out, as of his own.

Stella is still unmarried, and likely to remain so. She is not quite the ordinary type of girl. When she gave her heart to Rodney Elmore, it was given for ever; although she would probably be the last person in the world to admit it, he has it still. As, she declares, she will never marry save where her heart is, her prospects of remaining Stella Austin are stronger than either her father or her mother care to own. Tom is married; was married within six months of his heart being finally broken—to the girl with the mischievous eyes. And he is happy as a man may be; and he is a man, even up to his father's standard of manhood. He is practically the head of his father's firm, and a sufficiently effective and energetic head he makes. He declares that it is his wife who has done it, and that she has been and still is and ever will be the only woman in the world to him. He forgets; men—and women—sometimes do.

Nothing definite has ever been heard of Rodney Elmore; but among those who knew him in his youth there is a profound conviction that he still lives. One day, a month or so after his marriage, there came a postcard to Tom Austin from one of the northern States of America, with just these words on the back:

"Congratulations—good wishes—am delighted!

He was the only person who ever saw the card. He tore it up and burnt it. About him for nearly a week afterwards there was, at odd moments, an unusually reflective air. His wife asked him what he was thinking about.

"Why," he told her, "what should I think about but you."

He was thinking, wondering, how close to "M." was Rodney Elmore—his boyhood's friend!—as one result of what was very like a conspiracy of silence.

Richard Bernard Heldmann was born on 12th October 1857, in St Johns Wood, North London, to parents Joseph Heldmann and Emma Marsh.

Shortly after his birth his father became ensnared in a bankruptcy proceedings which enforced the abandonment of a career as a merchant for that of a schoolmaster at a school in Hammersmith, West London.

By his early 20's the young Heldmann, showing a talent for writing, began publishing fiction. In 1880, he began to publish works of boys' school and adventure stories for the myriad magazine publications all eager for good well-written content. The most important of these was Union Jack, one of the better quality boys' weekly magazine associated with the popular authors G. A. Henty and W.H.G. Kingston.

Heldmann was promoted to co-editor in October 1882, but his association with the publication ended suddenly in June 1883. After this, Heldmann published no further fiction under that name.

The reason at the time was not immediately apparent but in April 1884 Heldmann was sentenced to 18 months of hard labour for issuing a series of cheques, all forged, in France and Britain the year before.

In order to be well away from the scandal and damage this had caused to his reputation Heldmann adopted a pseudonym on his release from jail. Shortly thereafter the name 'Richard Marsh' began to appear in the literary periodicals. The use of his mother's maiden name seems both a release from the criminal record now associated with his given name and a lifeline to a fresh beginning.

A stroke of very good fortune arrived when his novel The Beetle was published in 1897. There had been more than a few previous publications of his works but The Beetle would turn out to be his greatest commercial success and added some much-needed gravitas to his literary reputation. The story concerns a mysterious oriental person who follows a British politician to London, and then wreaks havoc with his powers of hypnosis and shape-shifting. The Beetle has some similar aspects to certain other novels of the period, including those such as Bram Stoker's Dracula, George du Maurier's Trilby, and Sax Rohmer's many Fu Manchu novels. Like Dracula, and also the sensation novels written by Wilkie Collins and others during the 1860s, The Beetle is narrated from the various viewpoints of multiple characters to create suspense. The novel is also layered with many themes and issues of the Victorian era including women's rights, unemployment, urban poverty, radical politics, homosexuality, science, and Britain's imperial adventures, particularly in regard to Egypt and the Sudan. The Beetle sold out upon its initial print run and thereafter sold well for the next several decades. After Marsh's early death the novel's story was made into a film and adapted for the London stage, both in the 1920's.

It should also be noted that in the year of its first publication it outsold Dracula, then also in its first year of publication. In hindsight a remarkable achievement.

Marsh was a prolific writer and wrote almost 80 volumes of fiction as well as many short stories, across several genres from horror and crime to romance and humour.

However, at horror he was particularly adept. Works such as The Goddess: A Demon (1900), in which an Indian sacrificial idol comes to life with murderous resolve, and The Joss: A Reversion (1901), whose central premise is that of an Englishman who transforms himself into a hideous oriental idol are prime examples.

An important element of many of Marsh's novels is the investigation of the mystery. Several of his novels are centered on the crime and its subsequent detection. In the novel Philip Bennion's Death (1897) a bachelor is discovered dead the day after discussing Thomas De Quincey's essay on murder as a fine art, and his neighbour and friend begin efforts to solve his death. In The Datchet Diamonds (1898) a young man who has lost a fortune on the stock market mistakenly swaps bags with a diamond thief, and then find himself pursued by both the thieves and police. In A Spoiler of Men (1905), Marsh puts together crime and science-fiction; the gentleman-criminal villain renders people slaves to his will by a chemical injection.

As with many authors success with popular fiction was never quite enough. He also wanted to be regarded as a serious author. His novel A Second Coming (1900) imagines Christ's return to an early-20th century London and is his most well-handled attempt in that pursuit.

His prolific output of short stories ensured his being published in a plethora of magazines including Household Words, Cornhill Magazine, The Strand Magazine, and Belgravia, as well as in a number of short story book collections. These collections; The Seen and the Unseen (1900), Marvels and Mysteries (1900), Both Sides of the Veil (1901) and Between the Dark and the Daylight (1902) all feature an eclectic mix of humour, crime, romance and the occult.

He also published several serial short stories. Here he was able to develop characters whose adventures could be related in discrete stories across numerous editions of a magazine. An example is Mr. Pugh and Mr. Tress of Curios (1898). They are rival collectors between whom pass a series of bizarre and disturbing objects—poisoned rings, pipes which seem to come to life, a phonograph record on which a murdered woman seems to speak from the dead, and the severed hand of a 13th-century aristocrat.

During his career he sometimes came up with characters or stories ahead of their time. His character Miss Judith Lee, a young teacher of deaf pupils whose lip-reading ability involves her with mysteries that she solves by acting as a detective was very pro-active in this regard.

Richard Marsh died from heart disease in Haywards Heath in Sussex on 9th August 1915.

Several of his novels were published posthumously.

Richard Marsh – A Concise Bibliography

As Bernard Heldmann
Boxall School: A Tale of Schoolboy Life (1881)
Dorrincourt [Union Jack, April-September 1881]
Expelled: Being the Story of a Young Gentleman (1882)
Daintree (1883)

As Richard Marsh
Capturing a Convict (Strand Magazine 1893)

The Devil's Diamond (1893)
The Mahatma's Pupil (1893)
The Strange Wooing of Mary Bowler (1895)
Mrs Musgrave—and her Husband (1895)
The Mystery of Philip Bennion's Death (1897)
The Crime and the Criminal (1897)
The Duke and the Damsel (1897)
The Beetle: A Mystery (1897)
The House of Mystery (1898)
Under One Cover: Eleven Stories by S. Baring-Gould, Richard Marsh, Ernest G. Henham, Fergus Hume, Andrew Merry and A. St John Adcock (1898)
Curios: Some Strange Adventures of Two Bachelors (1898)
Tom Ossington's Ghost (1898)
The Datchet Diamonds (1898)
The Woman with One Hand and Mr Ely's Engagement (1899)
In Full Cry (1899)
Frivolities: Especially Addressed to Those Who Are Tired of Being Serious (1899)
The Purse Which Was Found
For One Night Only
Returning a Verdict
The Chancellor's Ward
A Honeymoon Trip
The Burglar's Blunder
Ninepence
A Battlefield Up-to-date
Mr. Harland's Pupils
A Burglar Alarm
A Lesson in Sculling
Outside
The Chase of the Ruby (1900)
An Aristocratic Detective (1900)
A Hero of Romance (1900)
The Seen and the Unseen (1900)
The Goddess: A Demon (1900)
Ada Vernham, Actress (1900)
A Second Coming (1900)
Marvels and Mysteries (1900)
The Long Arm of Coincidence
The Mask
An Experience
Pourquoipas
By Suggestion
A Silent Witness
To Be Used Against Him
The Words of a Little Child
How He Passed!
The Joss: A Reversion (1901)
Both Sides of the Veil (1901)

Amusement Only (1901)
The Twickenham Peerage (1902)
Between the Dark and the Daylight (1902)
The Adventures of Augustus Short: Things Which I Have Done for Others and Wish I Hadn't (1902)
A Metamorphosis (1903)
The Death Whistle (1903)
The Magnetic Girl (1903)
Miss Arnott's Marriage (1904)
Garnered (1904)
A Duel (1904)
A Spoiler of Men (1905)
The Marquis of Putney (1905)
The Confessions of a Young Lady (1905)
Under One Flag (1906)
In the Service of Love (1906)
The Garden of Mystery (1906)
A Woman Perfected (1907)
The Romance of a Maid of Honour (1907)
The Girl and the Miracle (1907)
The Surprising Husband (1908)
The Coward behind the Curtain (1908)
That Master of Ours (1908)
A Royal Indiscretion (1909)
The Interrupted Kiss (1909)
The Girl in the Blue Dress (1909)
The Lovely Mrs Blake (1910)
Live Men's Shoes (1910)
The Twin Sisters (1911)
A Drama of the Telephone (1911)
Violet Forster's Lover (1912)
Sam Briggs: His Book (1912)
Judith Lee: Some Pages from her Life (1912)
The Master of Deception (1913)
Justice—Suspended (1913)
If It Please You (1913)
The Woman in the Car (1914)
Molly's Husband (1914)
Margot—and her Judges (1914)
The Man with Nine Lives (1915)
Love in Fetters (1915)
His Love or his Life (1915)
The Flying Girl (1915)
Violet Forster's Lover (1916)
The Adventures of Judith Lee (1916)
Sam Briggs, V.C. (1916)
Coming of Age (1916)
The Great Temptation (1916)
The Deacon's Daughter (1917)

On the Jury (1918)
Orders to Marry ([1918)
Outwitted (1919)
Apron-Strings (1920)

For Debt, Windsor Magazine (January 1902)
Returning a Verdict, Cornhill Magazine (January 1896)
The Lost Duchess, Cornhill Magazine (January 1895)
Mrs Riddles Daughter, All the Year Round (17 March 1894)
An Episcopal Scandal, Cornhill Magazine (February 1894)
A Rubber or Two, All the Year Round (16 September 1893)
A First Night, Cornhill Magazine (April 1893)
The Mystery of Philip Bennion's Death, Household Words (3/10/17/24/31 December 1892)
The Princess Margaretta, Household Words (3 December 1892)
The Puzzle, Cornhill Magazine (November 1892)
A Victim to Art, All the Year Round (2 July 1892)
The Burglar's Blunder, Derby Mercury (24 June 1891)
Pourquoipas, All the Year Round (9/16 May 1891)
The Pipe, Cornhill Magazine (March 1891)
When Greek Joined Greek, Household Words (6 September 1890)
His First Experiment, Cornhill Magazine (September 1890)
"Mignonette", All the Year Round (9 August 1890)
The Long Arm of Coincidence, Household Words (24 May 1890)
The Match of the Season, Cornhill Magazine (May 1890)
A Set of Chessmen, Cornhill Magazine (April 1890)
A Dream of Diamonds, Household Words (7 December 1889)
My Uncle's Flirtation, Household Words (16 November 1889)
"Em", Household Words (2 November 1889)
The Barnes Mystery: An Adventure of Judith Lee, Strand Magazine (October 1916)
"Scandalous!", Strand Magazine (August 1916)
What Fell on her Hat, Strand Magazine (April 1916)
The Adventures of Sam Briggs: On the Film, Strand Magazine (March 1916)
A Set of Chessmen, Cassell's Magazine of Fiction and Popular Literature (Dec 1915)
Sam Briggs Becomes a Soldier: A Fighting Man, Strand Magazine (December 1915)
Sam Briggs Becomes a Soldier: On the Way Home, Strand Magazine (November 1915)
Sam Briggs Becomes a Soldier: An Official Mistake, Strand Magazine (October 1915)
Sam Briggs Becomes a Soldier: In their Own Gas, Strand Magazine (September 1915)
Sam Briggs Becomes a Soldier: Sanctuary, Strand Magazine (August 1915)
Sam Briggs Becomes a Soldier: In the Nick of Time, Strand Magazine (July 1915)
Sam Briggs Becomes a Soldier: A Night Surprise for the Germans, Strand Magazine (June 1915)
Sam Briggs Becomes a Soldier: In the Trenches, Strand Magazine (May 1915)
Sam Briggs Becomes a Soldier: Baptism of Fire, Strand Magazine (April 1915)
Sam Briggs Becomes a Soldier: Two Stripes, Strand Magazine (March 1915)

Life in the King's New Army: Jack Carpenter's True Story, VI: Career for our Boys, Daily Mail (27 February 1915)

Life in the King's New Army: Jack Carpenter's True Story, V: The Tailor and the Man, Daily Mail (26 February 1915)

Life in the King's New Army: Jack Carpenter's True Story, IV: Hutments', Daily Mail (25 February 1915)

Life in the King's New Army: Jack Carpenter's True Story, III: First-Rate Fighting Men', Daily Mail (24 February 1915)

Life in the King's New Army: Jack Carpenter's True Story, II: The Berwick Borderers, Daily Mail (23 February 1915)

Life in the King's New Army: Jack Carpenter's True Story, I: Crossed Swords, Daily Mail (22 February 1915)

Sam Briggs Becomes a Soldier: A Man in the Making, Strand Magazine (February 1915)

Sam Briggs Becomes a Soldier: Sam Briggs Becomes a Soldier, Strand Magazine (January 1915)

The Amazing Visitor, Strand Magazine (December 1914)

Looping the Loop: An Adventure of Sam Briggs, Strand Magazine (August 1914)

The Torch, Strand Magazine (October 1913)

"Gaiety" Abroad, Strand Magazine (September 1913), 274-82

A Self-Appointed Guardian, English Illustrated Magazine (August 1913)

For the Cause, Strand Magazine (April 1913)

The Adventures of Judith Lee: The Affair of the Montagu Diamonds, Strand Magazine (February 1913)

The Adventures of Judith Lee: Mandragora, Strand Magazine (August 1912)

The Adventures of Judith Lee: "8 Elm Grove—Back Entrance", Strand Magazine (July 1912)

The Adventures of Judith Lee: The Restaurant Napolitain, Strand Magazine (June 1912)

The Adventures of Judith Lee: Uncle Jack, Strand Magazine (May 1912)

The Adventures of Judith Lee: Was It by Chance Only? Strand Magazine (April 1912)

The Adventures of Judith Lee: Isolda, Strand Magazine (March 1912)

The Adventures of Judith Lee: "Auld Lang Syne", Strand Magazine (January 1912)

The Adventures of Judith Lee: The Miracle, Strand Magazine (December 1911)

The Adventures of Judith Lee: Matched

The Burglary in Berkeley Square, Pearson's Magazine (December 1908)

The River of Light, Strand Magazine (December 1908)

The Girl in the Light Blue Dress, Strand Magazine (October 1908)

O'Rourke of the Saucy Sixth, Grand Magazine (June 1908)

The Adventures of Sam Briggs: The Limerick, Strand Magazine (February 1908)

The Adventures of Sam Briggs: The Star of Romance, Strand Magazine (July 1907)

The Adventures of Sam Briggs: A Social Evening, Strand Magazine (April 1907)

My Best Story and Why I Think So No. 21: The Strange Occurrences in Canterstone Gaol, Grand Magazine (October 1906)

The Adventures of Sam Briggs: That Hansom, Strand Magazine (May 1906)

The Adventures of Sam Briggs: Her Fourth, Strand Magazine (December 1905)

The Adventures of Sam Briggs: A Modest Half-Crown, Strand Magazine (November 1905)

The Adventures of Sam Briggs: The Gift Horse, Strand Magazine (March 1905)

My Wedding Day, Strand Magazine (January 1905)

The Adventures of Sam Briggs: The Girl on the Sands, Strand Magazine (October 1904)

The Parson, the Soldier, and the Child, London Magazine (November 1903)

The Girl and the Boy, London Magazine (October 1903)

By Whose Hand? New Short Novel by Richard Marsh, Answers (1 August – 31 October 1903)

A Girl Who Couldn't, Strand Magazine (January 1903)

The Kit-Bag, Windsor Magazine, 17 (January 1903), 298-309

Their Reasons: Two Hitherto Unreported Conversations, House Annual (1902)

At Large: Being the Strange Perils and Experiences of George Otway, Suspect, Answers (12 July - 27 December 1902)

The Handwriting, Strand Magazine (June 1902)

La Haute Finance, Windsor Magazine (March 1902)

A Wonderful Girl, Strand Magazine (March 1902)

Skittles, English Illustrated Magazine, (February/March 1902)

Breaking the Ice, Strand Magazine (February 1902)

My Aunt's Excursion, Windsor Magazine (January 1902)

The Haunted Chair: The Story of a Strange Mystery, Harmsworth London Magazine (January 1902)

Miss Donne's Great Gamble, Strand Magazine (November 1901)

The Man in the Glass Cage; or The Strange Story of the Twickenham Peerage, Manchester Times, (6 September – 27 December 1901

The Adventures of Augustus Short: Things Which I Have Done for Others, and Wish I Hadn't: The Address Which I Gave for Rudman, Cassell's Magazine (November 1901)

The Adventures of Augustus Short: Things Which I Have Done for Others, and Wish I Hadn't: Jones's Love Affair, Cassell's Magazine (October 1901)

The Adventures of Augustus Short: Things Which I Have Done for Others, and Wish I Hadn't: The Duel I Fought of Jarvis, Cassell's Magazine (September 1901)

The Adventures of Augustus Short: Things Which I Have Done for Others, and Wish I Hadn't: Griffin's Offspring, Cassell's Magazine (August 1901)

The Adventures of Augustus Short: Things Which I Have Done for Others, and Wish I Hadn't: McCulloch's Shoes, Cassell's Magazine (July 1901)

The Adventures of Augustus Short: Things Which I Have Done for Others, and Wish I Hadn't: The Fitzroy-Jenkinsons' Rooms, Cassell's Magazine (June 1901)

Staggers, Windsor Magazine (April 1901)

How I Drove a Motor Car for Randal, Strand Magazine (April 1901)

The Disappearance of Mrs Macrecham: The Amazing Story of a Strange Cat, Harmsworth Monthly Pictorial Magazine (March 1901)

The Irregularity of the Juryman, Strand Magazine (December 1900)

The Strange Fortune of Pollie Blythe: The Story of a Chinese "God", Manchester Times (12 October 1900 – 8 February 1901)

Pugh's Poisoned Ring, Harmsworth Monthly Pictorial Magazine (October 1900)

Willyum, Penny Illustrated Paper and Illustrated Times, (26 May 1900)

Willyum, Hampshire Telegraph and Naval Chronicle (26 May 1900)

The Goddess: A Demon, Manchester Times (12 January – 30 March 1900)

The Stolen Treaty, Manchester Times (27 October 1899)

For One Night Only, Answers (8 April 1899)

In Full Cry, Manchester Times (3 March – 9 June 1899)

The Colonel's Cane, Cassell's Magazine (February 1899)

The Burglary at Azalea Villa, Manchester Times, (13 January 1899)

The Burglary at Azalea Villa, Newcastle Weekly Courant (14 January 1899)

Our Christmas Burglar, Answers (17 December 1898)

Something to his Advantage, Manchester Times (7 October – 4 November 1898)

A Lesson in Sculling, Newcastle Weekly Courant (October 1898)

That Five Hundred Pound Price, Harmsworth Monthly Pictorial Magazine (September 1898)

The Chancellor's Ward, Harmsworth Monthly Pictorial Magazine (August 1898)

The Ossington Mystery, Ipswich Journal (1 April – 17 June 1898)
The Duchess of Datchet's Diamonds, New Zealand Graphic and Ladies' Journal (New Zealand) (7 May – 25 June 1898)
The Peril of Paul Lessingham: The Story of a Haunted Man, Answers (13 March – 19 June 1897)
The Purse Which Was Found, Answers (17 April 1897)
The Rector and the Curate, Answers (19 December 1896)
An Illustration of Modern Science, Pall Mall Magazine (November 1896)
A Battlefield Up-to-Date, Idler Magazine (August 1896)
Twins, Idler Magazine (January 1896)
Lady Wishaw's Hand, Leeds Mercury (January 1895)
Young George, St Nicholas (March 1894)
Exchange Is Robbery, Idler Magazine (December 1893 - January 1894)
The Tipster: An Impossible Story, Home Chimes (December 1893)
The Influence of Women, Home Chimes (November 1893)
By Deputy: A Reminiscence of Travel, Home Chimes (October 1893)
Rivals, Home Chimes (September 1893)
Capturing a Convict, Strand Magazine (August 1893)
A Burglar Alarm, Home Chimes (June 1893)
Music Halls and Theatres, Home Chimes (March 1893)
A Strange Bride, Manchester Times (6/13 January 1893)
The Mask, Gentleman's Magazine (December 1892)
A Vision of the Night, Strand Magazine (December 1892)
Nelly, Home Chimes (November 1892)
A Prophet: A Story, New England Magazine (October - November 1892)
Mr Harland's Pupils, Home Chimes (August 1892)
The Brothers in Grey, Home Chimes (April 1892)
The Half-Back, Derby Mercury (March 1892)
The Half-Back, Home Chimes (February 1892)
The Violin, Home Chimes (December 1891)
The Short Story, Home Chimes (August 1891)
Magical Music, Gentleman's Magazine (May 1891)
A Honeymoon Trip, Home Chimes (April 1891)
Mitwaterstraand, Time (September 1890)
A Pack of Cards, Longman's Magazine (August 1890)
The Burglar's Blunder, Ladies' Journal (Canada) (1 July 1890)
The Strange Occurrences in Canterstone Jail, Blackwood's Edinburgh Magazine (June 1890)
A Substitute: The Story of My Last Cricket-Match, Longman's Magazine (June 1890)
The Burglar's Blunder, Gentleman's Magazine (May 1890)
A Silent Witness, Belgravia (October 1889)
A Bed for the Night, Belgravia (Summer 1889)
Payment for a Life, Belgravia (Summer 1888)